Mistletoe and Mayhem

"A terrific holiday cozy that contains more than one mystery . . . another entertaining yuletide whodunit."
—*Genre Go Round Reviews*

"Kate Kingsbury is the Queen of English cozy mysteries and her special Pennyfoot Christmas editions are always a special treat . . . Her gift of storytelling keeps the action and suspense moving along at a quick pace."   —*Fresh Fiction*

Decked with Folly

"Kingsbury expertly strews red herrings to suggest plenty of others had reason to wish Ian dead . . . This makes the perfect stocking stuffer for the cozy fan in your life."
—*Publishers Weekly*

Ringing in Murder

"*Ringing in Murder* combines the feel of an Agatha Christie whodunit with a taste of *Upstairs, Downstairs.*"
—*Cozy Library*

"Engaging . . . Cozy fans will be pleased to ring in the New Year with this cheerful Kingsbury trifle." —*Publishers Weekly*

Shrouds of Holly

"Charming . . . Will provide warm holiday entertainment."
—*Publishers Weekly*

"Delightful . . . Starring an intrepid heroine."
—*Midwest Book Review*

continued . . .

"Well crafted and surprising all the way to the last page, *Shrouds of Holly* is a pleasurable read that is sure to get you in the mood for the holidays!"   —*The Romance Readers Connection*

"Likable characters, charming surroundings, and eclectic guests continue to make this an enjoyable series. Bravo, Kate Kingsbury . . . for making this a holiday tradition."
—*MyShelf.com*

Slay Bells

"A pre–World War I whodunit in the classic style, furnished with amusing characters."   —*Kirkus Reviews*

"The author draws as much from *Fawlty Towers* as she does from Agatha Christie, crafting a charming . . . cozy delicately flavored with period details of pre–World War I rural England."   —*Publishers Weekly*

"A true holiday gem."   —*Mystery Scene*

**Visit Kate Kingsbury's website
at www.doreenrobertshight.com**

Berkley Prime Crime titles by Kate Kingsbury

Manor House Mysteries

A BICYCLE BUILT FOR MURDER
DEATH IS IN THE AIR
FOR WHOM DEATH TOLLS
DIG DEEP FOR MURDER
PAINT BY MURDER
BERRIED ALIVE
FIRE WHEN READY
WEDDING ROWS
AN UNMENTIONABLE MURDER

Pennyfoot Hotel Mysteries

ROOM WITH A CLUE
DO NOT DISTURB
SERVICE FOR TWO
EAT, DRINK, AND BE BURIED
CHECK-OUT TIME
GROUNDS FOR MURDER
PAY THE PIPER
CHIVALRY IS DEAD
RING FOR TOMB SERVICE
DEATH WITH RESERVATIONS
DYING ROOM ONLY
MAID TO MURDER

Holiday Pennyfoot Hotel Mysteries

NO CLUE AT THE INN
SLAY BELLS
SHROUDS OF HOLLY
RINGING IN MURDER
DECKED WITH FOLLY
MISTLETOE AND MAYHEM
HERALD OF DEATH

Titles by Kate Kingsbury writing as Rebecca Kent

HIGH MARKS FOR MURDER
FINISHED OFF
MURDER HAS NO CLASS

HERALD
OF DEATH

KATE KINGSBURY

BERKLEY PRIME CRIME, NEW YORK

THE BERKLEY PUBLISHING GROUP
Published by the Penguin Group
Penguin Group (USA) Inc.
375 Hudson Street, New York, New York 10014, USA
Penguin Group (Canada), 90 Eglinton Avenue East, Suite 700, Toronto, Ontario M4P 2Y3, Canada
(a division of Pearson Penguin Canada Inc.)
Penguin Books Ltd., 80 Strand, London WC2R 0RL, England
Penguin Group Ireland, 25 St. Stephen's Green, Dublin 2, Ireland (a division of Penguin Books Ltd.)
Penguin Group (Australia), 250 Camberwell Road, Camberwell, Victoria 3124, Australia
(a division of Pearson Australia Group Pty. Ltd.)
Penguin Books India Pvt. Ltd., 11 Community Centre, Panchsheel Park, New Delhi—110 017, India
Penguin Group (NZ), 67 Apollo Drive, Rosedale, Auckland 0632, New Zealand
(a division of Pearson New Zealand Ltd.)
Penguin Books (South Africa) (Pty.) Ltd., 24 Sturdee Avenue, Rosebank, Johannesburg 2196,
South Africa

Penguin Books Ltd., Registered Offices: 80 Strand, London WC2R 0RL, England

This book is an original publication of The Berkley Publishing Group.

FIRST EDITION: November 2011

Library of Congress Cataloging-in-Publication Data

Kingsbury, Kate.
    Herald of death / Kate Kingsbury.—1st ed.
        p. cm.
    ISBN 978-0-425-24335-0
    1. Baxter, Cecily Sinclair (Fictitious character)—Fiction. 2. Pennyfoot Hotel (England : Imaginary
place)—Fiction. 3. Murder—Investigation—Fiction. 4. Christmas stories. I. Title.
    PR9199.3.K44228H47 2011
    813'54—dc22   2011006679

PRINTED IN THE UNITED STATES OF AMERICA

10   9   8   7   6   5   4   3   2   1

To Bill, for understanding the true meaning of love.

ACKNOWLEDGMENTS

Once again I'm privileged to have worked with a wonderful editor, Faith Black. My deepest thanks for all your hard work, and for your enthusiasm and guidance. It means a lot to me.

My thanks, also, to my astute agent, Paige Wheeler. I truly appreciate all that you and Celeste Fine have done for me this year.

My dear friend in England, Ann Wraight, I thank you for your wonderful magazines that keep me in touch with my homeland.

As always, the art department has done an outstanding job on the cover. Truly brilliant. My grateful thanks to Judith Murello and her amazing team.

My apologies to all those wonderful fans who wrote with concerns about my health. I didn't mean to alarm you with the acknowledgments in my last book. I assure you, I am quite well, and looking forward to taking you for another visit to the Pennyfoot Country Club. Thank you all so much for your e-mails. You have no idea how much I enjoy them.

To my husband, who can always make me smile when I feel like crying. Thank you for always being there when I need you.

HERALD
OF DEATH

CHAPTER
❀ 1 ❀

The snow started falling the week before the first Christmas guest was due to arrive at the Pennyfoot Country Club. It began with just a few flakes that drifted on the wind and eventually disappeared into the gray ocean. Soon, however, the flakes grew thicker, fell faster, and a soft white carpet blanketed the sands.

Horses struggled along the Esplanade, dragging carriages that slid from side to side, until the icy ruts had worn deep enough to prevent the wheels from wandering.

Beyond the cliffs the snow clung to the bare branches of the oaks, gently covered the grass on Putney Downs, and partially buried the lifeless body of the elderly gentleman lying on the path, leaving only a bedraggled dog to mourn his departure.

* * *

At the far end of the Esplanade, Cecily Sinclair Baxter stood at the window of her sitting room overlooking the Pennyfoot grounds. The bowling greens resembled icing on a wedding cake—smooth, shiny, and begging for that first footprint to mar the surface. The sight brought her no pleasure, however.

"This storm couldn't have come at a worse time," she murmured, "with so much to be done. I have to go into town tomorrow. My gown for the Welcome Ball needs some alterations, and the snow looks very deep. I do hope Samuel won't have trouble with the carriage."

Across the room, her husband remained silent behind the pages of the *Daily Mirror*.

Cecily tried again. "I sincerely hope that all this snow goes away in the next few days. Our guests are not going to enjoy the Christmas season if they are floundering about with freezing noses and toes."

The rattle of a newspaper warned her that Baxter was deeply immersed in an article and did not wish to be disturbed. Since Cecily had never conformed to the adage that a woman should bow to her husband's wishes at all times, she turned to face him. "Did you not hear me?"

"I heard you."

The newspaper remained upright in front of Baxter's face, much to Cecily's annoyance. "Then please do me the courtesy of giving me a reply."

Baxter's sigh seemed to rebound off the walls. He lowered his newspaper and sent his wife a reproachful scowl. "What would you have me say?"

"That you agree that this snowstorm could be disastrous for our Christmas activities."

Baxter pursed his lips. "In the first place, snowstorms on the southeast coast of England rarely last more than a few days. We still have a week before our guests arrive. By then it will no doubt be as balmy as a spring day."

"But—"

He held up his hand. "In the second place, in the unlikely event that the snow is still with us, it should be a simple matter to organize activities that do not require our guests to go outside."

Cecily tossed her head. "Simple? *Simple?* Do you have the slightest idea what goes into planning events for the entire Christmas fortnight?"

He started to speak, but this time it was she who held up her hand. "In the first place, no, of course you do not know. You have never been involved in such matters. In the second place, I cannot imagine a Christmas without carol singers on the doorstep, or shoppers strolling down the Esplanade to gaze into the windows, or Boxing Day without the hunt, or—"

Apparently deciding that a raised hand was not going to silence his wife this time, Baxter folded his newspaper and stood. "My dear Cecily, you are borrowing trouble, as usual. As I said, it is highly unlikely the snow will still be with us in a week. Even if it should be, since you are the Pennyfoot's resourceful and proficient manager, I have no doubt that with the help of such brilliant and creative minds as those of your associates, the inimitable Phoebe Fortescue and the equally incomparable Madeline Prestwick, not to mention your own superior talents, this year's Christmas season will be every bit as memorable as the previous ones. If not more so."

Cecily gazed at him in awe. Baxter was usually sparse with his comments. Such a wordy compliment was rare indeed. Even so, at his words she couldn't help but suppress a shiver. "I sincerely hope not. I would like, for once, a Christmas without a corpse to ruin the festivities."

Baxter grunted. "I heartily agree. Dead bodies are hardly conducive to a merry Christmas. In any case—" Whatever he was about to say was cut off by a timid tapping on the door. Frowning, he called out, "Yes? What is it?"

The door opened, and a pert face beneath a white lace cap peeked in. "Begging your pardon, m'm, Mr. Baxter, but I have a message for you."

Cecily beckoned to the young girl. "Come in, Pansy. You are not disturbing anything."

"Yes, m'm." The maid ventured into the room with a wary eye on Baxter. "It's Police Constable Northcott, m'm. He's in the library, and he's asked to see you."

At the mention of the constable's name, Baxter emitted a low growl of disgust. "That numbskull can find numerous excuses to hang around this establishment at Christmastime. No doubt he is here solely to sample Michel's cooking and Mrs. Chubb's baking."

"Well, he's a little early for that." Cecily glanced at the calendar hanging over the marble mantelpiece. "Mrs. Chubb won't be making mince pies for at least another day or so." She smiled at Pansy, who had retreated at Baxter's grousing. "Did the constable say why he needed to speak to me?"

"No, m'm. He did say, though, that it was a matter of the utmost importance."

Baxter's scornful snort sent her back another two or three paces.

Cecily frowned at her husband before addressing the maid once more. "Thank you, Pansy. Please tell P.C. Northcott that I will be there in a short while."

She waited until the door had closed behind the maid before saying, "Really, Hugh, do you have to instill the fear of death in the members of our staff?"

The only time she ever used her husband's first name was when she was displeased with him, and he reacted at once by stiffening his back. "Is it my fault the maids have such a feeble disposition that they cringe at every word?"

"They don't cringe when I speak to them."

Baxter abandoned protocol and sat down. Picking up his newspaper, he shook it open with more force than necessary. "Then perhaps you should keep them out of my presence."

Cecily hesitated for a second or two, then walked over to her husband. Gently pushing the newspaper aside, she leaned forward and planted a kiss on his lips. "Whatever happened to your Christmas spirit, my love?"

"It vanished the moment I heard Northcott's name." He heaved such a sigh it lifted a strand of Cecily's hair. "I only hope he is not here on police business. For some odd reason, this time of year seems to attract bad news."

"He's probably here, as you say, on the off chance there's a stray mince pie or sausage roll lying about in the kitchen."

Baxter's frown intensified. "You will remember your promise, I trust?"

She drew back. "How could I possibly forget? You gave up a tremendously exciting career in exchange for it."

He held her gaze for a moment longer, then, seemingly satisfied, raised his newspaper once more. "Well, I'm relieved that it is you who must deal with him and not me."

"So is he, no doubt," Cecily murmured, as she crossed the room to the door. "I'll have Mrs. Chubb send up our midday meal, or would you prefer to eat in the dining room?"

"Too drafty," Baxter muttered. "I vastly prefer eating here by the fire." She was almost out of the door before he added, "With you."

Smiling, she made her way to the staircase and hurried downstairs.

Her smile faded by the time she reached the library. A visit from the constabulary was always unsettling, and she couldn't imagine what was so important as to bring P.C. Northcott to the Pennyfoot before his customary Christmas excursion to the country club's kitchen.

She could only hope, to echo Baxter's ominous words, that it wasn't bad news.

Mrs. Chubb stood in the middle of the kitchen, arms folded across her ample bosom and eyebrows drawn together. Glaring at the three cowering maids in front of her, she demanded, "Whose brilliant idea was it to put clean sheets on the beds without ironing them?"

Two of the maids glanced at the third standing between them, a gangly young woman with earnest eyes and rabbit teeth. She ignored their nudges and stared, speechless and trembling, at the irate housekeeper.

Mrs. Chubb, fast losing patience, raised her voice. "All right, Lizzie. Perhaps you'd care to explain why you put wrinkled sheets on the beds in three of our guest bedrooms?"

Lizzie ran her tongue over her lips, stammered a few indistinct words, and then lapsed once more into silence.

Mrs. Chubb raised her chin. "What did you say?"

"She said she thought it would save time," one of the other maids offered.

"Ho, indeed." Mrs. Chubb uncrossed her arms and dug her fists into her hips. "Well, listen to me, young lady. Your time-saving efforts means that the beds will have to be stripped, the sheets ironed, and the beds made up again. Now, tell me, is that saving time?"

Lizzie stared down at her shoe and traced a pattern with her toe on the tiled floor.

"So guess who's going to give up her afternoon off to get those sheets ironed and back where they belong."

Lizzie made a soft sound in the back of her throat.

"We have less than a week to get this place ready for our Christmas guests. So far we're running behind by almost that much. I expect extra effort from all of you, and that does not mean cutting corners. The Pennyfoot has a reputation to uphold, and if it means we all give up our time off to be ready for Christmas, then that's what we'll do. Do I make myself abundantly clear?"

A chorus of "Yes, Mrs. Chubb," answered her, and the housekeeper nodded. "Then be off with you." Just before the door closed behind the last maid's back, she called out, "Lizzie, I want to see those sheets perfectly ironed without a single crease."

"Bloody good luck with that."

The housekeeper swung around to face the voice that had spoken from the pantry. Leaning against the doorjamb, the sturdy young woman grinned. "Them flipping twits don't know how to warm a bleeding iron, let alone use one."

"Gertie Brown McBride!" Mrs. Chubb wagged a finger at

her chief housemaid. "I thought we'd agreed that you'd stop swearing for Christmas. You promised me."

Gertie shoved herself away from the doorway and tucked a thick strand of her black hair back under her cap. "It ain't Christmas yet, is it, and besides, I said I'd *try* to stop swearing. Doesn't mean I'll be able to bloody do it, does it."

The housekeeper thinned her lips. "I trust you'll try a lot harder than this. Madam's expecting some really important guests this year for Christmas."

Gertie raised her eyebrows. "Like who?"

"Never you mind who. You'll find out soon enough. Just watch your p's and q's, and for goodness' sake, Gertie, mind your mouth. If Mr. Baxter catches you swearing he'll throw a pink fit."

Gertie pouted. "It's not swearing. It's just the way I talk."

"Well, it sounds like swearing to me, and to everyone else who's within earshot. So watch it."

"I've been talking like this since I was a tot, and it's blinking hard to change it now."

Mrs. Chubb shook her head. She'd been having the same argument with Gertie for years, and she was no closer to winning it than she had been at the beginning, when a scruffy, big-boned, foul-mouthed child had shown up at the back door of the Pennyfoot begging for a job.

True, Gertie had made an effort since then, and had somewhat tempered the curses that sprinkled her conversation. There were still times, however, when she offended some of the more fastidious guests, and when word of it got back to Mr. Baxter, he not only scolded Gertie, he called

Mrs. Chubb to task for not controlling her rebellious house-maid.

Mrs. Chubb did not like being chastised. Especially when it was none of her fault. Gertie had to hold her tongue or Mrs. Chubb was fully prepared to wash the young woman's mouth out with soap.

The fact that the housemaid towered over her and out-weighed her by at least a stone did nothing to deter the housekeeper. Propriety had to be served at all costs. Even if it was an uphill battle with Gertie McBride.

P.C. Northcott stood with his back to the fire when Cecily entered the library. Hands behind his back, he was as close to the leaping flames as he could get without scorching his uniform. His domed helmet lay on the armchair next to him, together with a pair of worn leather gloves.

He greeted Cecily with a gruff, "Good morning, Mrs. Baxter. I trust you are well?"

Cecily eyed him with a touch of sympathy. His red nose and cheeks bore testimony to the bitter wind off the ocean. "Quite well. Thank you, Sam. And you?"

"A bit chilly, m'm. Can't feel me toes."

"It does look dreadfully wintry out there." Cecily looked at the tall windows that overlooked the rose garden. "I haven't seen this much snow in quite some time."

"Makes it a bit 'ard to ride me bike. That it does." The constable sniffed and drew a crumpled white handkerchief from his pocket. Burying his nose in it, he blew, producing a sound rather like that of a bad-tempered elephant.

Cecily winced. "I'll have Mrs. Chubb send up a drop of brandy. That might help warm you."

Northcott beamed and stuffed the handkerchief back in his pocket. "Awfully good of you, m'm, I'm sure."

"My pleasure, Sam." Cecily walked over to the bellpull and gave it a tug, then seated herself on a vacant armchair. "What else can I do for you today?"

Northcott sat down heavily and jumped up again just as swiftly. Tossing the helmet to one side, he muttered, "Forgot that was there." He sat down again, much more gingerly this time. "I'm here to ask for an h'enormous favor, m'm. I wouldn't be 'ere if I weren't desperate, and I have to ask you to be completely discreet about all this, if you know what I mean. No one can know I asked you, especially the h'inspector."

At the mention of Inspector Cranshaw, Cecily cringed. It was no secret to anyone that the dour police inspector would dearly love to shut down the country club.

The Pennyfoot had started out as a hotel, owned and run by Cecily, and much of its success had been due to the secret card rooms situated beneath the wine cellar.

Those rooms had entertained some of the most influential aristocrats in the country, including royalty. Patrons had enjoyed not only gambling to their hearts' content, but also dallying with damsels in the boudoirs, secure in the knowledge that their indiscretions would be kept strictly within the walls of the Pennyfoot Hotel.

Inspector Cranshaw was aware that all was not aboveboard under Cecily's reign, but without the proof he needed he was helpless to act upon it. He had vowed many times to close her down, and Cecily had no doubt that he waited with an eagle's eye for an opportunity to do so.

Now that the Pennyfoot was a country club, and licensed for card games, the inspector had lost his trump card. Cecily knew, however, that he still harbored resentment for the times she had outwitted him, and would stop at nothing to extract his revenge, should the chance arise.

"You have nothing to fear in that respect," she assured the anxious-looking constable. "I avoid contact with Inspector Cranshaw as much as possible. So, tell me, what is the favor?"

Northcott took out his handkerchief again and trumpeted into it before jamming it back in his pocket. He opened his mouth to speak, coughed, wiped his forehead as if he were now overly warm, and then cleared his throat.

Cecily watched all this with growing uneasiness. Whatever it was Sam Northcott wanted from her, it was apparently costing him a great deal to request it. What was more, she had a nasty feeling that it was about to cost her a great deal to accommodate him.

CHAPTER

❊ 2 ❊

"Well, m'm," Northcott began at last, "it's like this. I—" He broke off when a sharp tap on the door interrupted him.

Cecily called out, and a moment later the door opened. Gertie stuck her head inside and sent the constable a broad wink, which instantly sent him into a fit of coughing. "You sent for me, m'm?"

"Yes, Gertie. Police Constable Northcott would like a glass of brandy."

"Yes, m'm. Coming up right away." Gertie grinned at the red-faced policeman and withdrew her head.

"Very kind of you, m'm, I'm sure," Northcott muttered, once more fishing his handkerchief out of his pocket.

Cecily waited until the constable had everything under control again before prompting him with a polite, "You were saying?"

"Ah, yes, well, I was coming to that." Northcott harrumphed a couple of times, then said hoarsely, "I gather you've heard about young Jimmy Taylor?"

Cecily frowned. "Jimmy? The delivery boy from Rickman's Dairy? What about him?"

Northcott cleared his throat. "I'm sorry to h'inform you that he was found dead alongside his horse and cart last Sunday."

"Great heavens!" She gulped a couple of times, a hand at her throat. "I had no idea. That poor lad. He was so young. What happened to him?"

Northcott got a pained expression on his face, rather as if he urgently needed to use the facilities. "He was struck in the 'ead by a sharp object, namely a rock. The doctor didn't think that was what killed him, however."

"Then what did cause his death?"

"He fell and hit his head again on the wheel hub. Broke his neck, didn't he. That's what killed him."

Cecily was getting a nasty feeling in the pit of her stomach. "Where exactly did this rock come from?"

"Ah well, that's the thing, isn't it." Northcott ran a finger around the edge of his starched collar. "Dr. Prestwick is quite sure someone threw it at the lad, which makes the perpetrator responsible for Jimmy's death. We just don't know the identity of that person. Not at present, anyhow."

"I see." Actually, to be precise, she didn't see. It wasn't like Sam Northcott to come and inform her when a crime had been committed. He usually did his best to keep such things from her, wary of the inspector finding out about her "constant interference in police business," as he called it.

The fact that her "interference" invariably ended with

her solving the case and therefore enhancing Northcott's reputation with the inspector seemed to escape the constable, though he was always grudgingly grateful for her efforts.

The only reason she could think of as to why Sam Northcott was telling her about Jimmy was that his death somehow affected her, though she couldn't imagine why.

"I didn't know Jimmy all that well," she said, feeling her way. "I barely spoke to him. I'm dreadfully sorry to hear of his death, of course. His family must be devastated."

"They are, m'm. Devastated."

She waited through another long pause, wondering where all this was leading.

"Ah . . . that's not all, m'm."

Now she was becoming more than a little uneasy. "Then tell me, Sam. Why are you here? Why are you telling me about this dreadful incident?"

"There's been another murder, m'm. Up there on Putney Downs."

Her fingers clenched in her lap. "Go on."

"A passerby found him, lying on the path. Frozen stiff, he was. It were Thomas Willow, the shoemaker."

She shook her head. "I'm sorry, I've never met the man. I believe Baxter might have known him, but why—"

"He were whipped to death, Mrs. Baxter."

Shocked anew, her voice rose. "*Whipped?* Who would do such a thing?"

"There again, we don't know who did it. We do know, 'owever, that he was killed with Jimmy Taylor's whip."

A cold chill brushed across the back of Cecily's neck. "You think they were killed by the same person."

"Yes, m'm. It certainly looks that way. Especially since both victims had a gold angel stuck to their forehead."

She stared at him, wondering if she'd heard him correctly. "A gold angel?"

"Yes, m'm. Those little gold stamps that you lick and then stick 'em on Christmas cards? Well, both Jimmy and Thomas had one stuck to their foreheads."

"Oh, my."

"Down at the station they're calling the murderer the Christmas Angel."

Cecily winced. "That's a rather incongruous name for a killer."

"Yes, m'm. I don't think they mean anything by it. It's just a matter of reference, that's all. But there were something else you should know."

Given that she was already intrigued by the case, Cecily wasn't at all certain she wanted to know more.

Northcott, however, was already launching into his next revelation. "The killer left another mark behind." The constable leaned forward, dropping his voice to a conspiratorial whisper. "This is something the constabulary isn't letting on to the public, so I'd appreciate it if you'd keep mum about it, m'm, so to speak."

"Of course." Now wild horses wouldn't drag her away. "What is it?"

"Well, it seems that the perpetrator took a lock of hair from his victims before he left."

"A lock of hair?"

"Yes, m'm. Cut off nice and neat, it was."

Cecily drew in a sharp breath. How she would have loved to dig her teeth into this one. It took all her willpower to say

15

briskly, "Well, it sounds as if you have quite a case on your hands, Sam. I don't see, however, how this is any of my business."

"Well, I was coming to that, m'm."

The disquiet she'd been harboring ever since she'd walked into the room now intensified. "What exactly does all this have to do with me?"

"Well, that's the favor, you see." Once more Northcott dragged his handkerchief from his pocket and blew his nose. "It's like this, Mrs. B. As you know—" Once more he was interrupted by a tap on the door.

This time Gertie barely waited for a summons before opening the door. After bowing her head at Cecily, she carried the tray over to Northcott as if she were bearing a crown for the king.

Aware of the disdain the maids felt toward the inept constable, Cecily pursed her lips and hoped her chief housemaid wouldn't show him any disrespect in her presence. For then she'd be forced to reprimand Gertie in front of him.

To her relief, Gertie offered the brandy without comment and, apart from an overly enthusiastic curtsey when he took the glass, left the room without offending the man.

Nevertheless, Northcott had to resort to mopping his brow with his handkerchief before continuing. "H'anyway, as I was saying, as you know, Mrs. B., me and the missus always go away for the Christmas season. Well, not always, since we didn't go last year, what with the in-laws coming here for a change. Blinking disaster that were, too, m'm, if you'll pardon the h'expression."

"Yes, yes," Cecily said, finally succumbing to impatience. "Do get on with it, Sam. Why are you here?"

"I'm coming to that, aren't I." Sam fidgeted for a moment or two. "The inspector is tied up with some important job at Scotland Yard and wants me to take care of this case. He says as how I can't leave Badgers End until the killer is h'apprehended."

"I see," Cecily said yet again. Now she was, indeed, beginning to understand, and she didn't like what she was afraid was coming.

"Well, me and the other constables have been looking into it, and so far we've come up with nothing. If I don't find the killer in the next few days, I'm going to have to tell the missus that I can't go to London with her. She's going to raise merry hell if I do that."

"Yes," Cecily murmured. "I suppose she might."

"Not might, Mrs. B. She will. No doubt about it. I'll never hear the last of it. She'll be carrying on all year long until next Christmas, that's a fact."

"Well, I'm sorry to hear that, Sam, but I really don't know what I can do about it."

The constable fiddled with his helmet for a moment or two, then said in a rush, "I was rather hoping that you would help me out a bit. You've always been so good at finding out things, and people will talk to you, where they won't talk to me. I thought if you could just ask questions here and there, you know, like you usually do. . . ." He let his voice trail off, leaving Cecily no recourse but to answer.

There it was. The favor she'd been hoping he wasn't going to ask, fearing all the time that it was exactly what he had in mind.

This was the very first time Sam had ever asked for her help, and she was flattered. Intrigued by the gold angel stamps and missing locks of hair, she was also sorely tempted.

There was only one problem. After a lengthy and sometimes heated argument, Baxter had refused an important position abroad in order to allow her to remain in Badgers End as the Pennyfoot's manager. In exchange, she had promised never to get involved with another murder case.

It pained her a great deal to refuse Sam, especially since it meant he would most likely have to forgo his Christmas visit to London. More so, because she was already interested enough in the case to do some snooping, and most of all, because the threat of a murderer afoot in Badgers End could once more put a dampener on the Pennyfoot's Christmas season.

A promise was a promise, however, and she had broken enough of them in the past that it had taken a great deal of persuasion on her part for Baxter to accept the compromise.

"I'm dreadfully sorry, Sam." She squirmed at the dismay on the constable's face, but nevertheless pressed on. "My duties here in the country club prevent me from taking on any extra activities at present. I'm afraid you will have to hunt down this killer without me."

Sam shook his head in bewilderment. "But, Mrs. B., you've always jumped in before. Sometimes, or most of the time, you've done it despite the fact that I've asked you not to h'interfere. Now I'm asking you to help me with the sanction of the constabulary, albeit without the knowledge of the inspector. I don't understand."

She would have liked to enlighten him, but to admit to Sam Northcott that her hands were tied by a promise to her husband was utterly unthinkable. "I'm so sorry, Sam. If you come across any clues, I might be able to help you untangle them, but as far as questioning people and actively investigating, I'm afraid it's out of the question."

The constable's movements were slow and deliberate as he got to his feet, straightened his tunic, and reached for his helmet. "I'm sorry I inconvenienced you, m'm. I'll be off now."

Cecily followed him to the door, still murmuring apologies. "Perhaps you'd care to stop by the kitchen?" she offered, as an attempt to make up for disappointing him. "I'm sure Mrs. Chubb will be able to find something delicious for you."

He wavered, obviously torn between making a dignified exit and savoring some of Mrs. Chubb's mouthwatering baking. The baking won, and with a nod of thanks, he hurried off to the kitchen.

Cecily sat for some time after he'd left, gazing into the flickering flames from the coals. Once more violence had struck in the village. Fortunately, at least this time it hadn't happened inside the walls of the Pennyfoot. Yet.

She had to wonder what would happen if someone else died by another's hand and under her roof. How could she possibly stay out of it then?

Worse, how could she possibly break such a significant promise to her husband? He had given up so much so that she could stay in her beloved Pennyfoot. He would never forgive her if she betrayed him this time. All she could hope was that the killer had achieved his evil purpose and left the village. For if he still lingered there, she could envision all kinds of trouble ahead.

"I don't think we're ever going to be ready for Christmas," Pansy said, as she carefully fitted a serviette into its silver ring and laid it on the bleached white tablecloth. "Usually Mrs. Prestwick has all the decorations up by now."

Gertie gave a last critical glance around the dining room to make sure everything was in order. Although there were only a handful of guests in the hotel until the Christmas rush, every table in the dining room had to be laid as if expecting a visitor to be seated there.

Since every meal was laid differently, that meant clearing off the unused cutlery and china and replacing it with still more unused utensils, glasses, and dishes, all of which had to be washed and put away before being brought out again the next day.

Gertie had never seen the purpose of all that. If nobody was going to sit at the table, why go to all the trouble of putting clean dishes and silverware on it every day? Bloody stupid, it was. All that work for nothing. She had enough to do without having to blinking wash clean dishes and knives and forks.

Of course, when she'd told Chubby that, using her usual colorful expressions, all she'd got in answer was a box around the ears. Fat lot of good it did to complain.

"Are you all right?"

Pansy's anxious voice jerked her out of her thoughts. "Yea, I'm all right. Just thinking how much work we've got ahead of us with Christmas and all."

"Still missing Dan?" Pansy straightened a pair of silver condiment shakers and stood back to gauge her work.

"Nah." Gertie snorted. "I don't ever think of him anymore. After he went off to London I put him out of my mind." That wasn't exactly the truth. She'd missed the fun-loving, impulsive young man dreadfully the first few months, and the pain only gradually faded away until she could now say she didn't miss him and really mean it.

"You could have gone with him, you know. He wanted you to go."

"What? Leave my home and drag my twins all the way up to the city where they don't know nobody and there's no beach to play on and nothing but busy streets and all that smoke and noise? I don't think so. No man is worth all that. Even if he did have money."

"You could have lived in luxury up there."

"Yeah, and been unhappy. It would never have lasted."

Pansy picked up her tray of serviettes and moved over to the next table. "What about Clive? Would you go with him?"

For some strange reason, Gertie felt her stomach clench at the mention of the Pennyfoot's handyman. She managed a light laugh. "Clive? Whatever makes you think he'd ask?"

Pansy shrugged. "Everyone knows he's sweet on you."

"Everyone except me, then."

"Go on with you." Pansy looked up, her dark eyes sparkling with amusement. "You must know he likes you."

Gertie pulled in a deep breath. "Clive and me are just friends, that's all. If I ever get cozy with another man, it will be with someone what can provide for me and the twins in a manner much better than what I got now."

Pansy suddenly looked sad. "Does he know that?"

"We haven't discussed it."

"Maybe you should. It's not nice to lead a man on."

"I'm not leading him on," Gertie began hotly, then shut her mouth. Maybe she was, without realizing it. She knew Clive liked her, but as a friend. He'd never said anything to make her think differently. Maybe she was taking his friendship for granted. He was so good with the kids and all, and she really liked being in his company. That didn't mean she wanted to spend the rest of her life with him.

"Well," Pansy said, laying the serviettes neatly by the place settings, "I think you should make it clear to him how you feel. Just in case he should have any strong feelings for you."

Gertie glared at Pansy. "When I want your advice, missy, I'll bleeding ask for it. I know what I'm doing, and I ain't doing nothing wrong, so there."

"All right, all right." Pansy held up her hands. "I was just saying, that's all."

"Well, don't say."

"All right, I won't." Pansy tilted her head to one side and gave her a sly look. "I heard he was building a sleigh. A big one, pulled by a horse."

"He's already built it." A little stab of excitement caught Gertie under the ribs. "He's taking me and the twins for a ride on it on my afternoon off."

"Lucky you." Pansy pouted. "All I get to do with Samuel is walk the dog into the woods and back."

Gertie grinned. "Yeah, but I bet you have more fun in those woods with Samuel than I would ever want or need with Clive."

Pansy's cheeks glowed pink. "How do you know?"

"I can tell by the soppy look on your face when you come back." She glanced at the clock. "Blimey, we'd better get going. We've still got potatoes to peel for supper, and if Michel doesn't get his bloody cauliflower washed he'll be crashing saucepans around again."

She headed for the door, still feeling a little guilty about her friendship with Clive. It would not only devastate her to lose that companionship, the twins would never forgive her if she said something to break up what they had.

Still, she didn't want him thinking that their relationship was headed for something more permanent. Maybe she should sound him out and try to find out if he was expecting more from her than she was prepared to give.

Drat Pansy and her unwanted advice. Gertie stomped down the hallway to the kitchen, her enthusiasm for the sleigh ride fading fast.

CHAPTER
❄ 3 ❄

That evening Cecily waited until Baxter was settled in front of the fire with the latest copy of *Lloyd's Weekly* before putting down her book. "Do you have a moment to talk?"

Baxter eyed her over the top of the newspaper. "Is it bad news?"

"Not directly, though it is disturbing."

Baxter sighed, and lowered the newspaper. "Very well, we might as well get it over with."

Somewhat wary, she related her conversation with P.C. Northcott.

Baxter said nothing until she was finished talking. Then he shook the newspaper, raised it in front of his face, and murmured, "Well, I'm thankful you remembered your promise."

She wasn't sure why, but his indifference stung. "It wasn't easy."

He lowered the newspaper again. "Nor was it easy to refuse a position that would have been not only financially rewarding but immensely stimulating."

"Yes, I suppose—"

"To be charged with the installation and launching of hotels in various locations abroad was the most exciting opportunity I have ever been offered."

"Yes, dear, I do understand—"

"Only your obvious reluctance to accompany me on the venture could have persuaded me to turn it down."

Frowning, she muttered, "I am not questioning your sacrifice in order to please me. This is, however, the very first time Sam Northcott has openly asked for my help, and only dire circumstances would have prompted him to do so. I felt honored that he considered me capable of the task."

Obviously sensing an argument brewing, Baxter folded the newspaper and laid it on the arm of the chair. "Apart from the fact that the constable is anxious to visit his relatives for Christmas as usual, what is it about the case that so desperately requires your help?"

Cecily pursed her lips and stared at the smoldering coals in the fireplace. "I think he's afraid that we have a serial killer in the village, since both Jimmy Taylor and Thomas Willow were apparently killed by the same person."

"If you remember, you thought we had a serial killer in the Pennyfoot last year. It turned out he was killing people simply to throw you off the scent."

She threw him an uneasy glance. "Are you suggesting this could be the same scenario?"

"I'm not suggesting anything. I'm merely pointing out that you can't assume anything—something that Sam Northcott apparently hasn't learned yet."

She sighed. "He does have a tendency to jump to conclusions."

"That's not his only tendency." Baxter tapped the newspaper with his fingers. "I'm surprised Cranshaw isn't in charge of the case."

"So am I. There has to be something of vital importance to keep him in London at such a time."

"Nevertheless, I think Northcott has a blasted cheek asking you to help him do his duty."

"As I said, he must be desperate." She turned her gaze from the fireplace to her husband and found him watching her with a wary look in his gray eyes. "It *is* rather an intriguing case. I feel very sorry for Jimmy's family. How sad to lose someone so young. And then there's Thomas Willow, the shoemaker. I seem to remember you mentioning his name?"

"He made my last pair of shoes. Dratted nuisance, that. Now I shall have to go into Wellercombe to get new shoes fitted."

"What was he like?"

Baxter shrugged. "Old man, gray hair, gnarled hands. It amazed me how he could use those twisted fingers to make such remarkable shoes. He was a bit of a grouch, but I can't imagine why anyone would want to kill the old goat."

"He doesn't sound much like Jimmy Taylor."

"He wasn't. Couldn't have been more opposite, if you ask me."

"That's very strange."

Baxter's eyebrows drew together. "What is?"

"I just wonder what it was they had in common to cause their violent deaths." Cecily returned her gaze to the fireplace. "It would seem, from what Sam told me, that Jimmy's death was unintentional, yet someone used Jimmy's whip to beat an old man to death. Not only that, there's the gold angels and the missing locks of hair. There has to be a connection somewhere."

Baxter sounded worried when he answered. "I trust I don't have to remind you of your promise?"

"No, darling, you certainly don't."

"Glad to hear it."

Cecily sighed. This was one promise she wished heartily she hadn't had to make. For somewhere deep inside her, she had the uneasy feeling that she might break it.

The following morning, as she crossed the lobby on her way to the office, she heard the desk clerk calling her name.

Bowed at the shoulders and fast losing his gray hair, Philip seemed to age every time she saw him. His wrinkled forehead gave him a permanent frown, but he seemed even more anxious than usual as she approached the desk.

Still unsettled by her conversation with P.C. Northcott the day before, Cecily felt her nerves tightening. "What is it, Philip? Not bad news, I hope?"

Philip's eyes were clouded with apprehension. "I'm not sure, m'm. It's a telegram." His hand shook as he offered her the wrinkled yellow envelope.

Cecily smothered a cry of dismay. The news had to be something quite disastrous to arrive in such an exceptional fashion.

Her first thought was of her two sons, both abroad. Had

something dreadful happened to one of them? She stared at the envelope, too petrified to open it.

"Would you like me to read it, m'm?"

Philip's tremulous voice jolted her out of her trance. "No, thank you, Philip. I shall take it upstairs to Mr. Baxter. He can open it." If it contained the awful news she feared, she wanted her husband by her side when she heard it.

Her hasty return to her suite surprised Baxter, who was in the boudoir engaged in some activity that involved rustling paper. He seemed put out when she burst through the door, and immediately escorted her back to the sitting room, where he sat her down in her favorite armchair.

"Now," he said, smoothing back a lock of gray hair. "Please tell me the cause of all this agitation."

For answer, she held out the envelope, which shook even worse than when Philip had handed it over.

Frowning, Baxter took it from her, turning it over and back again. "What is it?"

"It's a telegram."

"I'm aware of that. What does it say?"

"I don't know. I was too afraid to open it." Her voice broke, and her words came out in a rush. "Oh, Bax, what if something has happened to one of the boys?"

"Hush, now." He stuck his thumb under the flap and slit it open. "You are borrowing trouble again."

She watched him anxiously as he scanned the lines. Her heart skipped when she saw his expression darken, and he swore under his breath.

"What is it?" She leaned forward, her heart now pounding like a sledgehammer.

"Are we never to escape this dratted curse?" Baxter thrust

the piece of paper into her hands. "Here. Read it for yourself."

She read it out loud, relief blended with dismay. "Cancel booking. Stop. Wife refuses to spend Christmas with murderer on the loose. Stop. With regret, Lord Chattenham. Stop. Oh, no!"

Baxter cursed again. "How the blazes did he get the news? Northcott only told you about the deaths yesterday."

"I have no idea." She stared at the faded letters pasted on the paper. "That's four people less for Christmas. Oh, Bax, what if more people do this? We'll be ruined!"

"Blasted cowards. We've had murders here before. It's never stopped people coming here."

"They don't usually get forewarning," Cecily reminded him. "What I don't understand is that this time, it had nothing to do with the hotel. Why should something that happened in the village scare them away?"

"I suppose they're worried the Pennyfoot might be next on the killer's list." Baxter began pacing back and forth. "I have to admit, with our record, it's a viable concern."

"Piffle." Cecily got up and walked over to the window. Staring outside at the wintry lawns, she murmured, "And I was worried about the snow. This is a vastly more serious problem."

"We'll just have to hope that idiot Northcott and his inept bobbies can find this killer and put him behind bars before the rest of our guest list evaporates."

Feeling a glimmer of hope, Cecily turned to face him. "He could certainly use some help, don't you think?"

Baxter's frown deepened. "I hope you're not contemplating what I suspect you are contemplating."

Cecily approached him, hands held out in appeal. "Bax, darling, I know I gave you my solemn promise, but this is an emergency. If we don't catch this killer soon, more of our guests may decide it would be safer to stay in London for the Christmas season. What if our special guest were to cancel? We'd never live down the scandal."

"He's a prominent London citizen. He can't afford to be perceived a coward."

"He could find some feasible excuse, I'm sure. We simply cannot sit by and do nothing."

"By we, I assume you mean yourself and that traitorous stable manager, Samuel."

Cecily smiled. "Actually, I was rather hoping you would contribute your intelligent opinions and ideas."

Baxter grunted. "You flatter me, my dear, but we both know I have no head for hunting down criminals. That takes a profound understanding of how those people's minds work, and that is something for which you alone have an aptitude."

"Why, thank you, sir!" Pleased with the unexpected compliment, her cheeks warmed.

"The fact remains, however, that the purpose of your promise to me was to keep you out of jeopardy, since you have a propensity to dive into danger without the slightest regard for your safety."

"If I swear to use extreme caution this time?"

He raised an eyebrow at her. "When has *that* ever happened?"

"Please, darling." She caught his hand and held it. "Our entire Christmas season is in jeopardy. At least this time I will have the sanction of the constabulary. Sam Northcott will be close at hand should there be any sign of peril."

Baxter's expression darkened. "That's what concerns me the most."

She smiled. "I shall be quite all right. All the constable needs is for me to ask a few questions in the village. Samuel will be with me, as always, and despite your displeasure at his willingness to help me, you will be the first to admit he is more than capable of taking care of me should the need arise."

She saw his scowl deepen and added hurriedly, "Not that it would, of course. I will make sure of that."

Baxter brushed a weary hand across his brow. "My dear Cecily, you will be the death of me yet. I refused a marvelous opportunity to work abroad so that you could continue your duties here at the Pennyfoot. In exchange, you promised to give me peace of mind by avoiding all contact with police business. Now here you are, proposing to actually assist the constabulary in a murder investigation. Is it any wonder my hair turns whiter by the day?"

Cecily gave him another sheepish smile. "It is very becoming, dear."

"Don't change the subject."

"No, dear." She held out her hands to him again. "What would you have me do? Sit here and do nothing while our guests cancel their bookings one by one?"

"That hasn't happened yet. We have lost only one booking."

"There could well be more."

Baxter raised his chin and stared at the ornate ceiling. "Once more I have been ambushed and overtaken. Very well. If you must. Have Samuel meet me in the library. I want a word with that young man."

"Thank you, darling." She wrapped her arms around his waist and gave him a hug. "I promise I shall use the utmost caution."

He rolled his eyes. "Where have I heard that before?"

She didn't answer him, being that she was already halfway out the door, on her way to call Sam Northcott to offer her services.

Pansy trudged across the courtyard, lifting her skirts clear of the snow that covered her ankles. She'd wrapped her shoulders with a shawl, but the icy wind stung her nose and ears, and she drew the soft woolen cloth over her head.

Snow was pretty, as long as you could look at it through the window of a warm kitchen. Walking through the stuff was not much fun. Her stockings were soaked, as was the hem of her navy blue skirt. Mrs. Chubb wouldn't be happy about that.

Reaching the door of the stables, she wrinkled her nose as the smell of horses invaded her nostrils. Samuel always said he didn't notice it anymore, which was just as well, seeing as how he worked in there most of the day.

He was somewhere at the other end. She could hear his voice, the soothing tones he always used while grooming one of the horses.

As always, her heart beat faster at the sound. Ever since Samuel had declared her to be "his girl," her world had grown bright with promise. Even though he'd impressed upon her that she was still too young for marriage, she was confident that one day she'd stand by his side as his bride, and she was content to wait for that day. No matter how long it took.

Samuel looked up as she drew close, his face splitting into a wide grin. "Hello, beautiful. What brings you in here?"

Pansy caught her breath. "I came to see you, didn't I."

"Well, that's always a pleasure." Samuel gave the horse a final pat and stepped away, rubbing his hands on his breeches. "Got time for a hug?"

"Always." She ran into his arms with a blissful smile. After a moment of pure pleasure, she murmured, "Actually, Mrs. Chubb sent me. Mr. Baxter wants to see you in the library."

Samuel let out a mournful sigh. "And here I thought you came just to be with me."

She tilted her head back to look at him. "I always want to be with you, Samuel."

He answered her with a quick kiss and let her go. "I'd better get over there. Mr. Baxter don't like to be kept waiting." He gently pushed stray hairs out of her eyes with his thumb, and then dashed off, leaving her to follow more slowly.

Somehow, the trip back through the snow seemed a lot less bothersome. In fact, Pansy practically skipped back across the kitchen yard and bumped smack into Gertie, who was on her way out the door with a coal scuttle in each hand.

"Here! What's your bleeding hurry?"

Gertie's scowl was fierce, and Pansy grabbed one of the coal scuttles. "Sorry. I was in a rush to help you, wasn't I."

"Yeah, not bloody likely. You just saw Samuel, didn't you."

Pansy blushed. "How did you know?"

"You got that soppy look on your face again, that's how." Gertie stomped across the yard to the coal shed, leaving Pansy to trail behind her.

Feeling sorry for her friend, Pansy followed her into the dark, musty shed. It was hard to be without someone to love, especially at Christmastime. She ought to know, she'd been through enough Christmases to know what it was like.

She'd watched couples kissing under the mistletoe, or standing close together at the carol-singing ceremony. She'd overheard whispers and shared laughter in the corridors. It had made the loneliness all the more painful.

How lucky she was to have Samuel. Someday, she silently vowed, Gertie would have that companionship again. It would be her Christmas wish for her friend. She'd do her level best to see that it came true.

"I have to go into town to see my dressmaker," Cecily told Samuel when he answered the summons to her office later.

"Yes, m'm. That's the house on Larch Lane, right?"

Cecily picked up her gloves and drew them on. "Actually, Miss Pauline Richards is out of town at present. We will be visiting her assistant, Miss Blanchard, and since her place of residence is quite close to the house where Jimmy Taylor's family lives, I thought we would pay the bereaved family a courtesy visit."

Samuel looked back at her, his eyes gleaming with expectation. "We're on the trail of another murderer, m'm?"

"Ah." Cecily edged around the desk and walked toward him. "I take it you have had a conversation with my husband."

"I have, m'm. Mr. Baxter told me about Jimmy Taylor dying and then that other bloke, the shoemaker, being killed with Jimmy's whip. Strange thing, that."

"It is, indeed."

"I was sort of surprised when Mr. Baxter told me you were going to look into it. I remember you telling me you promised him you wouldn't do that again."

"Yes, well, I did, but then I received a telegram canceling a booking because of the murders. Fortunately Mr. Baxter saw the necessity of solving this case before we endured more empty rooms for Christmas."

"It's not too late to invite someone else, m'm."

Alerted by his tone, Cecily narrowed her eyes. "You had someone in mind?"

Samuel shrugged. "I got a letter from Doris the other day. She seemed sort of down-in-the-mouth. She was talking about how she missed us all at the Pennyfoot, and I just thought, since the room is going to be empty anyway . . ." His voice trailed off as he looked hopefully at her.

"Samuel! That's a wonderful idea! I'll have Philip send her a note before we leave."

"She'll like that, m'm. She misses the days when she was a maid here, and now she's not on the stage anymore, she has more time to think about it."

"Daisy will love to see her, too. I know she misses her twin. It will be good for them to be together for Christmas. Although Daisy has her hands full being nanny to Gertie's twins. I hope she can find time to be with her sister."

"I'm sure they'll manage, m'm."

"Good. Well, we'd better be off. I'm anxious to get on the trail of our murderer."

Samuel gave her a sly look. "Mr. Baxter gave me all sorts of warnings, m'm."

"I imagine he did." Cecily regarded her stable manager, her head tilted to one side. Samuel had, at times in the past, been obliged to ignore Baxter's warnings. "I trust we understand each other in this matter?"

Samuel grinned. "You can count on me, m'm. As always."

"Thank you, Samuel. I never doubted it for a moment." She sailed out the door, leaving him to close it behind them.

CHAPTER

❀ 4 ❀

The assistant dressmaker's house lay on the far side of town. Normally Samuel would have taken the shortcut over Putney Downs, but since the snow had made the path along the cliffs somewhat treacherous, he'd insisted on the long route, taking them through town.

At first Cecily contented herself with watching the shop windows they passed along the Esplanade. The merchants had decorated for Christmas a month earlier, and their displays were a sight to behold.

Glistening snowflakes and stars hung from silver strings, while sparkling colored balls slowly twisted on invisible threads. Toy soldiers in bright red coats marched across one window, jostling for space among stuffed bears and dolls in pretty lace gowns. Another one harbored a dozen snowmen holding lengths of silks and satins, while behind them wide-brimmed hats covered in baubles and ribbons hung from the branches of a leafless tree.

Soon, however, too much bumping and rattling over the frozen streets took its toll, and by the time they reached Caroline Blanchard's cottage Cecily felt as if her neck were trapped in a vise.

She winced as Samuel helped her down from the carriage, and tried to stretch her back while they waited for Miss Blanchard to answer the door.

The seamstress greeted them with a rather stiff smile, as if she wasn't used to stretching her lips. She ushered them into the sitting room, which seemed to have been overtaken by numerous dogs and cats. She had to push two of the cats off armchairs before offering them to her guests.

Cecily's hesitance must have been noted, since Caroline was quick to apologize. Shooing the rest of the animals from the room, she murmured, "Please excuse the disorder. I occasionally pick up stray animals and try to find them a good home." She looked hopefully at Cecily. "I don't suppose . . . ?"

"Thank you, no," Cecily said hurriedly. "Animals are not allowed in the country club."

"The cats are good mousers." Caroline picked up a ginger striped cat and cradled it in her arms. "This one is very good at catching mice and killing them."

Cecily shuddered. "I'm sure it is, but no, thank you all the same."

"I think that's very commendable, what you're doing with the strays," Samuel assured the seamstress, much to Cecily's surprise. Her stable manager wasn't usually so forthcoming with strangers.

Caroline seemed unaffected by the compliment, however, and barely acknowledged him. In fact, she seemed discomforted by his presence and kept her distance.

With her auburn hair and creamy skin, she would have been a comely young woman were it not for her constant squinting, which Cecily attributed to a problem with the young woman's eyesight.

Even so, Samuel seemed quite taken with her, and put himself out to be at his most charming.

Since her stable manager rarely showed interest in female acquaintances, at least when in her company, Cecily found his behavior rather intriguing.

When Miss Blanchard grudgingly offered to bring a tray of tea and scones, Samuel leapt to his feet and insisted on carrying the tray for her. Although she thanked him, she seemed none too pleased by the gesture, though Samuel appeared not to notice.

Well aware of Pansy's passion for the young man, Cecily began to feel somewhat concerned. It seemed as though her stable manager wasn't quite as committed as Pansy would like.

She felt relieved when Miss Blanchard invited her to retire to another room where she could be measured for the alterations. Leaving Samuel huddled by the fire, Cecily picked up her gown and followed the slender Caroline down the hallway.

The seamstress led her into a room where several ball gowns hung from the picture rail. One in particular caught her eye—a marvelous creation of shot silk, in shades of maroon and black. Gleaming silver beads traced an intricate pattern down the bodice, and the neckline was trimmed in black lace. It was quite the most spectacular gown Cecily had ever seen.

"That gown is breathtaking," she said, as Caroline prepared to leave.

The seamstress nodded. "It's an original from Paris. Unfortunately it had a torn hem and was quite difficult to repair."

"I imagine it was, though I have no doubt you managed it." Cecily laid her gown on a chair. "Pauline tells me your needlework is quite extraordinary."

"Ms. Richards is very kind." Caroline opened the door. "I'll leave you to change into your gown," she said, and quietly closed the door behind her.

Left alone, Cecily took a moment to look around. The small parlor, with its poky little fireplace, tiny windows, and low ceiling, felt oppressive. An unpleasant odor reminded her of something, but she couldn't quite place it. Maybe it was the kitchen, late at night, when Mrs. Chubb burned chicken bones in the stove. The ashes did wonders for the rose garden in the spring, but the smell was atrocious. This smell, however, was more likely the dogs' wet fur, no doubt heated after running around in the snow.

A rather unusual sculpture graced the wall over the fireplace. It looked like a wooden wagon wheel, with brightly colored jewels in the shape of cats studding the rim where the spokes met. Captivated by the whimsical design, Cecily smiled as she moved over to another wall.

Several portraits hung there, and she moved closer to study them. Almost all of them were of cats or dogs, though one of them showed a fine-looking horse standing proudly in a field, head held high. A lover of horses herself, Cecily admired the picture for a moment or two before hurriedly donning the ball gown.

Caroline entered just as Cecily finished buttoning the bodice. Gazing at the ivory silk folds trimmed with coffee-colored lace, the seamstress murmured, "It's a lovely gown."

"Thank you. It does need a tuck or two taken out, though, as you can see."

Caroline frowned. "Maybe a smidgen at the waist, and the bodice does appear to be a little tight. I can let out the side seams to correct that."

"Thank goodness." Cecily patted the skirt. "I love the gown and I really don't have time to order another. I seem to have grown in all the wrong places this last year."

"Unfortunately age has a way of doing that to us."

Cecily raised an eyebrow, but refrained from commenting. Someone as young as Caroline Blanchard had no idea what it was to battle the changes the years wrought on a woman.

After the young woman had taken the measurements she needed, Cecily was once more left alone to change clothes. Fully dressed again, she made her way back to the living room, where Samuel was engaged in a somewhat one-sided conversation with the seamstress.

Seated across from him, the young woman's cheeks were flushed, though her expression when Cecily entered was more of relief than interest in Samuel's opinions.

Samuel, on the other hand, looked disappointed as he rose to his feet.

Cecily smiled at Caroline. "We must be on our way. I have another call to make before returning to the Pennyfoot."

"Oh, of course." She got up and led them to the door. "I will have your gown ready in a few days."

Samuel glanced at Cecily. "I can come by and pick up the gown for you, m'm."

Cecily hesitated, reluctant to foster what appeared to be a budding attraction for her stable manager. Then, deciding it was none of her business, and Pansy would simply have to fend for herself, she said lightly, "We shall see. Thank you, Miss Blanchard. Good day to you."

Samuel failed to comment as he handed her back into the carriage, and Cecily wisely held her tongue as well. If the young man was smitten with the seamstress, so be it. Though judging from what she had seen, Caroline Blanchard did not seem eager to reciprocate. If that were so, Samuel was doomed for disillusionment.

She soon forgot about the problem, however, as they neared the house where Jimmy Taylor's family lived.

The cottage was in darkness, the windows shrouded with green velvet curtains. The woman who answered the door looked as if she hadn't slept in quite a while. Her white face was drawn, with deep lines at the corners of her eyes and mouth. She wore a plain black frock, with a black lace cap over her graying curls.

Cecily felt a surge of sympathy for the woman, and quickly apologized for intruding. "I didn't know your son very well," she said, after Samuel had introduced them, "but he delivered almost daily to the Pennyfoot Country Club. I wanted to pay my respects and say how dreadfully sorry I am for your loss."

"Very kind of you, I'm sure," Mrs. Taylor murmured. "Won't you come in?"

HERALD OF DEATH

Following the woman into the sitting room, Cecily saw a large portrait of the young lad on the mantelpiece, bordered by a fluttering candle on either side. He looked happy in the picture, smiling broadly to show a row of uneven teeth.

She paused in front of it, shaking her head. "Such a dreadful thing to happen to one so young."

"He didn't deserve to die that way," Mrs. Taylor said, her voice breaking.

"No, indeed." Cecily seated herself on a worn sofa, while Samuel chose to hover near the door, one anxious eye on the clock. "Who do you think could have done such an awful thing?"

Mrs. Taylor sank onto the edge of an armchair. "I can't imagine. Jimmy wasn't always easy to get along with, but he had some good friends, and his customers always treated him well." She stared at the leaping flames in the fireplace. "Of course, there was Basil."

Her interest caught, Cecily leaned forward. "Basil?"

Mrs. Taylor nodded. "Basil Baker. Both he and Jimmy were sweet on the same girl. Gracie Peterson. Jimmy won her, though. They were talking about getting married and all." The woman's eyes filled with tears. "That won't happen now."

"I'm so sorry." Cecily paused to give the other woman time to compose herself, then added, "I imagine Basil was quite upset when Jimmy and Gracie made marriage plans."

Mrs. Taylor gave her a sharp look. "You're not suggesting that Basil killed my Jimmy? They might have been rivals, Mrs. Baxter, but Basil is not a murderer."

Cecily frowned. "It was my understanding that Jimmy's death was an accident. True, someone threw a rock at him,

43

but it was the fall and blow to his head on a wheel shaft that killed him, was it not? Isn't it possible that Basil, in his disappointment, lost his temper and threw the rock without meaning to cause Jimmy's death?"

Jimmy's mother briefly closed her eyes. "Possible, but not likely, to my way of thinking. Whoever threw that rock did so with enough force to knock our Jimmy right off his feet. I think that monster meant to kill my boy, and I shan't rest until I know who did this evil deed. I just can't bring myself to believe it was Basil. Those two were such good friends before that girl came along."

She showed signs of breaking down again, and Cecily rose to her feet. "I don't want to upset you further, Mrs. Taylor. I think I would like a word with Basil, however. He might be able to shed some light on this tragedy. Perhaps you can tell me where to find him?"

Mrs. Taylor looked up, her eyes wary. "You won't be getting him in any trouble, will you?"

"Let's just say I'd like to know why this happened."

The other woman gave her an address, and Samuel nodded. "I know where that is, m'm."

"Very well, then." Cecily walked to the door. "Rest assured, Mrs. Taylor, should I get at the truth, you will be the first to know."

Stepping outside, she took a good long breath of the chilly sea air. It was good to be on the trail of a killer again. When she'd given her promise to Baxter, she'd given up all thought of chasing down another murderer.

Her husband simply failed to understand that it wasn't so much catching a criminal that gave her so much satisfaction, it was bringing closure to the people left behind—the mourners, who needed answers in order to regain some sense of peace.

"Come, Samuel," she said, walking briskly toward the waiting carriage. "We have more questions to ask before we can go home."

"Mr. Baxter will be waiting for you to join him for the midday meal," Samuel reminded her. "He won't be pleased if you keep him waiting."

Cecily sighed. "I suppose you're right. It wouldn't do to upset him this early on in the investigation. Very well, then, Samuel. Home it is, and we will continue this quest this afternoon."

She settled back in the carriage, her thoughts replaying her conversation with Mrs. Taylor. It would be most interesting to find out exactly how Basil felt about losing his sweetheart to Jimmy. Even more interesting was how Gracie Peterson fit into the picture.

Cecily felt a small tug of excitement. She was really looking forward to talking to Basil Baker.

When she arrived back at the Pennyfoot, Gertie met her with the news that Phoebe Carter-Holmes Fortescue and her husband were in the library awaiting her return. Cecily had no recourse but to invite them to join her and Baxter for the midday meal.

This did little to improve her husband's sour mood, and throughout the meal Cecily struggled to keep Colonel Fortescue's attention away from him.

The colonel had an unfortunate habit of launching into one of his tedious war memoirs, thus sending his audience into a near stupor before his long-suffering wife managed to halt the saga. Given that the colonel, thanks to his war experiences, was also somewhat touched in the head, Baxter's tolerance of the gentleman was limited, at best.

Phoebe, as usual, was full of her plans for the annual Christmas pageant—a pantomime of *Peter Pan*. So enthusiastic was she, the crystal glassware was in imminent danger of being swept off the table by her effusive gestures.

Her face almost hidden by the enormous brim of her hat, which harbored a couple of robins among the ferns and ribbons, Phoebe spilled out a torrent of words. "We will have children flying across the stage"—she flung out an arm, nearly costing Baxter his sherry—"and pirates and a ship and—"

"How in blazes," Baxter asked, rudely interrupting, "are you going to get a ship on the stage?"

Phoebe's cheeks were red with excitement. "Your maintenance fellow, Clive, is building us one."

That was news to Cecily, but she managed to meet Baxter's glare with a serene nod. "Clive is so talented, and I'm sure it will be a marvelous addition to our Christmas celebrations."

Baxter grunted. "How do you propose to get rid of the thing when the show is over?"

Phoebe looked somewhat deflated. "I suppose we will have to break it up and let the dustmen take it away."

Seeing her husband's scowl darken, Cecily hurried to intervene. "We'll worry about that later. Think of it, Baxter, a real ship on our stage. We will be the talk of the town."

At her words, Colonel Fortescue, whose nose had been buried in a brandy glass, suddenly came alive. "A ship, you say? Jolly good fun, what? What? I remember when—"

"Not that kind of ship, dear," Phoebe said loudly, tapping her husband's arm to get his attention. "We were talking about my pageant and—"

Ignoring her, he stabbed at his chest with his thumb. "Got one of these for helping to take over the palace during the Zanzibar skirmish. Blighters were firing on our Royal Navy in the harbor and—"

"You're not wearing your medals, dear," Phoebe observed.

The colonel looked down at his chest. "I'm not? Well, I'll be blowed! Where the blazes are they, then?"

Phoebe squirmed in obvious discomfort. "We . . . You . . . ah . . . donated them, my precious."

The colonel's cheeks turned as red as his nose. "Donated . . . my . . . medals?"

Phoebe turned to Cecily. "Anyway, as I was saying—"

"Who's the blighter who stole them?" the colonel bellowed, turning the heads of the two other couples in the dining room.

"The Salvation Army, dear." Phoebe turned back to Cecily. "I was thinking—"

"Well, by George, we'll get them back!" The colonel leapt to his feet, waving his fist in the air. "I'll take my sword to them, the scoundrels. How dare they take my medals."

Baxter's face lit up. "Jolly good show, old man. Go get them. Right now, before they give them away to someone else."

Phoebe gasped in dismay. "Baxter, how could you? You know he'll stop at nothing when he gets like this." She grasped her husband's sleeve and tugged on it. "Sit *down,* Frederick, dearest. You agreed to . . . ah . . . get rid of the medals early this year. Remember?"

"Never!" the colonel roared. "I'm going after the blighters.

Out of my way, you peasant, I'm off to battle." This last was directed at Pansy, who had come to clear off the dishes.

Well used to Fortescue's antics, Pansy skipped aside to let him pass.

Brandishing an imaginary sword, the colonel charged across the dining room and out of the door.

Phoebe's hat bobbed up and down in her agitation. "Now look what you've done." She glared at Baxter. "He's probably going to attack the first person he sees in uniform."

"Let's hope it's not a constable," Baxter said, looking unusually serene. "Though I think it more likely your husband has taken refuge in the bar." He got up, stretched, and smiled at his wife. "I think I'll retire to our suite. I'll leave you both to discuss whatever it is you plan to subject our guests to this Christmas."

Cecily winced at the subtle reference to Phoebe's infamous disasters with her Christmas events. The woman put all she had into the presentations, but invariable something would go wrong, due largely to the inept group of performers under her wing. Fortunately, Phoebe was an eternal optimist and never doubted that the next performance would be a masterful triumph.

She seemed unperturbed by Baxter's comment and, indeed, watched him go with something close to admiration in her eyes. "He's right, of course. Frederick always ends up in the bar when he's upset."

She sighed and leaned back on her chair. "Quite the gentleman, your husband. You are fortunate, Cecily, to have such an intelligent and thoughtful companion."

Cecily pursed her lips. It was true that one never knew the true nature of a person unless one lived with them. Compared to Colonel Fortescue, however, she was forced to admit, Baxter was an angel. "I am, indeed. But what about the colonel? Should you not be hastening after him to see that he doesn't meet with some mishap?"

Phoebe shrugged. "Frederick is quite capable of looking after himself. In any case, if I were to wager on his whereabouts, I would say that he is at this moment downing a glass of your best brandy."

"And forgotten about his medals?"

"A good brandy can make him forget everything." She paused, then leaned forward and dropped her voice to a whisper. "I wouldn't tell this to another soul, but the truth is I sold the medals two years ago to a collector. He offered me a very good price for them."

Shocked, Cecily stared at her. "Phoebe! The colonel's medals? How could you?"

"We needed the money. Besides, he never wore them. He barely ever mentioned them. Today was the first time in at least a year or so. I didn't think he would miss them." She looked worried. "You won't tell him, will you? If he thinks we donated them for a good cause, he'll be much less likely to be upset about losing them."

"Of course I won't say anything." Cecily shook her head. "I just hope he never finds out. He'll never forgive you."

"Oh, poop. Frederick never remembers anything longer than a few minutes."

She didn't sound too convincing, and Cecily hoped for her friend's sake that the colonel never discovered the truth. Deciding to change the subject, she asked, "You mentioned children flying across the stage in your pantomime. I hope you didn't mean that literally."

Phoebe beamed. "Of course I did. I intend to ask Gertie if her twins would like to appear in the presentation, and several of the village children are eager to perform. My dance group will be on hand, of course. Deirdre is playing Peter Pan and Mabel is taking the role of Wendy." Phoebe clasped her hands. "This is going to be the most spectacular event I have ever presented."

Cecily was inclined to agree. Especially if the hefty Mabel hadn't lost any weight during the last twelve months. It was a trifle hard to visualize a pudgy Wendy, not to mention the problem of heaving that much weight around on a wire. Cecily's greatest concern, however, was for the children. "Are you sure that's a good idea, using children on a wire? That could be quite dangerous."

"I have complete faith in Clive." Phoebe straightened her hat with a little tug that dislodged a hat pin. Tutting, she picked it up off the table and stuck it back in her hat. "He's very good at building things, and he's assured me that the wiring will be completely safe."

Cecily privately vowed to have a word with her maintenance man before she allowed such risky maneuvers on her stage. "Isn't there another pantomime you'd rather do?" she asked hopefully. "Perhaps one that doesn't present such difficult construction?"

"We have already done most of the popular ones. Besides, I have wanted to do *Peter Pan* for years, but until I talked to Clive I didn't think we were capable of doing it." Phoebe tilted her head to one side, putting her hat at great peril. "He is a most unusual man. Very well educated for a janitor."

"Quite so. I just hope he has the knowledge for this undertaking."

"You worry too much, Cecily." Phoebe patted her arm. "We will take care of everything. You can just sit back on the night of the pantomime and enjoy the spectacle."

Cecily rather doubted that, though she refrained from voicing any more concerns. This was something she would take up with Clive, as soon as possible. Now, however, she had other pressing engagements. "I'm sure I will." She placed her serviette on the table and rose to her feet. "I'm sorry to put an end to this delightful conversation, Phoebe, but I have an appointment this afternoon."

"Oh, of course." Phoebe got up slowly, mindful of her hat rocking on her head. "I see that Madeline hasn't started the decorating for Christmas. Rather late, isn't she? Or is she not participating this year?"

"Madeline has promised to start work on them tomorrow." Cecily led the way to the door, speaking over her shoulder. "She has been occupied with the baby, who has been quite poorly lately."

"Oh, I'm sorry to hear that." Phoebe caught up with her in the corridor. "I do hope little Angelina feels better soon."

"I understand she's recovering nicely." Cecily caught sight of Samuel waiting for her in the lobby and raised her hand at him. "When will you begin rehearsals, then?"

"As soon as Clive has the stage set." Phoebe peered down the hallway leading to the bar. "I had better find my husband while he can still walk home." She waved a gloved hand at Cecily and scurried off.

Samuel waited for Cecily to cross the lobby before approaching her. "I have the carriage ready, m'm," he said, as he reached her.

"Good. Then let's make haste. I would like to be back here before it grows dark."

"Yes, m'm."

Samuel opened the door for her and she marched outside, all her thoughts now on the coming conversation with Basil Baker.

CHAPTER
❉ 5 ❉

Gertie hummed to herself as she climbed the stairs to the third floor. It was her responsibility to inspect the bedrooms and make sure that the beds had been made, the chamber pots emptied, the furniture dusted, and the windows opened to air out the rooms.

It was a task she enjoyed. She had too many memories of when she had to do all those things herself, and it felt good to just sail from room to room, looking things over, instead of slaving away at the jobs herself.

The Christmas season was always a good time at the Pennyfoot. Lots of things to look forward to, all the lovely smells of sugar, herbs, and spices coming from the kitchen, and Mrs. Prestwick's decorations making everything look colorful and bright.

She was still thinking about the decorations as she hur-

ried down the stairs, and almost bumped into Phoebe Fortescue, who was hovering at the bottom.

"Oh, there you are!"

The woman looked a little agitated, and Gertie wondered
what she'd done wrong. "S'cuse me, m'm? Is there something I can do for you?"

"Oh, I do hope so." Phoebe looked around the empty
lobby, and leaned forward. "I badly need children for the
Peter Pan pantomime. I was wondering if your twins would
like to be part of it. It would be a wonderful experience for
them."

Gertie hesitated. James wasn't known for his patience
and had trouble concentrating on anything for any length
of time. As for Lillian, she was a bit of a crybaby, and
would run away from anything that could upset her. "I
dunno," Gertie said slowly. "I don't know how they'd behave."

"I'm sure they would behave beautifully." Phoebe clasped
her hands. "I'll have lots of people around to make sure they
do what they're supposed to do. I know they would have lots
of fun, and think of the pride you'd feel, seeing them up on
the stage in one of my famous presentations."

Gertie frowned. She didn't know about pride. More like
worry, considering how Mrs. Fortescue's events never went
without something awful happening. "I'd have to ask them,"
she said at last. "If they want to do it, then I'll allow it, but
I wouldn't want to force them into doing something they
don't want to do."

"No, no, of course not." Phoebe looked relieved. "Ah . . .
would you mind if I did the asking? They might consider it
more if I'm the one to ask them."

Gertie wasn't fooled for a moment. No doubt Mrs. Fortescue would make it sound like a grand adventure, possibly even bribing them with promises of a reward of some kind. "I'd rather ask them myself, m'm, if you don't mind."

Phoebe looked disappointed. "Very well, then. Just be sure to tell them what a tremendously exciting experience this would be for them."

"I will, m'm." Gertie bobbed a curtsey and headed for the kitchen. She wasn't sure how she felt about letting her babies perform onstage. True, it would be an experience for them, and it would be exciting to watch them up there with all the toffs watching them and clapping for them.

Gertie smiled as she imagined the cheers and applause as the twins took their bows at center stage. Yeah, what harm could it do? She'd talk to them just as soon as she got off work. Humming again, she shoved the kitchen door open and went inside.

Arriving at the address Mrs. Taylor had given her, Cecily stepped down from the carriage, wincing as melting snow seeped over the rims of her boots. The wind whipped at the scarf she had tied over her hat, and she was grateful for the fur collar on her heavy serge coat.

Samuel opened the gate for her, and she trod her way carefully up the narrow pathway, mindful of the slippery surface beneath her feet.

The porch was dry, and she stamped her feet to remove the worst of the snow from her boots. Meanwhile, Samuel lifted the door knocker and smacked it down.

At first no one answered, and he had to rap again, louder this time.

"It seems as if no one is home," Cecily murmured. "We shall have to call another time."

She was about to turn away when the door creaked open, and a young man with a drooping mustache and stubble on his chin looked at her with sleepy eyes.

He was wrapped in a blanket that covered a dressing gown and nightshirt, the robe bunched closed by a tattered cord. "Whatcha want?" he demanded, not even bothering to put a hand over his mouth when he yawned.

"Here," Samuel said, stepping forward, "mind who you are talking to. This is Mrs. Baxter from the Pennyfoot Country Club and she's here to ask you some questions about Jimmy Taylor."

The young man's eyes sharpened at once, and his voice lost its drowsy tone. "What about him?"

Cecily forced a smile. "Mr. Baker? May we come in? Just for a moment? It's terribly cold out here."

Basil Baker looked over his shoulder, then back at her, his eyes now wary. "The place is in a mess."

"That's all right. I don't mind that at all. I'm sorry to disturb you, but this is rather important."

Losing patience, Samuel put a foot on the threshold. "Where's your manners, letting a lady stand out in the cold? Let her in, right now."

"I already told the bobby everything I know," Basil muttered, but nevertheless stood back to allow them to enter.

He hadn't exaggerated the condition of the living room.

Clothes and shoes littered the room, a half-eaten sandwich sat on a plate on the couch, and empty beer glasses lined the mantelpiece. No coals burned in the fireplace, and it didn't feel much warmer inside the house than it had outside.

"I was sleeping," Basil said, picking up the remains of the sandwich. "It's my day off, and I like to sleep late."

"Oh, I'm so sorry." Cecily felt a pang of guilt for disturbing the young man's rest. "I wouldn't be here if it wasn't important."

"I don't know what I can tell that I didn't tell the bobby," Basil said, tilting his head at the couch as signal for them to sit.

Cecily lowered herself gingerly on the edge of it, while Samuel contented himself with leaning against the fireplace. "I understand you were good friends with Jimmy Taylor," she said, doing her best to smile.

"Used to be, yeah." Basil hunched his shoulders. "Until he stole my girl. We was enemies after that." He coughed, and added quickly, "I wasn't the one what threw that rock at him, though. I swear it. I'll admit, I didn't like the bloke. We had a big scrap over Gracie. It was Jimmy what started it, though. I only finished it. I never went near him after that." He swiped his thumb in a cross on his chest, almost losing his blanket in the process. "I swear on the Bible I didn't."

He sounded sincere, and Cecily was inclined to believe him. "Do you remember where you were the day Jimmy died?"

"I was working, wasn't I. In the paper factory in Wellercombe. Twelve hours a day, hauling bloody big bundles of paper into the warehouse."

"It sounds like hard work."

"Yeah, it is. I hate the job." Basil dragged the slipping blanket closer over his shoulders. "I used to work on a farm, and I liked that a lot, but I can't get jobs on a farm no more. That's why I'm stuck doing factory work."

"It must have made it difficult for you to spend time with Gracie," Cecily said, digging her freezing hands deeper into her muff.

Basil gave her a sharp look. "What does that mean?"

"Oh, I was just wondering if that's why Gracie chose Jimmy, because you didn't have much time to spend with her."

Basil's brows drew together. "I don't know why she went with him. He was a nasty-tempered, ill-mannered pig, and I don't know what she saw in him."

"I imagine you were furious when she left you for him."

"Course I was. After the fight, though, I reckoned they deserved each other. I heard that he was slapping her around a bit, but she chose to stay with him. More fool her, that's what I say. Never did have no brains, that girl."

Cecily got up from the couch, wishing she could feel her toes. "I'd like to have a word with Gracie. Do you know where can I find her?"

"She lives where she works, over the toy shop in the High Street." Basil yawned again. "Now, if you don't mind, I'd like to get back to bed."

"Thank you for your help." Cecily nodded at Samuel, who was directing a stern glare at Basil. "Come, Samuel, we must leave this gentleman in peace."

Samuel snorted rather rudely and hurried to open the door for her.

Pausing on the doorstep, Cecily looked back at Basil. "How well did you know Thomas Willow?"

Basil frowned. "The shoemaker? Everyone in the village knows who he is, but I wasn't that friendly with him, if that's what you mean. What about him?"

"He was found whipped to death up on Putney Downs," Cecily said, keeping a close watch on Basil's face.

At first Basil's features seemed frozen in shock, then he looked scared. "I didn't know."

"Did Jimmy know him well?"

"Not that I know of. Jimmy couldn't afford to get his shoes custom-made. He bought his where I bought mine, at the market. What does all this have to do with me?"

"Nothing, I hope. Just as a matter of interest, though, someone used Jimmy Taylor's whip to kill Thomas Willow."

Basil's jaw dropped open. "Blinking heck. Who would be crazy enough to do something like that?"

Thoroughly chilled now, Cecily bid him good day. Climbing up into the carriage, she wished she'd brought a blanket herself as she sat down on the cold leather seat.

Frost had settled on the windows, painting a silvery pattern as they made their way to the High Street. All along the curb horses stamped impatiently, steam rising from their nostrils while they waited for their owners to return.

Samuel found a spot around the corner from the toy shop, and it was a short walk back for Cecily. Shop owners had cleared the pavements of snow, and it was quite a pleasure to tread on firm ground instead of slippery ice.

Customers filled the little shop, but it was blissfully warm inside, thanks to the large stove in the corner. Samuel made his way to the counter to ask about Gracie Petersen while Cecily paused by the stove, waiting for the blood to return to her extremities.

Glancing around, her gaze fell upon a display of Christmas cards. It wasn't the colorful pictures of decorated trees, snow scenes, and Father Christmas that caught her eye, however. It was a large box filled to the brim with shiny gold stamps.

Just at that moment a young lady approached her, asking, "May I be of help?"

Cecily gave her a quick smile. "I was just looking at these gold stamps." She picked up a sheet of them and studied it. "Angels, I believe."

"Yes, m'm. They're for sticking on the flap of Christmas card envelopes."

"Indeed." Cecily put the stamps back in the box. "Do you sell many of them?"

"Oh, yes, m'm." The assistant beamed. "That's the second box we put out today. Would you like some?"

"Perhaps later. Thank you."

The assistant melted away, just as Cecily spied Samuel hurrying toward her, followed by a young woman with bright red hair piled high and held in place with a black ribbon.

Her black frock was trimmed with lace and hung loosely on her slender frame, suggesting she had recently lost quite a bit of weight. She seemed nervous, and her curtsey was a trifle wobbly when she paused in front of Cecily. "You asked to speak with me, m'm?"

"Yes, dear, I did." Cecily glanced around the crowded shop. "Is there somewhere we can speak in private?"

Gracie looked frightened. "I don't know, m'm. I'm not supposed to leave the counter." She sent a worried glance over her shoulder. "I should be getting back there."

Cecily reached out to pick up a large spinning top. "Perhaps if I buy this, we could retire to a quiet corner to discuss the price?"

Gracie hesitated a moment longer, then nodded. "Over here, then, Mrs. Baxter."

She led the way to a corner of the shop that was partially hidden by a large display of dolls. Standing back in the shadows, Gracie poked a stray strand of hair underneath the ribbon. "Your footman said you wanted to talk about my Jimmy," she said, tears beginning to fill her eyes. "I don't like talking about it, him just being killed and all. What is it you want to know?"

"I'm so sorry for your loss," Cecily said quietly. "Actually I wanted to talk to you about Basil Baker. I talked to him a short while ago. He said he and Jimmy exchanged blows, and you were the cause."

Gracie gulped, struggling to control her voice. "Yes, they did. Basil kept pestering me to go back to him, and Jimmy told him to get out of town. He said he'd beat Basil up if he didn't leave and Basil said he wasn't going to leave and the next morning Jimmy waited for him to come home and jumped on him. They had a terrible fight, and Basil got the worst of it. Jimmy had a bit of a temper when he was crossed."

"So they were bitter enemies."

"I suppose so." She started, as if she'd just thought of

something. "You don't think Basil threw that rock at Jimmy?" She shook her head so violently a couple of pins flew out and pinged against the doll stand. "Basil might have hated Jimmy, but I know him. He wouldn't have done something like that. He could fight if he had to, but he'd never attack someone like that."

Cecily inspected the spinning top in her hand. "Who knows what people are capable of when under the influence of a terrible rage." She paused, then added quietly, "That's a nasty bruise on your cheek. It must be painful."

Gracie's hand flew to her face. "It's healing up nicely now, thank you."

Cecily nodded. "Very well." She held up the top. "How much is this?"

"One and fourpence, m'm."

"I'll take it, as well as that doll in the red velvet gown."

"Yes, m'm." Grace's smile was full of relief as she reached for the doll and carried it over to the counter.

Cecily followed more slowly, her thoughts on everything she'd heard that day. Basil certainly had a motive to want to hurt Jimmy, yet both Jimmy's mother and fiancée had assured her that Basil wasn't capable of such a violent act.

Could both of them have known him that well yet still be wrong about him? It was possible, and she didn't know Basil well enough herself to rule him out. For one thing, he'd lied about who had come off the worst in the fight. Of course, that could well have been pride talking, Cecily decided.

Also, there seemed to be no reason why Basil would want to kill Thomas Willow. In fact, until she knew what connection there was between Thomas and Jimmy Taylor, there didn't seem to be any way to solve the puzzle. Small wonder

Sam Northcott had asked for her help. This case was certainly intriguing. She would have to do a lot more digging if she was going to solve the puzzle in time to welcome her guests for Christmas.

"Did you hear about Jimmy Taylor?" Pansy leaned over a table to place a white candle into a brass candelabrum.

Across the dining room, Gertie paused in the act of bundling up a white tablecloth. "What about him?"

"I heard someone threw a rock at him and killed him."

"Go on! Who told you that?"

"Samuel. He heard it from madam."

Gertie shook her head. "I can't believe it. He weren't much older than you. Does Chubby know?"

"Yeah. She was there when Samuel told me. She was really upset. She liked Jimmy."

Gertie dumped the tablecloth into a wicker basket and shoved it with her foot over to the next table. "I don't know why. He was a miserable bugger, though I shouldn't be talking ill of the dead."

"No, you shouldn't."

"So who threw the rock?"

"I dunno." Pansy moved to the next table. "Nobody knows. It's all a big mystery."

"Yeah, well, we get a lot of mysteries around here, don't we." Deciding it was time to change the morbid subject, Gertie added, "Guess who's coming here for Christmas."

Pansy twisted around, a candelabrum in one hand and three white candles in the other. "You found out who the important guests are going to be?"

63

"What important guests?"

Pansy looked disappointed. "Mrs. Chubb says as how some really important guests are coming for Christmas, but she won't tell anyone who they are. She says it has to be a big secret, so no one's supposed to know."

"Well, nobody told me nothing about no important guests." Gertie dropped yet another tablecloth into a laundry basket. "Anyhow, I don't think anyone would call Doris important. Though I suppose she *is* a bit famous, having been on the stage and all."

Pansy uttered a little cry of dismay. "Doris is coming? Daisy's twin sister? *That* Doris?"

Gertie grinned. "Who else?" Pansy turned away, but not before Gertie saw the fear on her friend's face. "You're not worried about Samuel, are you?"

Pansy shrugged. "Course not."

"Good." Gertie dragged another cloth off the table.

"It's just, well, you know how Samuel felt about Doris. He moved all the way to London to be near her."

"And came all the way back when things didn't work out the way he wanted."

"I know, but . . ."

Gertie bundled up the tablecloth and threw it at her. "Don't be bleeding daft. Samuel loves you now. He's told you so, hasn't he?"

There was a long pause before Pansy answered with a note of defiance. "He hasn't actually said the words, but I know he does love me. He's always telling me I'm his girl, and he likes being with me."

"Well, then." Gertie picked the tablecloth up off the floor and tossed it into the basket. "Stop worrying about Doris.

Besides, Nigel is coming with her and they're bringing their daughter, Essie. So you've got no need to get in a bother about Samuel taking notice of her."

"I s'pose not." Pansy fitted the candles into the candlestick and stood back to inspect her work. "I just wish she'd picked somewhere else to spend Christmas."

"Well, what I'd like to know is who the important guests are that Chubby told you about." Gertie heaved up the basket and balanced it on her hip. "I'll have to get on to her about it. She'll let something slip sooner or later, you mark my words."

Pansy looked intrigued. "They must be really important if she won't tell us. Must be a really, really big, dark secret."

"Yeah." Gertie trudged over to the door, the basket bouncing on her hip. "I don't know why she hasn't said nothing to me. Chubby knows I know how to keep a bloody secret. I've kept enough of 'em since I've been here at the Pennyfoot."

Pansy followed her, eyes gleaming. "Like what?"

"If I told you, they wouldn't be bloody secrets anymore, would they." Gertie opened the door of the dumbwaiter and grunted as she dumped the basket inside. Tugging on the rope, she looked over her shoulder at Pansy. "I tell you one thing, whoever these important guests are, they're not going to be secret for long. They've got to eat and sleep and go to the lav like the rest of us, don't they. Sooner or later we'll spot them."

Pansy giggled. "Better not tell that to Mrs. Chubb. She'll have a pink fit."

Gertie wasn't listening. She was too busy thinking about who the important guests might be. Maybe some rich toff who would take one look at her and sweep her off her feet, like the blokes in the magazines Chubby hid under her mattress.

They would all live in a posh house like the ones on the hill above Putney Downs, where Lillian and James could play and ride horses and do all the things the rich kids did.

So deep was she into her fantasy that as she rounded the corner of the hallway she ran smack into a hard body. Two strong hands grasped her arms as she bounced backward, gasping for breath.

"Where's the fire?" a gruff voice demanded.

Looking up into Clive's amused face, she muttered, "Sorry. I didn't see you coming."

"Not often someone says that," Clive said, with laughter echoing in his voice.

She laughed with him, gently, knowing he was sensitive about his size. She never knew why. Clive was a big man with a husky build and massive shoulders, but he wasn't fat like some of the rich dandies who visited the Pennyfoot.

There weren't many men she had to lift her chin to look in the face. She liked that about Clive. He made her feel protected. Her and her children.

She knew that if any of them were in danger, Clive would be the first one to save them. He'd been there for all of them more than once, and she would always be grateful for that.

Remembering Pansy's words, she felt a stirring of guilt. What if Clive wanted more than gratitude? What if he thought she had those sorts of feelings for him? How could she let him down without hurting him?

She'd married once before to have security for her kids. It

wasn't an unhappy marriage, but Ross McBride had been a lot older than she, and they hadn't had much in common. She hadn't loved him the way she'd loved Dan.

But then, Dan had hurt her. Badly. When she'd told him she couldn't go to London with him, she'd nursed a faint hope that he wouldn't be able to leave her. She'd been wrong.

She'd been hurt too many times, and she wasn't getting involved with any man again unless she could truly love him and know, without a shadow of a doubt, that he loved her back.

"Why the frown?" Clive tilted her head back with a finger under her chin. "You look so pretty when you smile."

Gertie's grin spread all over her face. That was what she liked best about Clive. He knew how to lift her spirits when she was down. "The twins are looking forward to the sleigh ride," she said, as he dropped his hand. "So am I."

"Me, too. Tomorrow afternoon, two o'clock. Let's hope it stops snowing by then."

"I thought sleighs were made for riding in the snow."

"They are. It's the horse that has trouble with it."

"You'll be able to manage it."

He looked down at her, his dark eyes twinkling. "Nice to know you have such faith in me."

Something in his gaze unsettled her and she looked away, mumbling, "You're good at everything you do."

"Not everything."

He stepped back to let her pass, and she hurried by him, wondering what he meant by that. He often said things that intrigued her.

Not for the first time she wondered about his past. She knew so little about him. He'd told her he'd been married, but she didn't know what had happened to his wife, or if he had children, or why someone who seemed so clever would want to be a maintenance man at a seaside hotel.

Clive was a mystery, and the longer she knew him, the more she wanted to know about him. Tomorrow, she told herself. Tomorrow she'd try to find out about his past.

Feeling surprisingly excited at the prospect, she ran down the steps to the kitchen.

CHAPTER
❅ 6 ❅

Madeline arrived the next morning, prepared to start work on the decorating. It took two footmen to unload her carriage, carrying huge baskets of greenery and flowers, boxes of ribbons and garlands, and tubs filled with colored glass balls and a variety of ornaments for the tree.

Cecily met her in the lobby, disappointed that Angelina wasn't with her.

"I left her at home with the nanny," Madeline explained, floating across the carpet in her bare feet. She'd kicked off her boots the moment she'd stepped through the door. Her simple frock of pale green cotton, dotted with white daises, looked more suitable for summertime instead of the bitter cold outside.

Then again, Madeline defied convention in every possible way. She wore her long, black hair down her back instead of pinned up on her head, she wore no stockings or gloves, and the closest she ever came to a hat was a colorful scarf tied under her chin.

She was both loved and feared in the village. Her remedies, concocted from various herbs and wildflowers, cured everything from a cold to pneumonia, and more than one man had benefited from her "passion" potions.

There were those, however, who questioned her powers, convinced she was a witch. Even Cecily, who had seen Madeline upon occasion perform somewhat implausible deeds, wasn't entirely convinced they were wrong.

Today, however, Madeline was all smiles and sweetness as she directed the footmen to take her supplies to the ballroom. "This is my favorite time of the year," she exclaimed, as she watched the young men struggling under the weight of her boxes. "I just adore decorating the Pennyfoot."

"You always create such a wonderful setting for us," Cecily said, leading her friend up the stairs. "How is little Angelina? I do hope she's feeling better?"

"She's much better, thank goodness." Madeline pulled a face. "Kevin and I kept arguing over whose medicine would do her the most good, so it's quite a relief to be done with it."

Cecily gave her an anxious look. Kevin Prestwick, the respected village doctor, had great difficulty in coming to terms with his wife's healing powers. Although it was obvious to everyone that he loved Madeline dearly, it was equally obvious that he dismissed her beliefs as useless and potentially dangerous.

Cecily, on the other hand, relied a great deal on Madeline's perception and couldn't wait until they were in the suite and she could ask once more for her friend's help.

"I suppose Kevin told you about the incident that killed Jimmy Taylor," she said, as they settled themselves in front of the fireplace. "Such a tragedy to lose someone so young."

"Yes, Kevin was very upset about it all. He kept saying how senseless it was. If the lad hadn't fallen from the wagon, he'd be alive today."

"So he does think Jimmy's death was unintentional?"

Madeline gave her a shrewd look from under her long lashes. "Someone threw a rock at him. That was surely intentional."

"But perhaps that person didn't intend to kill Jimmy."

"Perhaps." Madeline paused, staring into the flames. "Then again, there's no doubt that someone meant to kill Thomas Willow. According to Kevin, the killer did a thorough job of it."

In spite of the warmth from the fire, Cecily shivered. "How awful."

"I knew Thomas Willow quite well," Madeline said, after another long pause. "I was shocked to hear of his death, though not exactly devastated. He was not a pleasant man, by any means."

Cecily raised her eyebrows. "Is that so? I hadn't heard that about him."

Madeline hesitated. "One shouldn't speak ill of the dead. All I will say is that he was a most unhappy man and tended to take out his misery on those around him."

"And Jimmy Taylor? You knew him, too?"

"I don't think we'd ever met."

"Jimmy was the young lad who delivered for Rickman's Dairy."

"Ah, well, I buy my milk, butter, and cheese at the market." Madeline frowned. "I find it strange that Thomas was killed with Jimmy's whip. Kevin told me about the missing locks of hair and the angel stamps. How bizarre. It seems likely they were killed by the same person, doesn't it. Did they know each other? Thomas and Jimmy, I mean."

"Not as far as I know."

"They must have had something in common. A common enemy, don't you think?"

"Exactly." Cecily leaned forward. "I was hoping you could help me with that."

"Me? But I didn't know . . . Oh!" Madeline's face cleared. "Well, I'll see what I can do, but I can't promise anything. After all, I didn't know Jimmy and I really didn't know Thomas all that well."

"Just do your best—that's all I ask."

Watching Madeline go into a trance was always an unsettling experience for Cecily. She had seen the transformation many times, but it never failed to raise goose pimples up her arms.

She sat quietly now as her friend closed her eyes and started to rock gently back and forth.

Madeline's eyelids began to quiver, her mouth twitched, and she made soft little sounds at the back of her throat. Suddenly she arched her back with a little cry, sending a cold chill down Cecily's back.

Madeline started whispering, words that made no sense, punctuated by low moans. Her hands rose, fingers outstretched as if warding off some kind of threat. Then, abruptly, it was over. Madeline fell back on her chair and opened her eyes.

Cecily waited until her friend's gaze focused on her, then asked anxiously, "What did you see?"

"An evil mind." Madeline looked shaken. "A dabbler in black magic. There is nothing more dangerous than a neophyte playing with the occult."

"Could you see him?"

"No. I saw only the black, boiling cloud that enveloped him." She shuddered. "You must stop this killer, Cecily. Soon. He is clever and extremely dangerous. His mind is filled with hate and revenge—a mind that will stop at nothing."

"Revenge for what?"

Madeline lifted her hands and let them drop. "That, I don't know."

"I need more." Cecily leaned forward. "What did Jimmy and Thomas have in common? Could it be that the two murders are not connected at all? That there are two killers?"

"I saw only one." Madeline sat up, her dark eyes gleaming with an intense light. "One thing I do know. It's not finished yet. There will be more. He must be stopped."

"That's all you can tell me?"

"I'm sorry." Madeline got up, shaking out her skirt to cover her bare toes. "I wish I could tell you more. Rest assured, Cecily, if I do see anything else I shall see that you know it."

Disappointed and more than a little fearful, Cecily rose and followed her friend to the door. "Thank you, Madeline. I know you don't feel comfortable using your powers this way, and I do appreciate it."

"You are a dear friend, Cecily. I would do anything for

you. I do have one suggestion that may be of help. Thomas had an assistant, who is now managing the shop. His name is Lester Salt, and he might be able to give you answers."

"That's an excellent idea!" Cecily hugged her friend. "Thank you, Madeline. I knew you would point me in the right direction."

"Just be careful—that's all I ask. You could be dealing with a very dangerous adversary." Madeline looked worried for a moment, then seemed to shrug off her concern. "If you want to repay me, please keep Phoebe and that idiot husband of hers out of my way."

Cecily smiled. Her two best friends had been bickering ever since they had met years ago. They couldn't be more opposite in nature or ideals, yet Cecily knew quite well they harbored a fondness for each other that neither of them would ever admit. "Don't worry. Phoebe will be busy with rehearsals, and the colonel will no doubt spend his time in the bar."

"Good. Then I shall be off to turn this decrepit old building into a Christmas wonderland."

"Do your best," Cecily said, laughing as she opened the door. "We will be overrun with children this year. Phoebe is presenting *Peter Pan* for her pantomime. There will be children in the cast, and I do believe she is asking Gertie's twins to participate. Doris will be here in the next day or two, and she's bringing her little daughter, Essie, so your hard work will be much appreciated and admired, I'm sure."

Madeline's face lit up. "Children! How marvelous. I shall make sure to include something just for them in my decorations." She sailed off, her frock billowing out behind her.

Cecily closed the door and walked slowly back to the fire. Madeline's vision worried her. If she hadn't known what her friend was capable of, she might have been able to dismiss the warning. After all, it had all sounded rather bizarre. *It's not finished yet. There will be more.*

Yet she did know Madeline's powers. She had seen them for herself. As close as she was to the fire, Cecily shivered. She had dealt with killers of all kinds, and in many forms, yet this one seemed to pose more threat than any of them.

Maybe Baxter was right. Maybe this time she was taking on more peril than was wise. Part of her wanted to heed her husband's warnings and let P.C. Northcott take care of the murders, as was his duty.

Cecily leaned back and closed her eyes. She must be getting old, to allow such weakness. This was one of the most interesting cases to come her way. Even if she did succumb to her caution, the intense desire to dig out the details and unravel the puzzle would not let her rest.

Besides, after all these years, Sam had asked for her help. She could not let this opportunity slip out of her hands. No, she must do what she could to bring this evil man to justice. If needs be, she would ask Madeline to help her. She was confident that her friend would be a match for anyone.

Thus resolved, she rose and tugged on the bell rope. She would have Samuel ready the carriage right away. With luck, Lester Salt would be able to send her on the right path.

* * *

Pansy picked her way through the snow, wincing as lumps of the cold white stuff found their way over the tops of her boots to sting her ankles.

On the first day of the storm she'd been excited to see the flakes falling so thick and fast, but now she'd had enough of it. She peered up at the gray sky, praying that the ocean winds would turn warm and bring the thaw.

Soon the Christmas guests would be arriving, and it wasn't much fun drying out boots and shoes, cleaning up the mess in the foyer, stoking the fires in the bedrooms, or heating the beds with bed warmers.

The summer guests were so much easier to take care of, and personally Pansy couldn't wait for the winter to be over with, Christmas and all.

She found Samuel in the stables as usual, romping with Tess. The big dog bounded over to her, ears flopping and tail wagging furiously.

Pansy crouched down to throw her arms around her furry neck. Samuel had found the stray wandering around the courtyard, half-starved, her coat matted and muddy.

Looking at her now, Pansy thought, as she stroked the silky head, it was like looking at a different dog. Samuel kept her bathed and fed, and she was quite the most beautiful animal Pansy had ever seen.

"Did you come to see me or my dog?" Samuel asked, his voice teasing as he approached them.

Pansy smiled up at him. "Both." She stood, giving Tess a final pat. "Madam wants the carriage readied and at the door as soon as possible." She tilted her head on one side. "She didn't say where she was going."

Samuel's face assumed the mask he always wore when she

questioned him about his jaunts with madam. "Most likely she wants to do some Christmas shopping." He opened the gate to one of the stalls and whistled to Tess. "Here, girl. In your kennel. You can stay warm there until I get back."

Pansy watched him close the gate, wishing she had somewhere warm and cozy to snuggle up in for a while. The question she wanted to ask him buzzed around in her head, but she didn't quite know how to ask it.

He was halfway across the stables before she called out, "I heard Doris is coming for Christmas."

She would have liked to have seen his expression when she told him, but he had his back turned toward her. He kept going for another step or two before turning to face her.

"Coming here to the Pennyfoot?"

"Yes." She walked toward him, trying to read his thoughts, but Samuel was very good at hiding them. "Her husband and little girl are coming with her."

"That's nice."

Pansy narrowed her eyes. "You still like her, don't you?"

"I still like her, yes. We worked together a long time, and she's a sweet lady. That doesn't mean I want to be with her. I've told you that over and over." Samuel spun around and marched over to the door, flinging words over his shoulder. "She's married, Pansy. Stop fretting about her."

He disappeared, leaving Pansy to nurse an ache that never quite went away. Samuel loved her, she knew that. He didn't have to say it, she could tell by the way he kissed her and all the nice things he said and did for her. Still, if only she could hear the words, just once, she'd know for certain, and all these nasty feelings about Doris would go away for good.

Dejected now, she plodded back to the kitchen, silently cursing the snow at every step. Would she ever be sure of Samuel's love? Right now, it didn't seem too likely.

Staring back at the sky, she changed her prayer. Let it snow. Hard. Piling up six or seven feet. That way, Doris wouldn't be able to come, and she could have Samuel all to herself for Christmas. Hunching her shoulders, she opened the kitchen door and went inside.

"His name is Lester Salt," Cecily said, as she climbed up onto the creaking, cold leather seat of the carriage. Shivering, she drew her scarf tighter under her chin. "He's the new manager of Thomas Willow's shoe shop."

"In the High Street," Samuel said, nodding. "I know where it is. It's going to be busy down there today, m'm. You might have a bit of a walk to the shop."

"That's all right, Samuel. I'm sure the shopkeepers will have cleared the pavements." She heard the big bay snorting as Samuel took the reins. She felt sorry for the poor animal. It wouldn't be easy for it to drag the carriage through all this snow.

If only the rain would start and wash the cold mess away. She was really becoming quite anxious about her guests. This had to be the worst Christmas season weather she could remember in many years.

The carriage jolted forward, sending her back against the seat. Her hat tipped in front of her eyes and she straightened it, securing it more firmly with a hat pin. Bracing herself for another rough ride, she thought about the questions she would ask Lester Salt. She needed answers and as soon as possible.

The gentleman who filled the doorway at the shoe shop was nothing like the assistant she had imagined. Dressed in a loudly striped suit with a red waistcoat, starched white collar, and bow tie, he looked more like a circus ringmaster than a shoemaker.

He extended a massive hand as if about to take her fingers in his, which Cecily managed to avoid by pretending to brush snowflakes from her cape.

Seemingly unaffected by the slight, Lester Salt boomed, "Welcome to Willow's shoe shop! How may we assist you this bright morning?"

Considering the sky was dark gray, Cecily thought the greeting a bit pompous. "I'm Mrs. Baxter, of the Pennyfoot Country Club," she announced, forestalling Samuel, who was about to introduce her. Judging from Lester Salt's demeanor, she decided, the man would not stand on protocol, and she had no time to waste. "I am here to ask you a few questions about Thomas Willow."

The shoemaker's change of expression hardly registered before it was wiped away by an effusive smile. "By all means, Mrs. Baxter! Come this way!"

He ushered her and Samuel into a small parlor at the back of the shop, leaving a couple of young lads to take care of any potential customers.

"It is indeed an honor to greet you, Mrs. Baxter," he gushed, as he beckoned her to sit down. "I know your husband well. Such a nice man. Very well-spoken, if I may say so."

Cecily wondered what Baxter would make of that.

"Thank you, Mr. Salt. My husband would appreciate your kind words."

"Not at all, m'm, and please, do call me Lester. Everyone does." He laughed, a rather harsh sound that grated on her nerves.

"Thank you, Lester." She chose a chair by the fire, where a pair of muddy boots sat next to a half-filled coal scuttle.

Samuel hovered near the door, looking anxious as always. Mindful of his sacred promise to take care of her, no doubt. Cecily was quite certain that Baxter had promised all sorts of dire consequences if Samuel failed to keep her safe.

She couldn't help noticing that the sofa and armchairs were of poor quality brocade, though the faded curtains at the window had once been very fine velvet. The sideboard and mantelpiece were bare of ornaments except for a large clock ticking above the fireplace. A small table at her side held only a book, its pages marked with a slim piece of paper.

The title intrigued her. *Tales of a Mystic.* It was the heading on the bookmark that held her attention, however, until Lester spoke.

"Now, then," he said, smoothing his drooping mustache with his fingers. "What can I do for you today, Mrs. Baxter? A nice pair of leather boots, perhaps, or a pretty pair of satin shoes to match a tea gown? I have a pair in black satin that are just exquisite."

Sorely tempted, Cecily had to focus on the task at hand. "Actually, Mr. Salt—"

"Lester." He shook a finger at her in mock disapproval. "Remember?"

"Pardon me. Lester." She crossed her ankles, beginning to

dislike this rather overbearing man. "As I said earlier, I'm here to talk to you about your former employer, Mr. Thomas Willow."

At the mention of the name, Lester's face momentarily darkened, then his expression changed to the false melancholy of a true salesman. "Ah, poor Thomas. He taught me all I know. Such a dreadful end. I can't imagine who would do such a thing to a defenseless old man." Lester wrung his hands. "I was simply devastated to hear the dreadful news. Left to die by the roadside in the bitter cold of a snowstorm. Whatever is this world coming to, I ask you?"

Cecily watched him closely. "Can you think of anyone who might have wanted to hurt him?"

Now Lester looked shocked. "Goodness, no. True, there weren't many people who liked him all that much, though I got along with him all right. He was rather a dour old devil, always seeing the worst in people. I used to say his only friend was his dog, and Thomas didn't treat *him* very well. He was always kicking or slapping him about."

He glanced over to a corner of the room, where for the first time, Cecily noticed a mangy-looking dog lay sleeping. "He's a bit of a mess right now, but as soon as I have time I'm going to give him a bath."

The dog looked as if it needed a lot more than a bath, Cecily thought, but she kept her comments to herself. "I understand you are managing the shop now," she said, looking back at Lester. "Do you happen to know the new owner?"

Lester's eyebrows twitched. "Oh, you haven't heard? Thomas left me the shop in his will." Again he uttered the brash laugh. "Of course, it will be a few weeks before everything is official, but I must keep the shop open for the customers."

"How very fortunate for you." Cecily paused, then added, "It must have been quite a pleasant surprise."

Lester locked his hands across his chest. "Nobody was more stunned than I to hear the news, Mrs. Baxter. Most unexpected. Thomas once told me he planned to leave the shop to me but I didn't believe him, of course. I thought he was merely saying that to keep me in his employ."

Cecily pursed her lips, wondering just how truthful was that statement. "So you are happy with the arrangement?"

"Well, of course!" Lester sent a hunted glance at the door, as if he wished the conversation were over. "It isn't every day someone gives away a thriving business. Of course, Thomas had no relatives, as far as I know. He never married, and there was no mention of siblings in his will."

"I see." She wondered how to phrase the next question, then decided to just ask it. "Can you remember where you were the morning Thomas died?"

As she'd suspected, Lester seemed offended by the question. He tossed his head, and smoothed back a lock of dark hair that fell across his forehead. "I was right here, Mrs. Baxter, where I've been ever since it happened, taking care of the shop as always. Thomas had taken Rex for his morning walk, and when he didn't return at the usual time I became concerned, particularly since the snow had been falling steadily all morning. When Rex wandered into the shop without Thomas, that's when I knew something was wrong. I was responsible for alerting the constables that he was missing."

"I see." Cecily glanced once again at the book by her side.

"I understand that Mr. Willow was killed with a whip belonging to Jimmy Taylor."

"So I understand."

Lester's mask of joviality had slipped considerably, and Cecily stepped carefully with her next words. "Was Mr. Willow acquainted with Jimmy?"

Lester blinked, then said quickly, "Ah, that I don't know. I, however, did know the boy. I didn't care for him. Rather a scrapper, if you ask me. Always looking for a fight. To be honest, if Jimmy hadn't died first, he would have been my first suspect on the list."

"Ah, but he did die first and, it would seem, killed by the same person who killed Mr. Willow."

"Precisely." Lester cleared his throat. "Well, if I can't do anything more for you, Mrs. Baxter, I must ask you to excuse me. This is a busy time of year for us, as you know, and if I leave the apprentices alone for too long they tend to make a mess of things."

"Oh, of course." Cecily rose and followed Lester to the door as Samuel snapped to attention. "Well, thank you, Mr. Salt. I appreciate your time."

"Not at all, Mrs. Baxter." Lester opened the door, looking at Samuel as if he were something the dog had dug up. "Anything to oblige such a good customer as your husband. Please tell him I shall be happy to provide him with new shoes when the time comes."

"I shall indeed."

She was about to walk through the door when Lester asked abruptly, "Tell me, Mrs. Baxter, do you have a personal interest in Thomas's death?"

Cecily smiled. "I take a personal interest in anyone in

83

Badgers End who dies by violence, Mr. Salt. I consider it my duty to do what I can to see the killer apprehended and punished for his crime."

"Very commendable, I'm sure." Lester gave her a toothy smile. "Well, good day to you, m'm. Please visit us again."

Not if I can help it, Cecily thought, as she stepped briskly outside and down the pavement to where the carriage waited. She had taken a dislike to Lester Salt, and while it was none of her business where Baxter had his shoes made, she sincerely hoped he would find another shoemaker to keep him well shod.

CHAPTER

❀ 7 ❀

Baxter was waiting for Cecily when she returned to the Pennyfoot. He had ordered their midday meal to be served in the suite, and together they enjoyed a large plate of ham, hard-boiled eggs, cheese, sweet pickle, sliced apple, and pickled onions, followed by a delicious pear tart and Devonshire cream.

"How is the investigation coming?" Baxter asked, as they sat on either side of the fireplace, sipping on a glass of delicious cream sherry.

Cecily, who had been anticipating the question, did her best to sound casual. "Quite well, thank you, though so far I have no answers. Other than the whip, I can't seem to find what links Jimmy Taylor to Thomas Willow."

Baxter grunted, took another sip of sherry, then murmured, "What surprises me is that no one saw either man killed. By all accounts, both men died in broad daylight. You would think someone would have seen something happening."

Cecily put down her glass. "I doubt if many people were out walking in all this snow."

"Maybe not when Thomas Willow was killed. But it wasn't snowing when Jimmy Taylor died."

Cecily stared at her husband. "You're right. It wasn't. I wonder . . ." She paused, considering his words.

Baxter raised his eyebrows. "You've thought of something?"

"I don't know." Cecily leaned back on her chair. "I was wondering if perhaps Thomas Willow saw who threw the rock at Jimmy, and therefore had to be silenced."

"Ah!" Baxter nodded. "That would certainly explain the connection between them, don't you think?"

"Perhaps. Then again, there's the little matter of the gold angels and the missing locks of hair." Madeline's words came back to haunt her. *A mind that will stop at nothing.*

Unwilling to tangle with such thoughts right then, she brushed them aside. "Someone went to a lot of trouble to connect the victims. I think our villain is trying to send us a message."

"Such as?"

Cecily shrugged. "I don't know. I suppose when I find that out, I shall be closer to finding the killer."

"Precisely, which begs the question: Why would he go to the trouble of giving you clues to his identity?"

"Perhaps," Cecily said quietly, "he's the kind of killer who enjoys playing a game."

Baxter stirred, his face creasing into a frown. "I don't like the sound of that. Perhaps you should think twice about helping out that confounded constable."

Annoyed with herself for saying too much, Cecily managed a light laugh. "Don't worry, Bax. I have no intention of playing games with a murderer."

"I certainly hope not." Baxter reached for the bell rope and gave it a tug. "I have some papers to take care of this afternoon. This blasted snow is preventing me from going into the city. I'm really considering moving my office down here permanently."

She looked at him in surprise. "You are? I know we've mentioned the possibility in the past, but you've always been so reluctant to move your work back here."

"That's because I didn't have an office of my own to work in." He glanced at the clock on the mantelpiece. "Since you are so seldom in yours, however, I might as well use that one, and I can simply leave on those occasions that you need it."

Cecily clasped her hands in delight. "I think that's an absolutely wonderful idea."

"I shall have to go into the city to clean out everything there, however." Baxter walked toward the door. "I thought I'd go tomorrow if the trains are running. I'll have everything transported down by the Royal Mail. I should get it all here before Christmas."

Cecily followed him to the door. "I'm so happy for you, Bax. There'll be no more getting up in the dark to catch the train, no more coming home late at night. You will be so much happier and rested working in the Pennyfoot."

"I hope so." He leaned over to drop a kiss on her cheek. "I haven't entirely given up the idea of taking that position abroad, you know. If that should transpire, it will be much easier to make the transition from here than from the city."

He was gone before she could respond. Worried now, she went back to the fireplace. She had assumed that he'd entirely dismissed the opportunity to open hotels in foreign lands. It seemed, however, that he was still harboring thoughts of such an enterprise.

She had weakened her situation considerably by asking him to release her from her promise. If he took that post now, she would have only herself to blame.

Miserably she stared into the flames. All she could hope was that finding this killer would be worth what it might cost her.

Gertie was in a fever of impatience for the midday meal to be over with, so she could get her twins ready for the great sleigh ride that afternoon.

There were only two guests still in the dining room—an elderly couple who seemed to take forever to eat their steak and kidney pie. Twice Gertie had been to their table to clear their plates away only to find them still piled high with pastry, meat, potatoes, and carrots.

"Are you going to finish all that?" she asked the woman, whose wrinkled face was so heavily powdered she looked like one of Lillian's dolls. "You won't have room for afters if you stuff all that in your blinking mouth."

The gentleman peered at Gertie over his spectacles. "You are an impertinent young woman, and I shall complain to the head of the household about your rude behavior."

Silently cursing her runaway tongue, Gertie tried to

make amends. "Please forgive me, sir, but Mrs. Chubb has made some delicious pear tarts, and she put a dollop of brandy in them. I was concerned your lovely wife might not have enough room to enjoy them."

"Oh, Wilfred, they do sound divine." The woman pushed her plate toward Gertie. "Take this away and bring me some of those tarts."

Her husband grunted and reluctantly surrendered his own half-finished plate. Gertie snatched them up and whisked them over to the dumbwaiter outside in the hallway.

"Two pear tarts," she called down, as the plates descended. Impatiently tapping her foot, she waited for the sweets to come up.

"Ah, there you are."

The deep voice behind her made her jump and she twisted around, breaking into a grin when she saw Clive. "What're you doing here? Looking for something to eat?"

Clive chuckled, a deep sound in his throat that always made her smile. "I came to see you."

"What about?" She looked at him anxiously. "Is something wrong?"

"No . . ." He hesitated, then added, "Well, yes. We'll have to postpone our sleigh ride."

"Oh." Her crushing sense of disappointment left her weak. "The twins will be upset. They were looking forward to it."

"I know." His frown deepened. "So was I. Mrs. Fortescue wants me to put up the sets and wiring for her pantomime. She's starting rehearsals in a day or so."

Gertie pouted. "That old bat always wants something. Can't the footmen do it?"

"They can and they will, but I have to supervise. Mrs.

Fortescue doesn't trust them to make the wiring safe." He bent his head to look closer into her eyes. "She told me the twins are going to be in the event."

Gertie shrugged. "Per'aps. I haven't asked them yet. I was going to do that on the ride this afternoon."

"Well, if they are going to perform, wouldn't you want to be sure that everything on that stage is really safe and secure?"

"I suppose so." She forced a smile. "You're right. Go and do what that fussy old Phoebe Fortescue wants. We'll go on the ride another time."

His big hand descended on her shoulder in a friendly pat. "I knew you'd understand."

She nodded. "Just hope the bloody snow doesn't melt."

He laughed, and she watched him walk all the way to the end of the hallway, the memory of his hand still warm on her shoulder.

Cecily hurried down the stairs, fastening her warm scarf under her chin. To her relief, Samuel was waiting for her in the foyer. Catching sight of her, he opened his mouth to speak, but she quickly silenced him with a finger at her lips.

Mindful of Philip watching them, she raised her hand, calling out, "If Mr. Baxter asks for me, Philip, please tell him I have gone into town and shall be returning shortly."

"Yes, m'm." Philip pulled a tablet toward himself, took a pencil from behind his ear, and scribbled something down.

Ignoring Samuel's curious stare, Cecily headed for the door, forcing him to dart around her to open it for her.

Once outside, she waited until he had handed her into

the carriage before asking him, "Do you happen to know a man by the name of Sid Tippens?"

Samuel's eyes widened. "I've heard of him, m'm. Never met the bloke, though."

"I believe he is a bookmaker?"

"Yes, m,'m, but—"

"Do you know where he lives?"

"No, m'm, but I do believe he has an office on one of the backstreets off the High Street."

"Then I need you to take me there, Samuel."

Her stable manager's face grew red. "I don't think Mr. Baxter would approve, m'm. I don't—"

"Never mind what Mr. Baxter will or will not approve." She leaned forward, fixing him with a hard stare. "I thought we had an understanding."

"Yes, m'm, but—"

"No buts, Samuel. Let's get on our way. I'd like to be back before Mr. Baxter finishes his work."

"Can't you ring the bookmaker on the telephone?"

"No, I can't. The operators at the exchange have a nasty habit of listening in to my business, and this isn't something I want to broadcast to everyone in the village."

Samuel looked as if he were about to suffer a heart attack. "From what I hear, m'm, this Tippens chap is not a good person. I don't think—"

"That's the trouble with you, Samuel. Sometimes you tend to think too much. Now, please do what I say and get going this minute."

Samuel's mouth clamped shut on whatever he was about to say next. Muttering something she didn't catch, he climbed up onto the driver's seat and shook the reins.

Kate Kingsbury

The carriage jerked forward, and Cecily leaned back with a sigh. She didn't like putting so much onto the back of her stable manager. Samuel had been a good and loyal worker all the years she had known him, and there was no question about his loyalty toward her. He had often faced Baxter's wrath while aiding her in her investigations, and had more than once risked his own life to protect her.

Well aware of the awkward position she put him in at times, she had to admit to strong feelings of guilt whenever one of her well-laid plans went wrong. She could only hope this visit to Sid Tippens would not turn out badly, for either of them.

Once they reached the High Street, Samuel left her alone in the carriage while he went to find out where the bookmaker had his office. While she waited, Cecily watched the people hurrying in and out of the shops on either side of the road.

Christmas was in full swing in the High Street. Geese and ducks hung in the windows of Abbitson's, the butcher's shop, naked of their feathers and necks hanging loosely as they swung from the hooks.

The haberdashery next door had a life-sized Father Christmas in the window, surrounded by elves bearing armfuls of socks, ties, handkerchiefs, and cravats.

She was admiring the colorful display of a snow scene in the clothier's when Samuel returned, out of breath and looking decidedly disapproving.

"I have to say this, m'm. If you're planning to place a bet on the horses, or something, you really need to know what you're doing. You could lose a lot of money gambling, and I know Mr. Baxter wouldn't like that at all. He'd blame me for taking you to a bookie and—"

"For heaven's sake, Samuel, I'm not going to gamble away my hard-earned money." Cecily climbed down from the carriage and shook out the folds of her blue serge skirt. "I happened to spot a betting slip from Mr. Tippens's office marking a book in Lester Salt's parlor. I simply want to have a word with the bookmaker, that's all."

For a moment Samuel looked vastly relieved, then his frown returned. "I'd be really careful what you ask him, if I were you, m'm. This bloke is a nasty bit of business, and I wouldn't want to upset him."

Cecily smiled. "I'll be the soul of discretion, don't worry. Besides, you'll be by my side, and I have every confidence that we shall be quite safe."

"I wish I did," Samuel muttered, as he reluctantly led the way around the corner and down a narrow street. He kept looking left and right, as if expecting trouble to leap out at them from every quarter, and Cecily was quite relieved when he paused in front of a door with a small leaded glass window in it.

"This is it, m'm. You're sure—"

"I'm quite sure, Samuel." Cecily turned the handle and pushed open the door, leaving her worried stable manager to follow her into the musty office.

At first it appeared to be empty, but the jingling of the doorbell had apparently alerted someone, as a swarthy-looking man with beady eyes, dark bushy eyebrows, and a scruffy beard stepped through a tattered curtain behind the counter.

His eyebrows shot up when he saw her, and he sent a questioning look at Samuel, who hovered right behind her. "What can I do for *you*?"

He'd phrased it so that it sounded as if he doubted he could do anything for them. Cecily stepped forward, putting as much authority into her voice as she could manage. "I'd like to speak to Mr. Tippens."

The man shifted his feet and glanced at the door. "Who's asking?"

Cecily took another step closer. "My name is Cecily Baxter, and I'm the manager of the Pennyfoot Country Club."

"All right." Again Tippens glanced at the door, as if expecting someone to walk through it at any moment. "I'm Tippens. So what do you want?"

Samuel made a guttural sound in his throat, and Cecily shot up a hand to silence him. "I would like to speak to you about Mr. Lester Salt. I believe you are acquainted with him?"

The bookmaker's heavy brows met across his nose. "How is that any of your business?"

"Here!"

Samuel stepped forward and again Cecily halted him. "I'm thinking of doing some business with Mr. Salt and I'd like to know if he is trustworthy, that's all. Does he pay promptly what he owes?"

Tippens stared at her for a moment, then laughed, and it wasn't a pleasant sound. "Take my advice, lady, stay away from that rotten sod. He's bad news. Pay his debts? That's a laugh. He owes me a bundle, and if he doesn't pay up soon, he's gonna be rotting away in a coffin. Like anyone else who upsets me." He gave Samuel a look obviously meant to intimidate him.

Throwing all protocol to the wind, Samuel grabbed her arm and started tugging her backward toward the door.

"I don't suppose you knew Thomas Willow or Jimmy

Taylor?" Cecily asked, her feet skittering on the wooden boards.

Tippens's face grew dark. "Never heard of 'em. Any more questions?"

"Thank you!" Cecily's last words were answered by the slam of the door in her face. She turned to Samuel, who looked as if he were about to be sick. "Really, Samuel, I'm quite capable of leaving the shop on my own two feet."

"Yes, m'm. Now, if you don't mind, we should get back to the carriage as fast as we can."

He rushed off, and she struggled to keep up with him, feeling rather sorry for him. It couldn't be easy for him, having to protect her from people like the seedy Sid Tippens.

On the way home, she mused on the short conversation she'd had with the desultory Mr. Tippens. So Lester Salt was in debt to the bookmaker. How fortunate for him to have inherited the shoemaker's shop. Now he should be able to pay back the money he owed. The inheritance couldn't have come at a more convenient time.

Could that have been a motive for murder? Lester needed money to pay the bookie. He knew Thomas was going to leave him the shop. He might have heard about Jimmy's death and decided to kill Thomas and make it look like the same person had killed both men.

Except that the constables had kept the missing locks of hair a secret. So how would he have known to take a lock of hair from Thomas? Unless he had actually seen what happened to Jimmy. Then again, he was in the shop when Thomas was killed. Or at least, that was what he'd said.

Sighing, she stared out the window at the white-capped

ocean. She was no closer to finding the killer, and time was running out.

There were two messages waiting for her when she walked into the Pennyfoot's foyer. Philip waved her over as soon as she stepped through the door.

"Police Constable Northcott rang, m'm," Philip said, sliding his tablet over to her. "He said to ring him as soon as possible. He said it was urgent."

Cecily felt a pang of apprehension. Sam Northcott never rang her unless it was of the utmost importance. He didn't trust the telephone operators any more than she did. Especially with police business. That worried her. Could it be something else—something personal, perhaps—that he needed to discuss with her? If so, she couldn't imagine what it could be. One thing she was certain of—it was unlikely to be good news.

Glancing down at the tablet, she murmured, "I'll ring him from my office." She scanned Philip's scribbled lines. "Oh, I see my dressmaker also rang."

"Yes, m'm. She said you needed to pay her another visit. She didn't say why."

"Thank you, Philip." Cecily tore off the sheet of paper and handed him the tablet. "Has Mr. Baxter finished his work in my office?"

"Yes, m'm. I saw him go upstairs about ten minutes ago."

Cecily pulled off her scarf and folded it over her arm. "I'll be in my office, then, if anyone needs me."

Heading down the hallway to her office, she unbuttoned her cape, her mind searching for a possible reason the constable would need to talk to her so urgently.

Once inside her office she snatched the receiver off its hook. The operator's nasal tone spoke in her ear.

"Number, please?"

"Put me through to the constabulary, please." She waited, tapping her fingers on her desk, while a series of buzzes followed.

After a moment or two, a harsh voice announced, "Badgers End Constabulary."

"P.C. Northcott, please."

"Who is this?"

"Cecily Baxter, from the Pennyfoot Country Club."

"Just a moment."

The buzzing sounded again. Cecily frowned. "Operator? Are you still on the line?"

A loud click answered her, and, shaking her head, she waited for Sam.

It seemed ages until she heard his voice, stumbling over his words as usual. "Mrs. Baxter? Is that you?"

"Yes, it's me, Sam. You asked me to ring you."

"Yes, m'm. I need to see you at the station. Right away, if you can. I crashed my bicycle and bent the front wheel so I have to wait now until it's mended before I can come out there. The inspector took the carriage and it's too far to walk in this snow."

Cecily uttered a cry of dismay. "Are you all right, Sam?"

"Yes, m'm. Thank you. Banged up me elbow a bit, but I'll be right as rain as soon as I get me bicycle back."

Mindful of the operator, Cecily asked cautiously, "Is this anything to do with the situation we discussed earlier?"

"Yes, m'm, it is."

She longed to ask him if he'd discovered anything new about the case, but it would have to wait until she was alone with him in his office. "I'll be there just as soon as possible." She hung the receiver back on its hook and pulled the bell rope to summon the carriage again.

All she could hope was that Sam had news for her that would lead them to the Christmas Angel. Or better yet, that the fiend who had done these terrible things had been caught.

Something told her that wasn't likely.

CHAPTER
❈ 8 ❈

Fortunately Samuel had not yet unharnessed the bay, and by the time Cecily had left instructions with Philip on what to tell Baxter, the carriage was waiting for her at the door.

Samuel seemed upset when she told him to take her to the police station. "We'll never be back in time for supper," he said, as once more she scrambled into the carriage. "Mr. Baxter will have my hide for this."

"Piffle." Cecily tied her scarf more securely under her chin. "We'll be there and back before he even knows I'm gone."

"I wouldn't take a wager on it," Samuel muttered. He closed the door and the carriage swayed as he climbed up on his seat.

Staring out the window, Cecily was relieved to see that the snow had stopped falling at last. With any luck, Baxter's prediction would be realized, and the snow would have gone by the time the guests were due to arrive.

Except for Doris. She and Nigel would be arriving tomorrow, bringing little Essie with them. Cecily could hardly wait. She had yet to see Doris's daughter. It hardly seemed any time at all had passed since the young woman was just a child herself.

Cecily smiled to herself as she remembered the frail little girl who had first arrived at the Pennyfoot.

Everyone had thought Doris was a little strange, since one day she would be struggling to lift things and jumping at every word spoken to her and the next day she would be belligerent and hauling heavy pans of water off the stove without any effort at all.

It was weeks before anyone realized there were actually two little girls sharing the same job—Doris and her twin sister, Daisy. Now Doris was married and living in London, and Daisy was still living at the Pennyfoot, taking care of Gertie's twins. It would be good to see them together again.

Perhaps by then this nasty business would be over with, and Cecily would be free to enjoy her beloved guest.

P.C. Northcott was waiting for Cecily when she arrived at the constabulary, impatiently hovering on the doorstep when she stepped out of the carriage. He ushered her into the inner office, leaving Samuel to wait outside at the main desk.

Cecily could sense the constable's agitation, which intensified her own anxiety. "For heaven's sake, Sam. What is it? What has happened?"

Northcott picked up a sheet of paper from the desk and fanned himself with it before answering. "There's been another murder. Out on Mackerbee's pig farm. His wife found him in the barn." Northcott swallowed. "He was stabbed to death with his own knife."

Cecily sat down hard on the nearest chair. "Was he . . . ? Did he . . . ?"

"Yes, m'm." Northcott ran a finger around his collar as if it were strangling him. "He'd lost a clump of his hair, and stuck to his forehead was a golden angel. It seems we have an honest-to-goodness real live serial killer in Badgers End." She could see the fear in his eyes when he looked at her. "The Lord only knows where all this is going to end."

"It will end with us capturing this fiend," Cecily declared, with a lot more confidence than she felt. "Have you uncovered anything about this case that might be helpful?"

Northcott shook his head. "We searched the barn from top to bottom and found nothing at all. I'm completely baffled, Mrs. B. I don't even know where to start looking." He buried his face in his hands. "The missus is going to kill me if I have to stay here over Christmas because of all this."

Cecily thought he had a lot more to worry about than missing a trip to visit relatives he didn't like in the first place, but she held her tongue.

She had quite enough to worry about herself without fretting over Sam Northcott's woes. She had another murder on her hands, and if word of it got back to London, there could well be a whole list of guests canceling for Christmas.

"Have you reported this to the inspector yet?" she asked, as the constable continued to mumble to himself.

Northcott shot up his chin. "No, I haven't. I was sort of hoping we could solve this case without bothering the inspector. He's got a lot on his plate right now."

Cecily knew quite well that Northcott was worried the inspector would come down hard on him for not solving the case sooner. "Well, perhaps we could keep this latest murder quiet for a little while? It might give us a little more time to sort all this out, don't you think?"

Northcott's frown cleared. "I do, indeed, Mrs. Baxter, and I have the utmost faith in your deductive talents. I feel quite sure that given enough time, so to speak, you will unravel this puzzle and find the monster that's doing this. Just one thing." He wagged a finger at her. "I trust that when the time comes, you will not take matters into your own hands and attempt to apprehend the criminal."

Cecily smiled. "Rest assured, Sam, I shall call upon your assistance, should I identify our killer."

"Good. Then I shall continue to investigate as usual, and I hope between us we can come up with some answers. And soon."

Cecily rose, gathering up her scarf. "I certainly hope so."

Northcott scrambled to open the door for her. "One last thing. If word got back to the inspector that I had asked you to . . . ah . . . assist in this case—"

Cecily silenced him with a raised hand. "As I said, Sam, I try to avoid the inspector as much as possible. He will never know."

"Thank you, m'm. Much obliged, I'm sure."

"You can thank me when we have the killer safely locked up in prison." She left him standing there and hurried across the lobby to the door.

Samuel was already waiting for her, one hand on the handle ready to open it.

The cold wind took her breath away as she stepped outside. Twilight had crept in while she was talking to the constable, and the lamplighter was making his way down the High Street, his long pole reaching up to set the lamps aglow.

Housewives hurried along the pavements, their bulging shopping bags swinging at their sides. It was almost closing time, and Baxter would most likely be chomping at the bit by now, wondering where she had gone.

"Tomorrow," she told Samuel, "we will visit the Mackerbee farm, and on the way back we will call on Caroline Blanchard again."

Samuel's face split into a grin. "Yes, m'm. I'll be more than happy to take you there."

Cecily had no doubt of that, and once more her thoughts flew to Pansy. For the sake of the young girl, she hoped that Samuel's interest in the seamstress was just a passing fancy. For if not, her young housemaid was in for a disappointing Christmas.

Doris arrived late the next morning, having caught the early train from London. Gertie happened to be passing through the foyer when Doris walked through the door, followed by a tall, thin-faced man sporting a luxuriant mustache and a young woman who carried a wiggling child in her arms.

The minute she spotted her friend, Gertie rushed over to welcome her. "Doris! You look bleeding gorgeous. Is that real fur?" She touched the fluffy collar with her fingers. "I've always wanted a coat with a fur collar."

Doris laughed. "It's so good to see you, Gertie." She turned to the nanny and held out her arms. "Give her to me,

Adelaide. She needs to meet her Auntie Gertie." Taking the child from her, she added, "This is my husband, Nigel, Gertie. Nigel, meet Gertie Brown McBride. The most efficient chief housemaid in England."

"Go on with you." Gertie felt her cheeks growing red as she dropped a quick curtsey to Doris's husband.

He smiled at her, and Gertie could see why Doris had fallen for him. He was a handsome devil, with kind eyes and a gentle mouth.

"This is Essie." Doris turned the little girl to face Gertie, but the child ducked her head and refused to look at her. "She's going through a shy stage," Doris said, hugging her daughter.

"She's beautiful." Gertie glanced at the grandfather clock in the corner of the lobby. "I have to scram right now, but I'll see you later." She turned to Philip, who was watching them with a somewhat jaded expression on his craggy face. "Take care of the Lansfields, Philip. They're very special guests."

"My pleasure," Philip murmured as he opened the register.

Gertie was almost at the bottom of the stairs when the front doors opened and Phoebe Fortescue swept in, pink feathers waving back and forth on her gray velvet hat.

Catching sight of her, Phoebe shouted out, "Gertie! I would like a word with you."

Smothering a groan, Gertie spun around. "Yes, Mrs. Fortescue?"

Phoebe winced as the door, apparently driven by the wind, slammed shut behind her. "I was wondering if your little ones had made up their minds yet? If they want to be in *Peter Pan* they will have to be ready to start rehearsals in the ballroom this afternoon."

Gertie sighed. Having felt compelled to keep her promise, she'd mentioned the pantomime to the twins the night before, trying to make it sound boring and difficult in the hopes they'd refuse.

They weren't fooled for an instant, however, and had excitedly agreed to be in the show. Gertie had tried a few weak arguments but there was no stopping her twins once they got their teeth into something. "They said they want to do it," she told Phoebe, "but don't be surprised if it all becomes too much for them and they throw a temper tantrum. They can be difficult when they're tired or upset."

Phoebe sniffed. "I know how to handle children." She tugged on her hat to straighten it. "Have no fear. Lillian and James will have the time of their lives up on the stage."

Gertie still had serious doubts about that, but it was out of her hands now. She just hoped the twins wouldn't cause any trouble. Phoebe's presentations usually ended in disaster as it was, and all Gertie could hope for was that her children wouldn't add to the confusion.

Promising to have them in the ballroom that afternoon, she started up the stairs. She had climbed three of them when Phoebe's shriek tore across the lobby.

"Doris! I had no idea you were coming down here this year!"

Gertie turned to watch Phoebe rush over to the little group at the desk. Completely ignoring Nigel, Phoebe grabbed Doris's arm. "You simply *have* to be in my pantomime! We're doing *Peter Pan* and you'd be the absolute *perfect* Wendy."

Doris started to protest, but Phoebe cut her off. "I simply *won't* take no for an answer! Rehearsals begin this afternoon in the ballroom. Two o'clock sharp. I expect you to be there." She leaned forward. "Oh, such a *beautiful* child! Hello, my precious little one!"

The little girl promptly howled and clung to her mother's neck. Doris started to explain, but Phoebe was far too excited about her pantomime to care. Raising her voice above the child's screams, she said something that Gertie couldn't hear.

Climbing the stairs, Gertie rolled her eyes at the ceiling. Phoebe had the cheek of the devil, and it would bloody serve her right if this pantomime ended up a flipping mess like all the rest of them.

In the next instant, she took it back. Her twins would be up there, and she didn't want nothing going wrong this time. Maybe, for once, Phoebe could pull off the perfect show. Gertie uttered a scornful laugh. Even she knew better than to expect miracles.

"You're going out *again*?" Baxter picked up the cushion from his chair and gave it a thumping. "Where to this time?"

"I'm sorry, darling, but I must pay another visit to my seamstress. She needs another fitting before she can finish my ball gown." Cecily took the cushion from him and put it back on the chair. "I shall try not to be too long. I thought you intended to go into the city today?"

"The trains are still running slow. I thought I'd wait until tomorrow. Maybe the thaw will have set in by then." He gave her a suspicious stare. "You haven't said much about your investigation."

She met his frown with a smile. "That's because there isn't much to tell. Oh, by the way, the new owner of Willow's shoe store, Lester Salt, hopes you will continue to shop there for your shoes. I have to tell you, though, he seems a little shifty to me. I don't know that I trust him all that much."

Baxter lifted an eyebrow. "Shifty?"

"Yes." She pulled on a glove and smoothed it up to her elbow. "I think perhaps you should find another shoemaker."

"I'll keep it under consideration." He continued to regard her with an intense frown. "What were you doing in the shoe shop, anyway?"

She gave him another expansive smile. "Buying Christmas presents, of course."

"Why do I have the feeling you're not telling me everything?"

She managed a light laugh. "Darling, you are far too concerned about me. I will tell you if there's anything significant happening."

"I wish I could believe that."

"I wish you could, too." She reached up to plant a kiss on his cheek. "I shall be home again soon. Oh, by the way, Phoebe will be holding rehearsals in the ballroom this afternoon, and I'm expecting Doris and her family to arrive any minute. Would you be a dear and take care of things for me until I return?"

"If you insist." He walked with her to the door. "I sincerely hope all this running back and forth will be over with by the time our Christmas guests arrive. I can't imagine how everything would get done without you."

"You give me entirely too much credit. We have admirable staff who are capable of keeping things running smoothly under the worst possible conditions."

"Ah, but they need supervision, and only you can manage that effectively."

She looked at him in surprise. "Why, Bax, darling, I cannot remember you ever being so effusive with your compliments. Perhaps it is you who is not telling me everything. Are you, by any chance, waiting for an opportunity to give me some unpleasant news?"

Both of Baxter's eyebrows shot up. "News? Not to my knowledge. I was merely attempting to stir up some of that Christmas spirit you're always talking about."

"Thank goodness." Cecily waved at her face with an imaginary fan. "I thought for a moment that you had accepted that position abroad."

An enigmatic expression that worried her crossed his face. "I would not do that without consulting you first, my dear. You must know that."

"Yes, but—"

He laid a finger over her lips, cutting off her words. "Hush, now. This is not the time to be making life-changing decisions. We can discuss the matter after Christmas, when there are few guests to worry about and we have time to think."

So, as she feared, the matter was not ended. She bid him good-bye and hurried down the stairs, her mind full of misgivings. It seemed that this opportunity would always be between them. Her husband dearly wanted to accept it, and she did not. It was as simple as that. If only the solution to the problem were as simple.

She put the matter out of her mind on the way out to Mackerbee's farm. There were other matters that had to take precedence over her personal worries.

Although no more snow had fallen, the icy ruts on the lane that led to the farmhouse had the carriage bouncing up and down hard enough to rattle Cecily's teeth.

Stepping at last onto the frozen ground, she wished she'd brought a pillow to sit on. Her bones ached as she followed Samuel up the redbrick path to the door.

The housekeeper who answered their knock seemed reluctant to allow them to enter. It wasn't until Cecily mentioned that P.C. Northcott had told her about the murder that she finally ushered them into a tidy parlor and asked them to wait.

Minutes later a puffy-eyed woman entered the room, continually dabbing at her nose with a man's white handkerchief. "I hope you will excuse me, Mrs. Baxter," she said, her voice catching on her words, "but I have just lost my husband, and I'm still feeling the shock."

"Of course," Cecily murmured, feeling guilt wash over her. Although questioning the recently bereaved was not new to her, it was never easy. She could imagine how she would feel if she lost Baxter under such circumstances.

She looked up at the woman, her voice registering her sympathy. "I'm dreadfully sorry for your loss. I humbly apologize for intruding at this time, but I'm sure you would want whoever did this dreadful deed caught and punished, and the sooner we can find him, the less chance there is of him depriving someone else of a loved one."

Mrs. Mackerbee sank onto the couch, tears running down her face. "I will tell you what I can, but like I told the constable, I don't know anything, really. Colin had been slaughtering pigs for the market. We'd had an exceptionally good year, and he was getting a good price for them." She stifled a sob. "The best year we've ever had, and he won't be here to enjoy the proceeds."

"I'm sorry." Cecily waited a moment for the woman to collect herself, then prompted, "You were saying?"

"Oh, yes." The widow hunted for a handkerchief, found one in her pocket, and blew her nose. "Well, like always when he's that busy, he wasn't home when I went to bed. I woke up in the night and he still wasn't home, so I went looking for him." She started to sob. "I'll never forget the sight of him lying there with that gold thing stuck on his face. . . ."

She was crying in earnest now, and Samuel, who had been standing by the window, took a step forward, concern written all over his face.

Cecily shook her head at him. Just at that moment, the door opened and the housekeeper walked in carrying a loaded tea tray. She took one look at the farmer's wife and glared at Cecily.

Mrs. Mackerbee, however, appeared to collect herself and ordered the housekeeper to lay the tray down on a small table.

Cecily suffered through an awkward silence while the disapproving woman poured the tea and handed her the cup and saucer.

Taking it from her, Cecily thanked her graciously, then waited until she had left the room before addressing the farmer's wife again.

"I know these questions might be painful," she said, as Mrs. Mackerbee sipped her tea, "but I believe they might help in the investigation. I would greatly appreciate it if you would try to answer them for me."

Mrs. Mackerbee nodded. "I'll do what I can."

"Very well. First of all, can you think of anyone who might want to hurt your husband?"

The widow's bottom lip trembled, and she struggled to hold back her tears. "Not a soul. Colin was a good man, a friend to everyone. He'd give his last crumb of bread to someone in need and go hungry himself. I never met anyone who didn't like him. Except perhaps . . ." She paused and shook her head. "No, never mind."

Cecily leaned forward. "You know of someone?"

Mrs. Mackerbee's cup rattled in the saucer as she put it down with a shaky hand. "No really, no. It's just . . ." Her voice trailed off, and she stared at the half-empty cup as if in a trance.

"Mrs. Mackerbee." Cecily reached out and touched the woman's arm. "I'd appreciate anything you can tell me about this dreadful matter. It's vitally important we capture this evil monster."

The widow started and gradually her eyes focused on Cecily's face. "Yes, I understand. I just don't want to get an innocent person in trouble."

"If he's innocent you have nothing to fear."

For another long, painful moment the other woman hesitated, then she said slowly, "There was a young lad working on the farm not too long ago. Nice boy, but completely useless for farmwork. Colin had to let him go. He was upset about it—Colin, I mean—because he really liked Basil, but

111

he had to be honest about it when the other farmers asked him for a reference. He told them Basil would never be any good on the farm. He just wasn't cut out for it."

Cecily could hardly wait for her to stop speaking before asking, "Would that be Basil Baker, by any chance?"

The widow widened her eyes. "Yes! It was! Do you know him?"

"I met him the other day." Cecily paused, then added, "Would you say he was hot-tempered?"

"No, no, not at all." Mrs. Mackerbee held out her hand in appeal. "Please, Mrs. Baxter, don't take anything I say the wrong way. Basil was upset when he lost his job, and there was a bit of an argument, but he would never hurt a fly, I'm sure of that. That's why he wasn't any good on the farm. He couldn't stand it when the pigs had to be slaughtered. Broke his heart, it did. He treated all the animals like they were his children. He was just too softhearted for this kind of work."

"But he was upset with your husband."

"I suppose so." She reached for her cup again, shaking her head. "No, it couldn't have been Basil. I just can't believe he would do that."

She didn't want to believe it, either, Cecily thought, but she'd been fooled too many times in the past to take anything for granted. She leaned back. "Was your husband acquainted with Thomas Willow, or Jimmy Taylor?"

"I don't know about the first gentleman, but I believe Colin knew Jimmy." Mrs. Mackerbee choked on the tea and quickly put down the cup. "Jimmy died last week. Are you saying there's some sort of coincidence?"

Cecily hesitated, then said reluctantly, "Not a coincidence. There's a possibility the deaths are linked."

"How very strange." The widow frowned. "You think the same person who killed my Colin killed Jimmy Taylor as well?"

"Yes, as well as Thomas Willow, the shoemaker. They all were found with gold stamps on their foreheads."

The fear was painfully evident on the widow's face. "The saints preserve us. I wonder who's next."

"Exactly. Which is why we have to be aggressive in our search for this killer." Cecily drained her cup and set it down in its saucer. Rising to her feet, she added, "Since you weren't acquainted with Mr. Willow, I assume you haven't met his former assistant, Lester Salt."

Mrs. Mackerbee struggled to her feet. "I'm not familiar with either name. Do they live in the village?"

"Mr. Willow owned Willow's shoe shop until he died and left the business to Mr. Salt."

"Oh! I know the shoe store. I pass it every time I go to the High Street." Mrs. Mackerbee led the way to the door, nodding at Samuel when he stepped forward and opened it for her. "I've never been inside, though. Colin goes . . . went in there occasionally to buy boots. In fact, he was just in there last week." Once more the mask of misery clouded her face. "I don't know what I'm going to do now. It's going to be hard without him."

Cecily impulsively put an arm about her shoulders. "It will take time, I know, but you will be strong and survive. I lost my husband many years ago, and at the time I wanted to die, too. I'm very glad I didn't, since I'm now married again and very happy. I hope you will be, too."

"Thank you, Mrs. Baxter." Mrs. Mackerbee paused by the front door as Samuel tugged it open. "I've heard that you're clever in finding murderers. Much cleverer than our constables, though they do their best, no doubt. Anyway, I just want to say I hope you find this horrible man before he kills someone else. I wouldn't wish this pain on anyone."

"I will certainly do my best." Cecily stepped outside, shivering as she dragged her coat collar closer around her neck. "Would you mind if I take a look around the barn where your husband died?"

The widow looked startled for a moment, then shook her head. "Not at all. It's the one closest to you, right over there." She pointed at a barn on the other side of the yard. "I could come with you if you like?"

Cecily could tell from the other woman's tentative tone that it was the last thing she wanted to do. Assuring her that they would be perfectly fine on their own, Cecily beckoned to Samuel and headed for the barn.

It was obvious, the moment she entered, that it was unlikely she'd find anything of value. The barn had been meticulously cleaned out, with new straw scattered over what must have been the place where Colin Mackerbee had died.

After searching around for only a few moments, Cecily gave up and led Samuel back to the carriage. The deeper she dug into this case, the more confusing it became.

Someone out there had managed to dispose of three men without leaving a single clue behind. Except for the gold stamps and the missing locks of hair—a rather deliberate attempt to link the murders.

What kind of strange mind would go to such lengths? Who were they dealing with, and what was the killer's purpose? Again she remembered Madeline's words. *He is clever and extremely dangerous.* Cecily shuddered. Could it be that, for the first time, she was up against a foe so formidable she was helpless to stop him?

Maybe they should call in the inspector, after all. It could take the full force and expertise of Scotland Yard to apprehend a killer this devious.

Not yet. P.C. Northcott had faith in her abilities, and she could not let him down now. She would find this madman and put him behind bars if it took all of Christmas to do so. She just hoped it wouldn't cost her marriage.

CHAPTER
❊ 9 ❊

Having wheedled an hour off from Mrs. Chubb, Gertie rushed her twins to the ballroom, where the rehearsal was already under way. As always, there was complete chaos as young women rushed to and fro, bumping into one another and arguing with wildly flapping arms, while Phoebe stood in their midst screeching instructions that everyone ignored.

Gertie was sorely tempted to take Lillian and James straight back to her quarters, but the twins dragged her over to the stage, loudly proclaiming their arrival.

Phoebe caught sight of them and yelled, "You're late! All children are to go to the green room and *stay* there until you are called."

Gertie felt like sticking out her tongue, but, mindful of her little ones, she contended herself with tossing her head before marching the twins backstage and into the green room.

The noise wasn't much better in there. Three boys and two girls, all close to the twins' age, were throwing stage props at one another, while one bored-looking mother sat knitting in a corner.

"The rest of the mums left me in charge of 'em," she told Gertie, nodding at the screaming children. "They won't take any notice of me."

Gertie let go of the twins' hands and yelled at the top of her voice. "*Qui-et!*"

The yelling subsided, and one of the boys stuck his nose in the air. "Who are you?"

Gertie dug her fists into her hips. "I'm the one with the blinking rolling pin, that's who. Any more noise from any of you and you'll get a bloody bonk on the head with it. So shut up and sit down. On the floor. All of you."

Ignoring the other woman, who sat staring at her with her mouth open, Gertie pointed at one of the boys. "You. Pick up this flipping mess and put it all back where it bloody belongs."

"It weren't my fault!" he protested, but Gertie took a threatening step toward him and he darted off, snatching up clothes and wigs from off the floor as he went.

"All right, that's better." Gertie crossed her arms and glared at the children, including her twins. "From now on, you all sit still and don't say a bloody word."

A muttered chorus answered her.

"Good." She dragged a chair from out of the corner and stuck it in front of her audience. "Now, you can all tell me your names, starting with you two." She nodded at the twins.

James and Lillian both promptly announced their names, and the rest meekly followed. Just as the last little girl spoke her name, the door opened and Phoebe rushed in.

"Where are they? Oh, there they are." She flapped her hands at the seated children. "Everyone up, up, up! It's time to go onstage. Now file out in a line, one behind the other. That's it! One, two, one, two . . ."

Gertie watched them all march out the door, then grinned at the mother. "I don't bloody envy her one bit. She's got her hands full, all right."

The other woman folded up her knitting and shoved it into a bag. "I think you should be the one in charge of them. They pay attention to you. I don't think they will behave that well with Mrs. Fortescue."

Gertie patted her on the shoulder. "She'll manage. She always does. Come on, let's go and watch them from the front. It's the first time mine have been in a pantomime. I can't wait to see how they get on."

She led the way out front, wondering just how long it would be before the children drove Phoebe crazy. That was always good for a bloody laugh, watching Phoebe Fortescue in one of her temper tantrums. It was usually the highlight of the whole flipping show.

Considering it was the first rehearsal, it didn't go half-bad in Gertie's opinion. Lillian burst into tears when told she was supposed to be a boy, but after romping around on the pirate ship for a while, she soon settled down.

Gertie was amazed at how fast Lillian and James took direction and remembered their parts. Phoebe strode about the stage giving orders and getting in everyone's way, but somehow they all got through the scene without any huge mishaps.

Just as Phoebe called a halt to the rehearsal, Gertie felt a hand on her shoulder. She didn't have to turn around to know who stood behind her.

"You did a lovely job on the pirate ship," she said, smiling up at Clive. "It looks bloody real. Especially when it moves."

He smiled back at her. "I'm still not happy with the wiring. It will take some more work before I allow anyone on it."

"I'm just glad my twins don't have to fly." Gertie looked up at the harnesses hanging from the rafters. "It's not that I don't trust your work, but Mrs. Fortescue has a history of bad luck on this stage."

"I know." Clive followed her gaze. "That's why I'm going to be extra careful."

"Well, maybe this time nothing will go wrong." She turned her head as Lillian called out Clive's name and ran toward him.

He swept the child up in his arms and gave her a hug before setting her down.

Once again Gertie longed to know if he had children of his own. She knew, however, that this wasn't the place or time to ask him. It would just have to wait until the sleigh ride. That was, if the snow didn't all melt away before they could go.

To her amazement, he seemed to read her mind. "I think we should take that sleigh ride tomorrow," he said, laughing as both Lillian and James let out a shriek of excitement. "If we wait too long there won't be any snow left to ride on."

"I'll have to see if I can switch my afternoon off with someone." Gertie saw the expressions of alarm on her children's faces. "Don't worry," she told them. "I'll manage it somehow." She glanced at Clive out of the corner of her eye. "This time nothing is going to stop us going."

Clive put his hand over his heart. "I promise. Tomorrow we go."

Gertie watched the twins jump up and down and knew exactly how they felt. It had been a long time since she'd looked forward to something this much. All her previous doubts seemed to have melted away. Now tomorrow couldn't come soon enough for her.

Cecily arrived at Caroline Blanchard's home just as dusk was settling in over the countryside. The windows of the seamstress's cottage glowed from the light of oil lamps, and a cheerful fire danced in the fireplace as she ushered her guests into the parlor.

After shooing out what seemed like a hoard of cats and dogs from the room, Caroline offered Cecily a cup of tea, which was hastily declined.

"I am in rather a hurry to get back to the Pennyfoot," she told Caroline, ignoring Samuel's look of disappointment. "I'm expecting guests to arrive, and I'm anxious to welcome them."

"Oh, of course. Then we will go at once to the fitting room." She headed for the door, nearly colliding with Samuel in his haste to open the door for her.

She gave him a stiff, "Thank you," and sailed through,

leaving him staring after her with a dazed expression on his face.

Cecily coughed, and he sprang back to let her pass. She thanked him and received a sheepish smile as she hurried out the door after Caroline.

Entering the fitting room, she noticed that all but two of the gowns had gone. Caroline must have been busy since Cecily last visited.

She soon forgot about it when Caroline helped her slip the ball gown over her head and button it up.

It fit perfectly, making her look almost slim in the long mirror. She turned this way and that, well satisfied with the way the silky folds fell smoothly from her hips to her ankles.

Caroline, however, seemed hesitant. "The latest fashions from Paris indicate a shorter hem this year," she said, studying the gown. "I think I should shorten it just a little. I'm really busy right now but I could have it ready in the next two or three days."

Cecily considered it, staring at her image in the mirror. The gown looked perfect to her, but on the other hand, if the ladies were wearing shorter hems this year she certainly didn't want to look out of date, and it was too late now to order a new gown.

"Very well," she said at last. "I still have some shopping to do. I can pick it up on the way back the next time I go into town." She turned, looking over her shoulder for another view. "You have done an excellent job," she told Caroline, who actually smiled at the compliment. "It looks wonderful, and now I can hardly wait to wear it."

In fact, it pleased her so much she couldn't resist adding,

"Would you like to come to the Welcome Ball? It is usually reserved for the Pennyfoot guests, but you have made me look so elegant, I feel I should reward you in some manner. I would be most happy if you could join us."

Caroline's smile wavered. "Thank you, Mrs. Baxter. It is most kind of you, I'm sure, but I have no one to escort me, so I must decline."

"Oh, that's a shame." Cecily turned her back so that Caroline could unbutton the gown. "If you should change your mind and can think of someone to escort you, then you will be more than welcome."

Caroline bowed her head. "I doubt that will happen. I am quite content to spend my days here with my animals to keep me company. I find them more congenial than most people I meet."

Cecily thought she heard a wistful note in the seamstress's voice and felt sad for the woman. She was too young to be spending her life alone with only cats and dogs for companionship.

If it wasn't for Pansy, she might have encouraged Samuel to court Caroline. Samuel loved animals, too, and had rescued a stray dog himself, so they had something in common.

Shaking off the thought, she returned to the parlor. Baxter was always chiding her for meddling in others' affairs, and he would no doubt point out that in order for Samuel to make Caroline happy, he would have to break Pansy's heart.

And that wouldn't do at all.

She found Samuel petting a dog that looked vaguely familiar. Her stable manager looked up with an air of expectancy as Caroline entered, only to be disappointed when she deliberately ignored him.

"Come, Samuel, we must be on our way." She waited for him to give the dog a final pat and then, with a hasty farewell to Caroline, hurried out the door.

Anxious now to return home, Cecily urged Samuel to hurry as they rattled and bounced over the country roads. She was thankful when they entered the Esplanade where the ride was a little smoother, thanks to the wheels of carriages and the occasional motorcar that had worn down the ruts.

The moment she entered the foyer she noticed the Christmas tree by the stairs. The footmen must have brought it in for Madeline. Its branches were bare right now, but Cecily knew the kind of magic Madeline was capable of, and had no doubt that she would turn the tree into a breathtaking vision of splendor.

Smiling, she crossed the carpet to the reception desk, where Philip was snoozing on his chair. Punching the bell to wake him up, she asked, "Have Mr. and Mrs. Lansfield arrived yet?"

Philip started, jerked his hand, and knocked over the penholder. Scrabbling to right it, he muttered, "Ah . . . yes, m'm. The Lansfield party arrived this morning."

"Do you know where they are now?"

"I saw Mr. Lansfield pass by a short while ago. Mrs. Lansfield wasn't with him."

"She is probably in her room. Thank you, Philip." Cecily headed for the stairs and hurried up them to the second floor.

The young woman who answered her knock seemed a little tense, no doubt due to the child crying somewhere inside the room. "Mrs. Lansfield is in the ballroom," she said, in answer to Cecily's inquiry. "I believe she's rehearsing for a presentation of some kind."

Taken aback, Cecily thanked her and once more headed for the stairs. What was Phoebe thinking of, asking Doris to perform in her pantomime? True, the songstress had obliged her before, but that was when she was still appearing on the stage. Doris was married now, with a child. Phoebe had absolutely no right to pester the woman now.

Cecily stormed down the steps, rehearsing exactly what she would say to Phoebe when she saw her.

She never reached the ballroom, however. Just as she arrived at the bottom of the stairs, Doris appeared in the foyer, followed by Daisy and Gertie's twins, all chattering at once.

Lillian ran over to Cecily and threw her skinny arms around Cecily's hips. "We had such fun," she said, her eyes sparkling with excitement. "We learned to dance and sing and everything!"

Cecily patted her godchild on the head. "I'm so glad you're having a good time, precious."

At her words James came rushing over to her and tugged on her skirt. "I'm having a good time, too!"

Cecily put an arm around each of her godchildren and gave them both a peck on the cheek. "I shall look forward to seeing you both perform," she told them.

Daisy broke away from her sister and hurried over to take the children by the hand. "I promised Gertie I'd have them back in their room before she had to serve supper," she said, looking worried.

Cecily glanced at the clock. "You have a few minutes yet. Tell Gertie I kept them talking."

Daisy grinned. "Yes, m'm." She waved at Doris, then led the twins to the kitchen stairs.

Doris, who had followed her sister, watched them leave, then turned to Cecily. "It's wonderful to see you again, m'm."

"Oh, Doris, this is such a delight. It's always so lovely to see you. Where is your husband? I'm dying to meet him. And little Essie." Cecily waved a hand at the stairs. "I was just up at your room and I heard her when your nanny answered the door, but I didn't like to disturb them without seeing you first."

Doris looked anxious. "Was she crying? She cries a lot when I'm not there."

Avoiding a direct answer, Cecily murmured, "Your nanny seems very capable. It's probably just a phase the child is going through."

Doris sighed. "She seems to have a lot of phases. Daisy offered to take care of her, but she has her hands full with the twins, and Essie isn't used to her. Besides, what would Adelaide do all day without Essie to look after?"

"What, indeed." Cecily glanced at the grandfather clock. "In fact, you should be spending this time with your family instead of performing just to please Phoebe. I'm most annoyed with her for demanding such an obligation from you. Shame on her."

Doris laughed. "It's quite all right, m'm, honestly. I'm really enjoying being onstage again. I haven't done any singing since I got married and I do miss it."

"But what about your husband? How does he feel about it?"

Doris shrugged. "Well, to tell the truth, he wasn't all that happy about it at first. I think he was afraid that I'd have such a good time I'd want to go back to it. I couldn't do that, of course. Not now. Once I told him that, he was all right with it."

"Well, as long as you don't mind. As for Daisy, I think she'd enjoy taking care of Essie now and then, if you wanted to give your nanny a little time to herself. Daisy is wonderful with the twins. I'm sure she could handle Essie beautifully."

Doris nodded. "Maybe I will. You're right, m'm. Daisy is good with children. I told her she should have some of her own instead of taking care of other people's children."

Cecily smiled. "Don't let Gertie hear you say that. I don't know what she'd do without Daisy."

"Oh, Daisy would never leave the twins, m'm. I really think that if she were to get married, she'd want to take them with her."

Cecily was still smiling about that as she made her way to the ballroom.

There was no sign of Phoebe when she entered, but Madeline was over by the windows, perched on a ladder high enough to make Cecily's blood run cold.

"What are you doing?" She sped over to the ladder, hands outstretched. "Why aren't the footmen doing that for you?"

Madeline turned her head to look down at her, her arms full of red velvet ribbons. "The footmen don't know the difference between a bow and a loop, that's why." She tilted her head to one side. "You seem tense, my friend."

"Tense? I'm practically rigid. Do come down from there before you hurt yourself."

Madeline's melodious laugh echoed up to the ceiling. "You know me better than that, Cecily dear. I can take good care of myself. Nevertheless, since it disturbs you so much, I'll come down. I'm just about finished here, anyway."

She leaned back to survey the gold and silver garlands she'd strung above the tall windows and looped all the way across the balconies.

"It looks marvelous," Cecily declared. "Absolutely perfect. Now come down and I'll have the footmen put up the bows tomorrow."

Madeline descended the ladder far too swiftly in Cecily's opinion and landed lightly on her feet at the bottom. "I have to gather holly and mistletoe from the woods in the next day or two. Kevin can bring them here in the carriage before he goes on his rounds."

"I could have Samuel take you, if you'd prefer." Cecily took the ribbons from her and laid them on a nearby table. "Just tell me when you want to go."

"That would be wonderful, thank you. I hate asking Kevin when he's so busy. This cold weather has filled his surgery with patients." Madeline gave her a sharp, intense scrutiny. "Something else has happened, hasn't it. Another victim of the Christmas Angel."

Her friend's remarkable ability to read her mind never failed to impress Cecily. "Yes, I'm afraid you're right." She went on to recount her visit to the Mackerbee farm.

"Everything seems to come back to Basil Baker," Cecily added, as Madeline wound the ribbons up into balls and fitted them into a basket. "Yet everyone I talk to insists that he simply isn't capable of murder."

"And what do *you* think?"

Cecily picked up a ribbon and began winding it. "I don't

know what to think. I do know that given enough incentive, we are all capable of taking another's life. But these seem such senseless, cold-blooded killings. I just can't imagine the young man I spoke with being responsible for such evil."

"What I find most disturbing is the locks of hair being taken from the victims." Madeline took the ribbon ball from her and placed it in the basket. "It suggests that our killer is dabbling in the occult. There are certain . . . rituals that can be performed with locks of hair belonging to the deceased."

Cecily felt a chill. "Such as?"

"Well, there are fortunate ones, such as passing on inherited talents to the descendants, and there are evil ones, such as sending souls to the devil."

"You think our killer is performing one of these rituals?"

Madeline shrugged. "I can't think of any other reason why he would take a lock of hair from all of his victims."

"He could simply be trying to confuse everyone into thinking the murders were committed by an evil spirit or something."

"He could. On the other hand, the murders could have really been committed by someone in league with an evil spirit."

Cecily shivered. "If that's so, I am at a distinct disadvantage."

Madeline paused, one long ribbon dangling from her hand. "Whoever your killer is, Cecily, be warned. There is a diabolical mind behind these acts of violence, and such hatred has destroyed all reason. I beg you, be careful."

"I shall, never fear." Shaking off a surge of apprehension,

Cecily smiled. "Now come, share a glass of sherry with me before you go out in the cold. I'll have one of the footmen take you home."

"No need." Madeline packed the last ribbon away and shut the lid on the basket. "Kevin is stopping by to fetch me. He should be here any minute."

"Oh, good." Cecily led the way to the door, pausing to admire the golden garlands and silver bells hanging above the stage. "I would like a word with him, if he has time."

"He always has time for you, my dear."

Something in the way she said it made Cecily wonder if her friend knew that at one time, Dr. Kevin Prestwick had paid a great deal of attention to Cecily.

That was long before he'd married Madeline, of course, and even he must have forgotten about it by now. The one person who hadn't forgotten was Baxter. He always acted somewhat antagonistic when in the presence of the good doctor, yet whenever Kevin needed help, Baxter was always the first one there to offer it to him.

As it was, Kevin was talking to Baxter in the foyer when she and Madeline arrived there.

"Ah," Baxter said, when he spotted Cecily. "I do believe this is my wife, though I see her so rarely these days I'm not sure I recognize her."

"Piffle." Cecily smiled at the doctor. "Take no notice of him, Kevin. He's still having trouble finding the Christmas spirit."

Kevin reached for her hand and pressed it to his lips. "It is indeed a great pleasure to see you again, Cecily."

Baxter muttered something under his breath, and she warned him with a quick frown.

"Likewise." She pulled her hand from Kevin's fingers. "I was wondering if you have time for a quick word or two?"

Kevin glanced around the empty foyer and lowered his voice. "About the recent murders, I presume?"

Cecily also looked over her shoulder. Satisfied they were alone, she asked, "What can you tell me about them?"

"Not much." Kevin hunched his shoulders. "They were brutal. The victims were obviously attacked by someone in a great rage. All three had a chunk of hair missing and a stamp stuck on their forehead."

"All three?" Baxter's sharp voice interrupted. "There's another one?"

Cecily cursed herself for forgetting she hadn't told him. "Yes, dear." She laid a hand on his arm. "I'm sorry, I should have mentioned it. Mr. Mackerbee from Mackerbee's pig farm. His wife found him stabbed to death."

Baxter eyed her with suspicion. "When did you come by this information?"

"Last night, dear. I didn't want to spoil the evening by bringing up such a morbid subject, and I quite forgot to mention it this morning." She sent Madeline a meaningful glance, hoping that her friend would interpret it. It would save a lot of awkwardness if Baxter wasn't informed of her visit to the Mackerbee farm.

True, he had grudgingly given his blessing for her investigation, but the less he knew, the less he worried, and the more freedom she'd have to continue.

Even so, he eyed her now with alarm. "This is beginning to sound as though we have an exceptionally dangerous criminal lurking out there."

Cecily patted his arm. "They are all dangerous, my love. Until they are caught, which they usually are in the end."

Baxter's mouth had pulled into a thin line. "Yes, but this is different. From what I hear, the victims are random, with no obvious reason for their murders and no connection to each other. Which means anyone could be the killer's next target. Including you."

Cecily shook her head. "I disagree. The fact that all three victims had locks of hair missing and gold angels stuck to their heads is symbolic of something. There's a connection there somewhere, and once we find that, we'll find the killer."

Baxter looked to Kevin for help. "What do *you* think? Just how dangerous is this killer?"

Kevin shrugged. "This person is obviously greatly disturbed and therefore highly unpredictable. I tend to agree with Cecily, however, that there is a link between the victims. All we have to do is find it."

Baxter nodded. "That's *all* you have to do. Never mind the danger."

Afraid she was losing this argument, Cecily tugged on his arm. "Darling, you know I promised you to take the utmost care. The people I question have nothing to do with the murders. They are the victims. They have all lost loved ones. I'm here to help them and try to prevent someone else losing someone they love. They will not hurt me."

Madeline finally spoke up. "Don't worry, Baxter. Your wife is an intrepid and clever sleuth. No one will get the better of her, I promise you."

Cecily smiled her thanks, while Baxter looked unconvinced.

"Well, my dear, we should be getting home," Kevin announced, taking his wife's arm. "We must spend a little time with our daughter before she lies down to sleep."

Cecily walked with them to the door. "I know I don't have to remind you," she said, "that it's imperative we keep quiet about all this murder business. We don't want to start a panic in the village, though I suppose it will only be a matter of time before word gets out."

Kevin looked grave. "I'm afraid the rumors have already started. Two of my patients have asked me what I know about the Christmas Angel. I've done my best to reassure them but, as you say, it's only a matter of time."

"Then we must find this killer, and soon."

"I agree." He stood aside to allow Madeline to exit.

"I'll see you in the morning, Cecily!" With a wave of her hand, Madeline stepped out into the cold night followed by her husband.

Cecily watched them go, Madeline's words ringing in her ears. *No one will get the better of her, I promise you*. She could only hope that would prove to be true.

CHAPTER

❋ 10 ❋

Baxter left for London early the next day, leaving Cecily alone with her thoughts. She had lain awake for at least an hour that morning, going over in her mind everything she had learned so far.

The only link to the murders was Basil Baker. He knew all three of the victims and had good reason to resent two of them. There was, however, one way to possibly rule him out.

It was almost noon before she finally sat down in her office. She wasted no time in picking up the telephone and asking the operator to put her through to the paper factory in Wellercombe.

It took a while before the operator finally reached someone, and the gentleman who spoke to her seemed irritated to be disturbed. He spoke very fast and very abruptly, as if he wanted to put an end to the conversation as soon as possible.

"Yes," he said, in answer to Cecily's question, "Basil Baker works here, and yes, he's been here all week. His day off is Sunday, that's all."

Cecily frowned. "*Every* Sunday?"

The man sounded even more annoyed. "Yes, madam. Every Sunday. Now if you will excuse me, I have work to do."

The loud click in her ear told her the conversation was at an end. Cecily replaced the receiver, her brows knitted together. Basil could not have killed Colin, since he was in Wellercombe all day. Unless he'd found a way to sneak out and return without anyone seeing him.

On the other hand, Jimmy had died on a Sunday. Basil's day off. Yet when she'd asked Basil, he'd told her he was working the day Jimmy died. It would seem that Basil had not told the truth. The question now was why he'd found it necessary to lie.

Could it be that her theory was correct—that Basil had thrown the rock at Jimmy after all? And that someone had seen the incident and taken advantage of the situation?

She leaned back in her chair, closing her eyes. Maybe she was wrong about there being a connection. Maybe they were all wrong. The memory of her last skirmish with a killer remained clear in her mind.

They had all been so certain it was a serial killer, never dreaming that the murderer was killing random victims to place the blame on a notorious London mass murderer.

Maybe these present victims, as Baxter had suggested, were all random, with nothing in common. After all, Badgers End was only a small village. It wasn't that surprising that Basil knew them all.

If so, her chances of catching the killer would have to rely on luck. And that, as Cecily knew well, was a very long shot.

She was about to get up from her desk when the telephone rang. After the second ring it was silent, meaning that Philip had picked it up at the reception desk.

Hoping that it wasn't another cancellation, Cecily left the office and went in search of Samuel. It seemed that another visit to Basil Baker was in order, and although she didn't expect to gain much more insight into the case, she dearly wanted to know why Basil had lied about being at work the day Jimmy Taylor died.

She encountered Pansy in the hallway and sent her to order the carriage, then continued on to the foyer, to find out if the telephone message was bad news.

Philip assured her that it was simply a guest inquiring about the weather. "I told the gentleman that it has stopped snowing and that a thaw is on the way." He smirked. "He seemed quite pleased about that."

Cecily looked at him in surprise. "Where did you get the news about a thaw?"

Philip shrugged. "I didn't. But sooner or later it's going to thaw, isn't it? I just didn't say when."

Cecily pinched her lips. She was about to chide her desk clerk when a blast of cold air announced the opening of the front door.

Sam Northcott's bellow echoed all the way across the foyer. "Mrs. Baxter! I want a word with you!"

"Blimey," Philip muttered. "Can't he wait until he's a bit closer?"

Cecily was inclined to agree, though she could see that

the constable appeared to be highly agitated. He had forgotten to remove his helmet, and his hand fluttered up and down as though he were trying to shake something nasty from it.

Watching him rush toward her, Cecily felt a stab of anxiety. "Philip," she said, "have a bottle of brandy sent to my office. Right away."

She didn't wait for him to reply. Sam Northcott reached her while she was still talking, his eyes brightening when she mentioned the brandy. "My office, Sam," she said, and led the way down the hallway.

Northcott barely waited for her to take her seat behind her desk before he plopped down on a chair. Suddenly remembering his helmet, he snatched it off and dropped it on the floor. "This is terrible," he muttered. "This is really, really terrible."

Her own heart beating twice as fast as it should be, Cecily clutched the edge of her desk. "Tell me, Sam. What's happened now?"

He looked at her, perspiration gleaming on his forehead. "There's been another one." His voice rose, becoming almost unrecognizable. "They're coming thick and fast, Mrs. B. 'Orrible, it is. When's it going to stop, I ask you? Who's going to be next?"

Cecily's stomach churned and she placed a hand over her midriff. "Oh, my. Who is it this time?"

"It's Henry Farnsworth. He's the gamekeeper up at the Bellevue estate. Or he was, more like it. Lord Bellevue sent us the message. Luckily I got my bicycle mended so I can get around again. I got right on it and went up there."

"Did he tell you what happened?"

"No, m'm. The butler did. Seems Henry was out there early this morning shooting pheasants for a dinner party tonight. One of the gardeners found him. He'd been shot with his own gun."

Cecily felt a chill course over her entire body. "I suppose there was a gold angel on his forehead?"

Sam nodded.

"And a missing lock of hair?"

"Yes, m'm. Not that Henry had much hair to begin with. Just about took it all, that maniac did." Northcott ran a hand over his own bald head. "He wouldn't have much luck with me, would he, m'm."

His laugh held no humor, and Cecily couldn't even raise a smile. "Did you speak with the gardeners? Did they see anything?"

"Not a thing. They heard the shots, but since they knew Henry was shooting at pheasants, they took no notice. It wasn't until one of them went to cut some holly for the mansion that he found Henry."

"What about Lord Bellevue and his wife? Did they see anything?"

"I couldn't talk to them, m'm. The butler said they were too upset to speak with me. Which is why I came up here."

Cecily thought she understood. "Would you like me to speak to them?"

Northcott looked relieved. "Yes, m'm. They won't turn you away, being as you're a lady. I'd be most grateful if you could see what you can find out."

"I'll do my best, Sam. I suppose you searched the area thoroughly?"

"I put my best men on it. They didn't find nothing,

though." He shook his head. "They didn't find nothing at all at the other murders, neither. Whoever did this is really good at picking up after himself."

"So it would seem," Cecily murmured. "It seems we are dealing with an exceptionally clever killer."

Northcott drew a handkerchief from his pocket and mopped his brow. "I'm never going to get away for Christmas at this rate. I might as well tell the missus to go without me."

Personally, Cecily thought, the constable was entirely too concerned with his holiday, but she refrained from saying so. "Don't give up just yet, Sam." She stood, forcing the constable to leap to his feet. "Our killer has committed four murders now without being detected, or thinks he has, and sooner or later he will make a mistake and give himself away."

"I hope you're right, m'm." Northcott bent down to retrieve his helmet. "And I certainly hope it's sooner rather than later. The inspector is going to find out about all this any minute now, and he'll be breathing fire down my neck, make no mistake about that." A light tap on the door turned his head. "Would that be the brandy, by any chance?"

"No doubt." Cecily crossed the room and opened the door. Pansy held a tray containing a brandy bottle and two glasses. "Your carriage is on the way, m'm," she announced, bending her knees in a curtsey.

"Thank you, Pansy." Cecily reached for the tray. "I'll take this. Go back to the foyer and watch for the carriage. Let me know the minute it arrives."

"Yes, m'm." Pansy disappeared, and Cecily carried the tray to her desk and set it down. "Help yourself, Sam. I must go up to my suite and get ready for my visit to the Bellevue mansion."

"You don't have time to join me, m'm?"

He didn't look too disappointed when she shook her head. "Not this time. I think perhaps Mrs. Chubb might have some mince pies in the kitchen, if you'd like to call in there on your way out."

"Yes, m'm. Much obliged, I'm sure."

She was about to leave when he added, "Thank you, Mrs. B. I'm really glad of your help. This is a nasty one, to be sure. Just be careful, all right?"

"I will, Sam. You must be careful, too." She closed the door and walked slowly down the hallway, deep in thought. This latest murder would seem to exonerate Basil. He could hardly have committed the crime while he was working at the factory.

Whether or not he was responsible for Jimmy Taylor's death remained to be seen, but that was not her concern right now. The murders were piling up at an alarming rate. Her immediate objective was to find this diabolical monster and halt his terrible rampage.

If she and the constables couldn't apprehend the killer, the news would be all over London, and Inspector Cranshaw would waste no time in getting to Badgers End.

Not only would Sam Northcott be in deep trouble, the Pennyfoot's Christmas season could be a total disaster. Even she would think twice about spending a week or so in a village with a murderous maniac on the loose. The Christmas Angel had to be stopped, and there was no time to lose.

*   *   *

"I can't believe we're actually going on the sleigh ride," Gertie said, wrapping a scarf around Lillian's head. "I was so blinking sure the snow would all be melted before we could get out there." She smiled at Daisy. "Now you can have some time off to spend with Doris."

Daisy bent down to button James's coat. "Doris is really busy with the pantomime. I think I'll take Essie out for a walk in the pram. She looks like she needs some fresh air. Her skin is as pale as a lily."

Gertie laughed. "That's because she lives in London. You can't get fresh air with all that smoke and dirt."

Daisy patted James's head and stood. "Yeah, I know. You're lucky the twins live down here at the seaside. It's a lot better for them."

"Don't I know it." Gertie glanced in the mirror. Her cheeks were flushed, and her eyes seemed to be sparkling. It had to be all that rushing around to get out. "I was lucky Lizzie didn't have nothing to do today. She swapped her afternoon off with me. I promised her I'd bring her back some mistletoe, so I hope we find some."

"What about the pantomime rehearsal this afternoon? Aren't the twins supposed to be there?"

"Yeah, but it won't hurt for them to miss one. I told Pansy to tell Mrs. Fortescue that I had an urgent appointment and had to take them with me."

"Well, you'll all have fun, I know," Daisy said, sounding just a little bit envious.

Gertie gave her a sharp look. "Don't you ever get tired of taking care of other people's kiddies?"

Daisy shrugged. "What else would I be doing? It's a lot

more fun than being a housemaid. I never did like that job. Too much like hard work."

"Well, I mean, don't you ever wish you could meet someone and get married and have children of your own?"

Daisy's face clouded over. "Not anymore. I did meet someone once, but I didn't fit into his world, and he didn't fit into mine."

Gertie felt a pang of sympathy. "I remember. He was a toff, weren't he? A bloody lord, of all things. Of course it wouldn't work. Poor sods like us can't mix with the toffs. That's why I couldn't go to London with Dan. He was used to all that high-society stuff. I'd have been bleeding miserable, just like you would have been, married to a lord." She grinned. "Lady Daisy. Just doesn't sound right, does it."

"No, it doesn't." Daisy bent over to kiss Lillian's cheek. "Be good, little ones. Behave yourselves this afternoon, and be nice to Mr. Russell."

"We will," the twins sang out together. Lillian grabbed hold of Gertie's hand. "Come on, Mama. We don't want to be late."

James rushed to the door. "No! Mr. Clive might go without us!"

Daisy raised her eyebrows. "Mr. Clive?"

"They've heard me call him Clive for so long," Gertie explained as she allowed her daughter to drag her to the door. "I'm surprised they remember to put the mister in front of it."

Daisy laughed. "Have a lovely afternoon."

She planned to do just that, Gertie told herself, as she hurried down the hallway after her children.

Clive was waiting for them in the lobby, nervously twisting a fur hat around and around in his hands. He grinned when he saw the twins and held out his arms.

Both children rushed forward and were swept up to his chest, each receiving a kiss before being set down on the floor again.

Clive turned to Gertie and swept her a deep bow. "Your carriage awaits, madam."

Hearing Philip's snort of derision behind the reception desk, Gertie sent him a glare before smiling at Clive. "We are ready, sir."

James let out a howl of protest. "A carriage? I thought we were going riding on a sleigh!"

"We are," Clive hurriedly assured him. "We have to go through the kitchen to it, though. I had to harness it up in the courtyard and leave it there. We'll go out the back way."

Gertie felt a little letdown. She would have loved to leave from the front of the country club, driving away from the entrance in high style with everyone watching her.

She soon forgot her disappointment, however, in the excitement of climbing aboard the sleigh. Touching the red leather seats, she thought it was the most beautiful thing she'd ever seen. Made of strong oak, the sides had been painted white with a wide red stripe curling along the sides.

Shiny brass fittings sparkled in the frosty sunlight, and the chestnut impatiently stamping its feet at the front wore red ribbons in its mane. Clive had even provided blankets— thick red fluffy ones to wrap around their knees.

The whole thing looked like it had been plucked from one of the twins' picture books. James's and Lillian's faces glowed with excitement, and Gertie felt like hugging Clive for giving them such a special treat. She sat with an arm around each of her children as he climbed aboard.

"It's good that we're going today," he said, gazing up at the clouds. I think the thaw is just about ready to settle in."

"Then we're going to enjoy the snow while it's still here, aren't we?"

The twins answered her with an enthusiastic "Yeah!" as the horse took off, dragging the sleigh behind him.

It was a bit bumpy, but once they got onto the Esplanade the sleigh ran smoothly over the packed snow. Gertie pointed out the Christmas goods in the shop windows as they sped by, and to her great delight, people on the street turned to wave at them.

The twins waved back, shouting, "Happy Christmas!" at the top of their voices, nearly deafening Gertie, though after a while she was calling out, too. She felt like a queen, riding along and waving to her subjects.

Before long they had left the town, headed for the path leading up to the Downs. Gertie began to get a bit nervous as they climbed higher, following the path as it ran along the cliffs.

The twins were not a bit scared. They hung over the edge to watch the waves rushing onto the beach, and waved at the seagulls that swooped overhead.

Gertie hung on to them both, terrified they would fall and plunge down the cliffs to the rocks below. She breathed a huge sigh of relief when Clive turned the horse off the path and followed the trail into the woods.

Once inside the trees, he pulled up and brought the

143

sleigh to a stop. "You wanted to get some mistletoe," he said, as the twins scrambled down to the ground. "This is the best place to find it."

Smiling her thanks, Gertie let him help her down. Standing beside the sleigh, she ran her hand along the smooth side. "This is lovely, Clive. You're so blinking clever with your hands. You should be doing it for a living. It must have cost a bloody fortune to build, though."

Clive laughed. "Mrs. Baxter helped out with the fittings. The leather seats came out of a motorcar that Samuel had in the back of the stables."

Gertie stared at him. "Was that the one what was given him last year by one of our guests?"

"Yes, it was." Clive watched James dart off into the trees. "The guest gave the motorcar to him because it had broken down and he was getting a new one. Samuel thought he could fix it, but it was beyond repair." He started forward. "James? Come back here! You'll get lost if you stray too far."

James's voice drifted back to them. "I'm right over here."

Clive shook his head. "I'd better go and fetch him. It's too easy to get lost in these woods."

He rushed off, leaving Gertie alone with Lillian. The little girl's shoulders were hunched, and she hugged her muff close to her chest.

"Are you cold, sweetheart?" Gertie put an arm around the shivering child.

Lillian nodded her head, her teeth chattering. Gertie shoved her back into the sleigh. "Here, cover yourself up with the blanket. I'll go and look for some mistletoe and I'll be back right away, so you stay here until I get back, all right?"

144

Lillian nodded again and snuggled down under the blanket. Satisfied the child was all right, Gertie trudged off after Clive and James.

When she caught up with them, she was surprised to see they had collected several bunches of mistletoe. "Where did you find all that?" she demanded. "It's not easy to find."

Clive grinned. "It is when you know where to look."

She made a face at him. "Well, I'm glad you found some. Lillian's feeling the cold, so I think we should be getting along."

"Look what I found!"

Gertie turned around to look at her son. He held a thick walking stick in his hand and he waved it at her in his excitement. "I can keep it, can't I?"

"I don't know. Let me look at it." Gertie took it from him and examined it more closely. The knob of the walking stick gleamed like gold, and it had some sort of military cross on it. "This looks like the walking stick Colonel Fortescue always carries," she murmured, turning it around in her hands. "Though what would it be doing out here?"

"Those military sticks are quite common," Clive said, taking it from her. He held it up to the light. "This one has initials carved into it." He squinted. "F.G.F."

"Frederick G. Fortescue." Gertie frowned. "I bet it's his."

"He must have lost it when he was out walking." Clive ran his fingers down the stick. "It doesn't look as if it's been here too long, though."

"Can I keep it, Mama? Can I?" James reached for the stick, but Gertie pulled his hand away.

"No, luvvy, we have to take it back to the Pennyfoot to see if it belongs to the colonel."

"But—"

James's words were cut off by Clive, who had thrust up his hand. "Shshsh! Listen."

Gertie looked at him in alarm. "What's the matter?"

"Listen!"

Gertie listened, and heard what Clive must have heard—the sounds of snapping twigs and crackling leaves. Scared, she clutched James close with one hand and Clive's arm with the other. "Is it a wild animal?"

"Not unless one has escaped from a zoo." Clive tilted his head to one side. "That sounds too big for an animal in these woods. That's a man crashing around out there." He thrust the mistletoe and walking stick at her and then snatched James up in his arms. "Where's Lillian?"

Something in his voice scared her even more. "She's in the sleigh. I tucked her up to get warm."

"Quickly. We have to get back to her." Clive surged forward, brushing aside branches and shrubs as he ran back to where they'd left the sleigh.

Clutching the mistletoe and walking stick, Gertie stumbled after him. *Panic.* That was what she'd heard in his voice. She'd never seen Clive scared of anything before. She couldn't imagine what had scared him now, but she wasn't going to wait around to find out. Picking up her skirts, she tore after him.

CHAPTER

❈ 11 ❈

Pansy scuffed her feet as she walked slowly down the hallway to the ballroom. From the far end she could hear music
and a chorus of out-of-tune vocalists. The pianist sounded as
if he was taking his anger out on the piano. That didn't surprise Pansy. Every year Phoebe Fortescue had to hire a different pianist. They never came twice.

Pansy heard one say that he wouldn't work with that
screaming witch again if his life depended on it. And now
she had to tell that witch that Gertie's twins would not be at
rehearsal.

Pansy knew what that meant. It meant she'd get screamed
at, that was what. Phoebe Fortescue wasn't all that friendly
at the best of times, but when she was working on one of her
events, she'd tear someone apart if they didn't do what she
wanted when she wanted it.

Pansy was not looking forward to being torn apart.

She reached the doors of the ballroom and slowly eased one of them open. Phoebe was marching back and forth in front of the stage, shouting directions at everyone while the scarlet-faced pianist thumped the keys in a desperate effort to drown her out.

The women up on the stage completely ignored Phoebe as usual. They were used to her tantrums and blithely turned a deaf ear, much to Pansy's admiration. They were all singing, but it sounded as if they were singing different songs. Some were singing faster than others, and some were so off-key it hurt Pansy's ears to listen.

Phoebe leapt up and down, shrieking, "Stop! Stop!"

No one listened, and the women went on warbling their awful medley until finally Phoebe stalked over to the pianist. "I said, *stop*!" she yelled in his ear. Apparently running out of patience, she grabbed the lid and slammed it down.

The poor man snatched his hands off the keys and out of the way just in time. "I say!" he said, in a pained voice. "You don't have to be so vicious. I heard you."

"Then why didn't you stop?" Phoebe leaned forward so sharply her hat toppled over her eyes.

Giggles erupted on the stage, interrupting the singing. One by one the voices faded into blissful silence.

Struggling to straighten her hat, Phoebe's voice cut across the room like ice. "If any of you want to appear in this prestigious event, I suggest you pay attention and obey instructions. I should hate to have to dismiss you for insubordination."

The women looked at one another, whispering and shrugging.

Phoebe walked to the front of the stage. "The word means *disobedience*!" she yelled.

"Oh," said one of the performers, a hefty woman with ginger hair and a double chin. "Why the flipping heck didn't you say so, then? I thought it meant not being able to sing."

"If I were going to dismiss any of you for that," Phoebe shrilly declared, "none of you would be *in . . . this . . . pantomime*!"

She'd shouted the last three words, making Pansy wince. Deciding that to prolong the wait would only make matters worse, she crept forward until she was within three feet of the woman.

Phoebe raised a hand, obviously about to deliver another scathing remark.

Pansy coughed. "Er . . . Mrs. F-Fortescue?"

Slowly lowering her hand, Phoebe turned. "*Yes?*"

Pansy swallowed. There was more venom in that one word than in a dozen vipers. "I . . . er . . . I have a message for you, m'm." She hurriedly curtsied, hoping that would earn her points.

Phoebe seemed unmoved. "What is it, child? Speak up!"

"It's Gertie . . . I mean, Mrs. McBride. She says to tell you the twins can't come to rehearsal this afternoon."

Phoebe's eyes seemed to glow with hostility. "And why not, pray? Are they ill?"

"No, m'm." Pansy curtsied again for good measure. "Mrs. McBride had an urgent appointment, and she took the twins with her."

"An urgent appointment." Now Phoebe's voice was full of disdain. "What appointment could possibly be more urgent than this rehearsal?" She advanced on Pansy, her hand raised. "Does she not realize that we have less than a week to present this pantomime? How am I supposed to put on my best achievement if my performers are not here to rehearse? Tell me that!"

Pansy backed up a few steps. "I'm sorry, Mrs. Fortescue. "I don't know—"

"It's not her fault!"

The voice had come from backstage and everyone turned to look as Doris appeared. She walked out to the center of the stage and looked down at Phoebe. "This young lady is simply bringing you a message. It isn't fair of you to rant and rave at her for something that is none of her fault."

Pansy drew a sharp breath. Doris, the woman she'd feared and despised, had come to her rescue. Tears pricked her eyes as she gazed up at her. How could she hate her now?

Phoebe seemed at a loss for words for once. She blinked a couple of times, coughed, then turned her steely gaze on Pansy again. "Thank you," she muttered, too low for anyone else to hear. "You may go."

"Yes, m'm." Pansy dropped one last curtsey and turned to flee.

Once more Doris's clear voice rang out. "Just a moment, Pansy!"

Pansy halted, wondering what was coming. Should she have thanked her? Was Doris offended? She turned to face the stage but the songstress had disappeared.

Phoebe, meanwhile, was tapping the piano with her baton. "From the beginning, if you please." She whisked around to face the stage. "Ladies, in time, if you please. All together now . . . and one and two and one and two . . ." She pumped her baton up and down, while a few voices started the first notes of the song. After a few nudges from their companions, the rest hastily caught up, and the ragged chorus limped painfully along.

Pansy resisted the urge to put her hands over her ears. Just then Doris appeared from the backstage door and walked over to her.

Up close the songstress was even prettier than Pansy had thought. She'd seen Doris only once before, and that was from the back of the ballroom the last time she had visited the Pennyfoot.

Doris was the image of her sister, Daisy, but there was something about her that made her seem different. More worldly, with a sort of glowing confidence and poise that Daisy had never had.

Doris wore her hair fluffed up in the front with little tendrils curling at her cheeks, not scraped back like Daisy's, and she'd done something to her eyes to make them shine. Her cheeks were a delicate shade of pink and her mouth was painted red. When she smiled, she showed a row of perfectly even teeth. She was so gorgeous, Pansy couldn't help staring at her. No wonder Samuel had fallen in love with her.

Doris seemed uncomfortable with the scrutiny. She took Pansy's arm with gentle fingers and led her to the rear of the ballroom. "I have a huge favor to ask of you," she said, raising her voice to be heard above the racket going on onstage.

Overwhelmed by this dazzling creature's presence, Pansy could only nod.

Doris rolled her eyes as the caterwauling got louder. "I know you have duties that keep you busy, and believe me, I know how hard you work. I was a maid here once myself."

Kate Kingsbury

Wondering what all this was leading up to, again Pansy nodded.

"What I need is someone to assist me with the costume changes." Doris waved a hand at the stage. "Phoebe won't have time to do it, and I don't trust anyone else. I was wondering if you'd have time to help me."

Pansy swallowed. To be asked to assist a real-life music hall star onstage was an honor that would make her the envy of the Pennyfoot staff.

On the other hand, this was *Doris*. The love of Samuel's life. Did she really want to spend time with her, perhaps throwing her into Samuel's path again?

Doris looked uncertain. "If it would interfere with your duties I quite understand."

Pansy made a quick, if rather rash, decision. "I'm sure madam will allow me time to assist you, since it's for the benefit of the guests. I'll be happy to do it."

Doris smiled, showing her perfect teeth again. "Well, I don't know how much benefit it will be"—she nodded at the stage—"but we'll do our best, and thank you. Perhaps, if you're not too busy, you could manage to attend the two dress rehearsals?"

"I'll try to be at all the rehearsals from now on. That's if Mrs. Chubb can do without me."

"I'll have a word with her and Mrs. Baxter. I'm sure we can arrange something to everyone's satisfaction. Thank you, Pansy."

"Thank you, m'm." Pansy dipped a curtsey. "I'd better get back to the kitchen now and ask Mrs. Chubb about it." She turned and fled before Doris could change her mind.

She still wasn't sure how she felt about it all, but one

thing she did know. All the maids were going to wish they were her, being an assistant to a famous West End performer. She couldn't wait to tell them all.

Mrs. Chubb looked up in surprise as Pansy burst into the kitchen a few minutes later. "Goodness, child, what's got into you? You're not usually in such a hurry."

"Doris has asked me to assist her with her costumes!" Pansy got the words out between gasps for breath. "Can I have time off to go to rehearsals? She said she'd ask you herself, but I thought I'd ask you first so you won't be surprised."

Mrs. Chubb laid her rolling pin down on the pastry board and wiped her hands on her apron. "We're getting ready for the Christmas guests, Pansy. You know it's a busy time for all of us."

Now that it seemed there could be obstacles to her big chance, Pansy wanted it more than she'd ever wanted anything before. "I know, Mrs. Chubb, but I'll try to make up for it, I really will."

"Well, we'll see." Mrs. Chubb picked up her rolling pin again and began pushing it back and forth across the slab of pastry.

"There's a rehearsal tomorrow," Pansy said hopefully.

"I said, we'll see." Mrs. Chubb raised her chin. "Now go and get those tables ready for supper. With Gertie gone we're getting behind again."

"Yes, Mrs. Chubb." Pansy trailed out of the kitchen, all the excitement draining out of her. Maybe it was just as well. She didn't want to like Doris, and she had the feeling that if she was around her long enough, she'd end up liking her a lot.

* * *

Arriving at the Bellevue mansion, Cecily had to use all her powers of persuasion before the butler would allow her to enter.

At first the portly gentleman insisted that Lady Marion was indisposed and unable to rise from her bed. Lord Bellevue was tending to her and did not wish to be disturbed.

"I understand their distress over this terrible tragedy," Cecily said, smiling at the stern face of the butler, "but I am here not only to offer condolences, but hopefully to shed some light on the matter. After all, it is in all of our best interests to find this evil killer and incarcerate him, is it not? We must stop him before he attacks again. Who knows who might be next." She gave him a meaningful look, and saw a flash of alarm in his eyes.

He seemed to think it over, then abruptly pulled the door open wider. "Very well. If you will come this way, I will see if Lord Bellevue will speak with you." He looked down his nose at Samuel. "You may wait in the kitchen until your mistress is ready to leave."

Cecily opened her mouth to protest, but Samuel was too quick for her. "I prefer to wait in the carriage," he said stiffly.

"Suit yourself." The butler turned and headed across the wide entrance hall to a narrow passage beyond.

"Samuel, see if you can find a gardener to show you where the gamekeeper died," Cecily whispered. "Take a good look around and see if you can see anything out of the ordinary."

"Very well, m'm." Samuel marched off, his head held high.

Glowering at the butler's back, Cecily followed him to a

154

small room off the library. Left alone, she studied the china figurines in the curio close by her chair. The delicate pieces were quite beautiful, and she was still staring at them when the butler opened the door.

"Lady Marion," he announced, and stood aside to allow the woman to enter.

Surprised that the lord's wife had come in the place of her husband, Cecily sprang to her feet. "Please forgive me for this intrusion, Lady Marion. If it were not for the dire circumstances I would not have disturbed you at this time."

"I quite understand. My husband thought it better if I talk to you." Lady Marion seemed a little pale but otherwise quite in control of her emotions. With her auburn hair and wide green eyes she was an attractive woman, regal in her stature and graceful in her movements.

"Please," she said, taking a seat on the davenport, "tell me how I can help you. I'm told you are assisting in the investigation of this dreadful spate of crimes."

"Yes, I am." Cecily sat down and folded her hands in her lap. "I was hoping you could tell me more about what happened. I know it's all terribly upsetting but—"

"It's all right, my dear. I'll do the best I can. I really don't know that much, however. Harry . . ." Her voice broke and she took a moment to compose herself. "My gamekeeper was shooting pheasants for a dinner party I'd planned for this evening. Apparently one of the gardeners found him. . . ." Again she paused. "Please excuse me. The shock, you know."

"Of course." Cecily gave her a moment, then added, "I heard he was shot with his own gun."

"Yes, I believe he was."

"And the gardeners saw no one lurking around the grounds? No sign of a horse, or a carriage?"

"No one." She shuddered. "This is all so terrifying."

Cecily could see the conversation was causing the woman some pain and hurried to bring it to an end. "Do you know if Mr. Farnsworth was acquainted with a man named Thomas Willow?"

Lady Marion seemed startled. "Thomas? Yes, of course. He made Harry's shoes as well as my husband's." She shook her head. "It's hard to believe Thomas has gone as well. He's been a mainstay in the High Street for so many years. I never liked the man, too caustic by far, but he had his reasons. I suppose anyone would be ill-tempered trying to keep a struggling business running." She looked up. "I understand Lester Salt is taking over for him."

"So I heard."

"Such a capable man, though I feel sorry for him. The poor man has inherited nothing but debts. I must say, he seemed to be handling everything quite well when I spoke to him."

Cecily raised her eyebrows. "When was that?"

"Just the other day. He brought my husband's new shoes." Lady Marion frowned. "He's all right, isn't he? I mean, he's not . . ."

"No, no. Lester is quite well as far as I know."

"Thank goodness." Lady Marion patted her throat. "This is all such a terrible nightmare. With everything that's been happening, one wonders if anyone is safe. My husband has been keeping one of Harry's shotguns by his side ever since we heard the dreadful news."

"Did Mr. Farnsworth know Colin Mackerbee, the pig farmer?"

Lady Marion looked confused. "I don't understand. What does any of this have to do with Harry's murder?"

"Maybe nothing." Cecily paused, then added, "Though there's a possibility that all these men died by the same hand."

Lady Marion sat up, her eyes wide with fear. "Great heavens! What kind of maniac do we have in our midst?"

Cecily did her best to reassure her. "I don't wish to alarm you, Lady Marion. I'm quite sure that whoever killed your gamekeeper is far from here by now."

Fanning her face with her hand, Lady Marion sank back on the davenport. "I certainly hope you are right."

"Can you think of anyone who might have wanted to hurt Mr. Farnsworth?"

Lady Marion's eyes filled with tears. "He was the gentlest man I know. He had the wit of a joker and the soul of a child. All those who knew him loved him. I shall miss him dreadfully."

Something in the way she said it made Cecily wonder if the woman's fondness for her gamekeeper went beyond a normal relationship between an employer and a member of her staff.

In the next moment she decided she was being uncharitable and unnecessarily suspicious. "Well, thank you, Lady Marion. I will pass your comments on to P.C. Northcott in the hopes that it might help in his investigation."

Lady Marion rose, steadying herself with one hand on the arm of the davenport. "You will let me know if this beast is caught? I shall not have a moment's peace until I know he is safely behind bars."

"Of course. I shall make sure you are notified." Cecily sent a last glance at the curio. "I've been admiring your figurines. They are quite beautiful."

The other woman managed a wan smile. "Thank you. They are from Royal Doulton, in Staffordshire. I started to collect them while on holiday there."

Cecily was about to turn away when her glance fell on a photograph of Lady Marion and her husband dressed in evening clothes. "What a lovely gown! I saw one just like it at my dressmaker's house the other day."

"That was most likely my gown." Lady Marion picked up the silver frame. "Was it in shades of maroon and black?"

"Yes, it was." Cecily took another look at the photograph. "Of course, I should have known. Caroline said it was a Paris original."

"It's my favorite gown." Lady Marion put down the frame and walked to the door, prompting Cecily to follow her. "Caroline is a very good seamstress. She's a nervous little thing but has an excellent command of her talent. Most accommodating, as well. She delivered the gown herself. I must admit, when Pauline told me she would be spending the month in London I was quite dismayed, since I had torn the hem and it needed expert attention. Caroline, however, came to my rescue." She paused at the door, one hand on the bell rope. "I shan't be wearing it this evening, after all. I have canceled the dinner party. I just couldn't face it with Harry gone."

She pulled the rope, saying, "Jarvis will see you out. Thank you for your efforts in finding who did this. I hope you are successful in your quest."

"I hope so, too."

The door opened to reveal the butler, his face still stark with disapproval.

Cecily turned once more to Lady Marion. "Thank you for your help in this. I just have one more question. Was your husband as fond of Mr. Farnsworth as you were?"

Her question was directed at the other woman, but out of the corner of her eye she watched the butler. She thought she saw a flicker of alarm cross his face, but it was gone so quickly she couldn't be sure.

"Of course he was." Lady Marion's voice had sharpened. "As I said, everyone loved Harry. Including my husband."

Cecily nodded. "Then good day to you. I shall see that you are informed when there is any news." She followed the butler to the door, and quickly stepped outside.

Samuel was pacing around the carriage when she reached it. Despite his hat and warm scarf, his face was pinched and his shoulders hunched against the wind.

"You would have done better to wait in the warm kitchen," Cecily said, as she stepped up into the carriage.

"I don't like being ordered about by a butler," Samuel said stiffly.

Cecily could understand how he felt. Most people didn't understand the relationship she had with her stable manager. Especially people like Lord Bellevue's butler. She felt she owed Samuel some kind of compensation for his discomfort. "I think I'd like to stop by the Fox and Hounds for a drop of sherry."

Samuel's eyes lit up. "Now?"

"I don't see why not." Cecily glanced up at the darkening sky. "Mr. Baxter won't be home for a while and we have time

159

before supper. It must be opening time at the public house by now. Besides, I would like a word with Mr. Collins. As a publican, he has more access to gossip than anyone I know. We might be able to pick up a tidbit or two to help us in our investigation. Did you manage to see where Harry Farnsworth died?"

"Yes, m'm. I found the bloke that found Harry dead. I looked all around but couldn't see nothing but stones and twigs and trodden-down bushes. The constables must have trampled around quite a bit. It was all flattened down around where he was killed."

Cecily nodded. "I rather thought the constables would have searched the area pretty thoroughly. You never know, though. Sometimes they miss something." She looked up at the sky. "We had better make haste to the Fox and Hounds if we are to be home before dark."

Samuel needed no further encouragement. He slammed the door shut and leapt up on his seat before Cecily could draw another breath.

The ride down to the village pub seemed to take forever with the bumping and swaying of the carriage. At times it rocked from side to side, causing Cecily to grasp the door handle to steady herself.

The reason for it was clear as she made ready to step down into the courtyard of the Fox and Hounds. The thaw had begun to set in at last, and as usual for that part of the coast, the westerly winds had brought warm rain to melt the packed snow.

The sheen of water lying on top of ice made walking even more treacherous, and Cecily was glad of Samuel's hand under her arm as they made their way gingerly to the door of the private bar.

Barry Collins, the publican, greeted them with a cheery bellow. Waving his arm around the empty room, he added, "You're the first customers I've seen in here all day. This weather is killing my business."

Listening to the clamor of voices above the piano chords next door, Cecily smiled. "It sounds as though you are making up for it in the public bar."

Collins nodded. "Darts match going on. They'd march through fire to get here for that."

"Well, I'm glad it's quiet in here. I was hoping you'd have time to talk."

Without being asked, Collins reached for a small glass and a bottle of cream sherry. "I thought you might be calling in here. I heard about the Christmas Angel. Nasty goings-on, that. We're trying to keep it quiet around here. Business is bad enough, what with the weather and all." He put down the bottle and carried the brimming glass over to her table.

"I don't blame you." Cecily accepted the sherry with a smile. "A serial killer is not to be taken lightly. This man is extremely dangerous and unpredictable."

Collins raised his eyebrows at Samuel, who promptly ordered a mild and bitter. The publican stuck a pint mug under the spout of the beer barrel and pulled the brass-tipped handle. Watching the white foam rise halfway up the glass, he asked, "Do you have any ideas who might be behind all this?"

"Not as yet." Cecily sipped the sherry, closing her eyes as the dark liquid slid down her throat to warm her stomach. "I don't suppose you've heard anything that might help?"

"Sorry, Mrs. B. From what I've heard, and it isn't much, there seems no reason for it all." The publican switched the glass to another barrel and topped it up, allowing some of the foam to pour over the edges of the glass.

Samuel got up to fetch it, nodding his thanks before taking his seat again.

Collins poured a small glass of light ale and brought it over to the table. "All right if I join you?"

"Oh, please do!" Cecily waved a hand at the empty chair.

Sitting down, Collins murmured, "I might as well, seeing as the place is empty." He glanced at Samuel. "How's it looking out there?"

"Slushy," Samuel said, picking up his glass. "The carriage was all over the road."

"Well, at least it looks like it's thawing fast." He looked back at Cecily. "Good job, too, I reckon, seeing as how you have a hotel full of guests for Christmas."

"Indeed." Cecily took another sip of the sherry. "I must say I'm most relieved to see the weather warming up. Now, if only I could find the Christmas Angel, my troubles would be over."

Collins nodded. "Bad business, that's for sure. I heard that Harry Farnsworth bought it this morning. Nice chap, he was. I can't imagine why anyone would want to do him in."

"Yes, I'm afraid that's the whole point." Cecily sighed. "It's all very puzzling. I just can't seem to pinpoint a motive for all this. It all seems so senseless. None of the victims have anything in common. They are young and old, married and unmarried. Two were known for their bad temper, the other two were gentle as lambs according to the people I spoke to, and they came from all walks of life. It's quite the most challenging crime I've ever come across."

"Ah, but you have a great reputation for catching criminals, Mrs. B." Collins raised his glass. "I have great faith in you. You'll find him. I'm sure of it."

"Hear, hear!" Samuel said, raising his glass.

Cecily stared at her sherry. "I'm not so sure. I have a horrible, hopeless feeling that this time a madman will go on killing innocent victims and there's nothing anyone can do to stop him." She looked up into Barry Collins's worried face. "If that's so, God help us all."

CHAPTER
❀ 12 ❀

Panting and gasping for breath, Gertie stumbled up to the sleigh. Clive waited for her, clutching Lillian in his arms with James tugging at his coat.

"Get in," he said, as she reached him. It was an order, not a request. Normally Gertie would have told him what to do with his orders, but something in his voice scared her so much she scrambled up onto the seat without a word.

Clive thrust Lillian onto her lap and picked up James, tossing him onto the other seat like a sack of grain. Before she could draw breath to protest, the janitor leapt up onto his seat and flicked the reins.

Stamping its feet, the chestnut snorted, then took off, sending Gertie back against the cold leather seat. The jolt snapped her teeth on the tip of her tongue.

Eyes watering, she yelled, "What the bloody hell is the

matter with you? Why are you in so much of a blinking hurry?"

Clive said something over his shoulder, but she couldn't hear what he'd said. Lillian had started crying, and James was hanging over the edge of the sleigh, shouting at Clive to go faster.

Gertie hugged Lillian closer and yelled at her son. "Sit back! You'll fall out and break your bloody neck!"

"No, I won't!" Still hanging over the side, James turned his head to grin at her. Just then the sleigh hit a bump.

Gertie cried out and clutched Lillian tighter as she felt her seat rise up in the air. Clive called out something, but at that moment the sleigh thumped down hard on the ground.

Gertie looked around just in time to see James disappear over the side. She screamed, making Lillian yell louder.

Clive shot a startled look over his shoulder and reined in the horse. The sleigh came to a sliding halt, and before it had stopped, Gertie was scrambling off it.

She landed on her knees in the snow and struggled to her feet. Clive jumped down and came slipping and sliding toward her. Together they ran back to where a huddled heap lay on the side of the road.

"James!" Gertie's desperate cry scared the seagulls. They fluttered up from the beach, screeching their indignation as Gertie dropped to her son's side.

To her soaring relief he had his eyes open, and the moment he saw her he started crying—quiet sobs that tore at her heart. "Are you hurt, luvvy? Tell Mama where you hurt."

"My—my arm hurts!" His sobs grew louder.

Clive bent down by her side and ran his hands over the boy. When he touched James's right arm, the boy let out a scream. "It looks like it's broken." He looked at Gertie and she was shocked to see tears in his eyes. "I'm so very sorry."

Struggling against tears herself, she said roughly, "It's not your fault. I told him not to hang over the side." She shuddered as the wind whipped her scarf against her cheek. "What do we do now?"

"Give me your scarf." He unwound his own scarf and held out his hand for hers.

She gave it to him, aware of her heart pounding in her chest. She couldn't bear to see her little boy in so much pain. She would give anything to take his place. It was her fault. She should have been more strict with him. She was a rotten mother. Daisy would never have let this happen.

Somehow Clive must have sensed what was going on in her tortured mind. He put an arm about her shoulders and hugged her against his big body. "Cheer up, luv. We'll get him to the doctor and he'll take care of him."

He let her go and turned to the boy. "Now, James, this is going to hurt a little, so I want you to be really, really brave, all right? Let's show your mama what a brave boy you are."

James gave him a scared nod, tears still running down his cheeks.

Gertie watched in awe as Clive eased the broken arm against her son's chest and tied the two scarves tightly around him to hold it in place.

Apart from a whimper or two, James hardly made a sound, though he couldn't stop the tears from soaking the collar of his coat.

Gertie ached to hold him, but she was afraid of hurting him more. Instead, she stood back and let Clive pick him up. Stepping carefully through the slushy snow, he carried the boy to the sleigh and sat him down next to his sister.

Lillian was shivering and crying, and Gertie quickly scrambled onto the seat and put her arm around the little girl. Being careful not to touch her son's injured arm, she hugged him close, and held on to them both as Clive drove the sleigh carefully down the path to the town below.

Luckily, Dr. Prestwick was in his surgery when they arrived. He gave James some medicine to dull the pain and set the arm in a plaster cast—a procedure that seemed to take forever and made poor James cry out in pain. Gertie felt sick by the time it was all over.

Dr. Prestwick assured her that the fracture was a simple one and that James would heal in time. "Thanks to Mr. Russell," he added, as Gertie thanked him. "If he hadn't bound the arm just the way he did, it might have been a different story."

Still drowsy from the medicine, James fell asleep on the ride back to the Pennyfoot. Anxious to get the children back to the comfort of their room, Gertie had little time to express her thanks.

"I don't know what I would have done if you hadn't been there," she said, as Clive carried James down the kitchen steps. "You saved his life."

Clive shook his head. "It wasn't that bad, though I know you must have been terrified. I feel responsible for what happened."

"Please, don't." She took James from him at the door. "It

wasn't your fault. James was being a bloody twerp and I wasn't firm enough with him."

"Well, I hope his arm doesn't give him too much pain." He started to move away, then added, "I'm so sorry the afternoon turned out so badly. I know how much the twins were looking forward to the sleigh ride."

Gertie smiled. "It was a lovely sleigh ride. And your sleigh is beautiful. Thank you, Clive."

He looked at her for a long moment, making her feel self-conscious. "It was my pleasure, Gertie." With a swift wave of his hand, he walked briskly away from her and up the stairs.

It wasn't until he disappeared that she realized she'd forgotten to ask him two things. One was about his past. The other was why he'd acted as if the devil was after him in the woods.

Pansy dumped a pile of serviettes onto the nearest dining room table and grabbed up a silver serviette ring. Here was her one chance for doing something really exciting and old Chubby had to go and spoil it all. It wasn't fair.

She snatched up one of the white linen squares and rolled it into a thin sausage before shoving it through the ring. Throwing it down on the table, she was about to reach for another ring when Gertie's voice spun her around.

"Whatcha doing?"

"What does it look like I'm doing?" Pansy waved the ring at her. "I'm playing Ring a Ring o' Roses with the serviettes."

"All right, you don't have to be cheeky. I was just asking." Gertie walked over to the next table. "Here, give me some. I'll help you."

Feeling sorry for snapping at her friend, Pansy handed over a pile of serviettes. "Did you have a nice sleigh ride?"

"Yeah, we did." Gertie gave her a sharp look. "You're not cross with me because I took the time off, are you?"

Pansy shook her head. "Sorry. I'm upset at Mrs. Chubb. She won't let me help Doris with her costumes in the pantomime."

Gertie gasped. "Phoebe Fortescue asked you to help her?"

Pansy turned to her, all her resentment flooding to the surface. "No, it was *Doris* what asked me! She said she needed help with her costumes and didn't trust nobody else. She trusted *me* to help her, and now Mrs. Chubb says we're too busy and she'd have to think about it. You know what *that* means. It means she's not going to let me do it." Pansy blinked back a tear. "And I *want* to do it! I really do!"

"All right, all right, don't get your flipping knickers in a twist." Gertie started threading the rolled-up serviettes through the rings. "I'll have a word with Chubby. We'll find a way for you to do it."

"It'll mean going to rehearsals. At least the dress rehearsals, as well as the pantomime."

"Leave it to me." Gertie smiled at her. "Don't worry. You know I can get around old Chubby."

Pansy sniffed. "Thank you, Gertie—you're a real friend." Feeling much better, she moved on to the next table. "So tell me what happened on the sleigh ride."

Gertie shrugged. "Not a lot. We went up to the woods to get some mistletoe, and James fell out of the sleigh and broke his arm."

Pansy paused, a serviette dangling from her fingers. "You're joking."

"No, I'm not." Gertie sighed. "It was awful, seeing him disappear over the side like that. I thought he was dead. Scared me to bloody death, I can tell you."

"Is he all right?"

Gertie rolled up another serviette. "Well, he's got a plaster cast on his arm. Solid as a rock, it is. He has to keep it on for weeks. That'll bloody slow him down a bit. It will probably mean he won't be in the pantomime."

"Oh, Gertie, I'm so sorry." Pansy rushed over to give her friend a hug. "Poor James. I hope this doesn't spoil Christmas for him."

Gertie snorted. "Once he sets eyes on what Clive is making for him he'll forget all about his blinking arm." She shook her head. "That man is so clever with his hands. Too bloody good he is to be working here."

Pansy gave her a sly smile. "You really like him, don't you?"

Gertie turned away with a careless shrug. "He's all right. I don't really know him, do I. I mean, just when I think I know him well, he goes and does something really strange. Like in the woods this afternoon. He acted as if he was really scared of something. Took off in the sleigh like a bleeding bat out of hell. We were going so fast we hit a bump and that's when James went flying. Mind you, he was hanging out of the sleigh, so it wasn't really Clive's fault, but I never did find out why Clive had acted so strange."

Pansy put the serviette down on the right side of the place setting. "P'raps he was scared of the Christmas Angel." She caught her breath, silently cursing the slip of her tongue.

Gertie raised her head. "The who?"

"Never mind. Forget I said anything." Pansy hurriedly moved to the next table.

Gertie walked over to her, her hands on her hips. "Tell me what you're talking about."

"I shouldn't have said nothing. Samuel told me not to say nothing to nobody."

"I'm not nobody." Gertie leaned forward. "So bloody well tell me."

Pansy held out a moment or so longer, then gave in. It was only a matter of time before everyone knew, anyway. Samuel had said that himself. "The Christmas Angel. He's going around Badgers End killing all sorts of people. He leaves golden angels on their foreheads and chops off lumps of their hair."

A loud gasp echoed across the room. Pansy swung around, just in time to get a glimpse of Lizzie's terrified face before the maid rushed from the room.

"Now you've gone and done it," Gertie said, looking a little frightened herself. "It'll be all over the Pennyfoot. You'd better tell me the rest of it."

Pansy shivered. "I don't know any more than that. Madam and Samuel have been going around asking questions, but Samuel says nobody knows why he's killing people. They think he's loony and just does it because he feels like it."

Gertie's face had turned pale. "Where is he killing people? Not here in the hotel?"

Pansy felt sick. "No, no, not here. All over Badgers End. Remember Jimmy, the dairy farm boy?"

Gertie nodded.

"Well, it were the Christmas Angel what killed him. He killed a shoemaker and a farmer as well."

Gertie looked as if she was about to cry. "I don't believe it."

"Well, it's true. Samuel wouldn't joke about a thing like that. Ask him yourself."

"Does Chubby know?"

"I don't think so."

"Well, we'd better tell her, before Lizzie spreads it all over the Pennyfoot. Maybe we can stop her. Come on!"

Gertie sped across the room to the door, and Pansy followed, certain now that she'd never get the chance to help Doris in the pantomime. Mrs. Chubb was never going to forgive her for spreading the word about the Christmas Angel.

Worse, Samuel was going to be really cross with her, too. This was turning out to be a horrible Christmas season.

Cecily arrived back at the Pennyfoot to find the entire place in an uproar. The lobby was full of young women and a half dozen children all milling about, some crying, some shouting, and all of them acting as if the world were about to come to an end.

Spying one woman huddled on the staircase, clinging to a banister, Cecily hurried over to her. "Mabel! Whatever has happened? Has someone been hurt?" *Don't let it be Phoebe,* she prayed silently, as the frightened woman stared up at her.

Mabel let go of the banister and clutched Cecily's skirt. Loud enough for the entire population of Badgers End to hear, she yelled, "There's a madman loose in the village! He's going around chopping off people's heads!"

Loud screams greeted her words, adding to the chaos in the lobby. Cecily rolled her eyes at the ceiling, then waded into the hysterical crowd, searching for someone, anyone, who could help her restore order.

As if in answer to her thoughts, a bellow erupted from the stairs, quieting the frightened women. "What the blue blazes is going on here?"

A few whimpers answered, but Baxter put an end to that with a raised hand. "Silence! This is a respectful country club. I will not tolerate such raucous behavior. You will leave the premises immediately. All of you."

Cries of fear greeted his command and Cecily sped back to the stairs. Bounding up them to stand by his side, she called out, "Quiet, everyone. I have something important to say."

It took a few moments of grumblings and whimpering before the group fell silent. Cecily made an effort to sound calm and confident. "Please, listen to me. The person they are calling the Christmas Angel is not chopping off people's heads, I can assure you. Neither is he running around killing off everyone he sees. It is true one or two men have died recently, but at the moment we have no way of knowing who killed them or why. In any case, no women have been killed, so none of you has cause to worry. You can go home now. You will all be perfectly safe, I promise you."

Praying that was true, she watched the women file fearfully out of the door.

Baxter said nothing until the door had closed behind the last performer. "You managed to calm them down. Well-done," he said, rubbing his fingers across is brow. "That caterwauling was giving me a blasted headache."

Cecily followed him up the stairs. "How did they find out about the murders?"

"I don't know. I had just arrived home and was reading when I heard the racket below and came down to see what was going on. I was surprised to see you in their midst."

"I walked in on them." Cecily frowned. "Someone must have told them."

She reached the turn of the staircase just as a voice called out from below.

"Oh, there you are, Cecily! A word with you, please?"

Baxter groaned. "I was wondering where she had gone."

Cecily turned to look down at Phoebe. "She must have stayed behind in the ballroom. She probably wants to know what all the ruckus was about."

"Just don't bring her up to the suite." Baxter left her, climbing rapidly to the top of the stairs.

Grimacing, Cecily hurried down to where Phoebe stood by the Christmas tree. Cecily had been so focused on the group of hysterical women she'd failed to notice that Madeline had decorated the tree.

Colored glass balls hung from the branches, while lacy white snowflakes and red and gold bells added color. Cecily saw gold garlands and silver ribbons, but nowhere on the tree were the golden angels that usually hung there. Madeline obviously had decided they would be inappropriate.

Phoebe looked at the tree with an air of disdain. "It's not up to her usual standards."

"I think it's lovely." Cecily relaxed her shoulders. Phoebe must not have heard the uproar in the lobby or the news of the Christmas Angel, or she would most likely have been beside herself with terror.

"Well, to each his own." Phoebe tucked her hands inside her fur muff. "Have you seen Frederick? I looked in the bar, but he's not there. I was wondering if perhaps he was visiting Mr. Baxter in your suite."

Cecily almost laughed. The idea of Baxter entertaining the addle-headed colonel was ludicrous. "I just left Baxter and he made no mention of the colonel. Have you looked in the library? Sometimes he takes a brandy in there to sip by the fireplace."

Phoebe clicked her tongue in annoyance. "I suppose he could be there. Now I shall have to go all the way back there to look."

Just then Cecily caught sight of Gertie and Pansy emerging from the hallway. She beckoned to them, and they rushed over to her.

"I'm so sorry, m'm," Pansy said, dropping a shaky curtsey. "I had no idea Lizzie was there. I wouldn't have said nothing otherwise. It just sort of slipped out."

Cecily realized at once to what she referred.

Before she could signal to her to be quiet, however, Gertie added, "That bloody twerp told everyone about the Christmas Angel. I told her he was just chopping off locks of hair, but she went running around saying he was killing people and chopping off their heads, and I . . ." Gertie's voice trailed off as she finally noticed Cecily's eyebrows frantically twitching up and down.

It was too late, however. Phoebe turned slowly to Cecily, her voice pitched an octave higher. "Chopping off people's heads?"

Cecily took hold of her arm and felt it shaking beneath her fingers. "Now, now, Phoebe, it's quite all right. No one is chopping off heads."

"No, course not," Gertie said helpfully. "The crazy bugger cuts off a lock of their hair after he kills them and sticks a gold angel on their foreheads. That's why they call him the Christmas Angel."

"Oh, my." Phoebe's eyes rolled up in her head and her knees sagged.

Supporting her friend as best she could, Cecily glared at Gertie. "Bring a chair over here and don't say another word."

"Yes, m'm." Gertie hustled across the foyer and dragged a chair out from behind the reception desk.

Phoebe moaned, and her eyes fluttered open. "Oh, my goodness. What happened?"

"You had rather a nasty shock," Cecily said, seating her on the chair. "Pansy, fetch a glass of brandy from the bar, and while you're there look for Colonel Fortescue and ask him to come to the foyer right away. If he's not in the bar, look in the library on your way back."

"Yes, m'm." Pansy sped off, leaving Gertie standing there with a sick look on her face.

Looking at her, Cecily felt a sense of impending doom. "What is it?"

"I just remembered something, m'm."

"What is it?"

Gertie sent a worried glance at Phoebe, then said quickly, "We found a walking stick stuck in a holly bush in the woods this afternoon. I think it belonged to the colonel, m'm."

Phoebe uttered a little cry, while Cecily asked sharply, "Are you sure?"

"Well, it had his initials on it, F.G.F., and what looked like a military cross. Didn't see the colonel anywhere, though."

Phoebe uttered a shrill scream. "The Christmas Angel! He's killed my Freddie!" With that she slumped into a dead faint.

CHAPTER
❋ 13 ❋

A few moments later, while Cecily and Gertie were still trying to revive Phoebe, Pansy returned with the brandy.

Cecily took it from her, and tried to dribble a few drops in between Phoebe's lips. Making things difficult was the wide brim of Phoebe's hat, which kept getting in the way.

Cecily would have taken it off her head, except that Phoebe never removed her hat in public. Although she had never openly admitted it, it was generally believed by her peers that she was completely bald and wore a wig. Cecily wasn't about to prove or disprove that theory.

Having no luck with the brandy, she decided to wait it out. Eventually Phoebe would recover. She looked at Pansy, who was hovering close to Gertie, her face creased with worry.

"I looked for the colonel, m'm," she said, plucking at the

folds of her skirt. "I couldn't see him anywhere. I asked in the bar and no one's seen him all afternoon."

"Oh, bugger," Gertie muttered. "That's why Clive was so scared. He must have seen the Christmas Angel."

Cecily carefully put the brandy down on the hallstand. "What are you talking about, Gertie?"

The housemaid shivered, and hugged her arms. "It were in the woods, m'm. Up on Putney Downs. We were looking for mistletoe when we found the walking stick, and then Clive thought he heard something and the next moment he was off and running with James back to the sleigh where we left Lillian and then he took off so fast like he was scared or something and we hit a bump and James was leaning out and he fell out of the sleigh and broke his arm and—"

"What!" Cecily halted the torrent of words with a sharp gesture of her hand. "James has broken his arm?"

"Yes, m'm. He fell out of the sleigh. But Clive bound his arm up and we took him to Dr. Prestwick and he put it in a cast."

"Oh, for heaven's sake." Cecily considered for a moment taking a gulp of brandy, then thought better of it. "How is the child now?"

"Well, he's hurting a bit but he was playing with his soldiers when I left him with Daisy. I think he's going to be all right."

Hearing a moan, Cecily turned her head. Phoebe's eyes were open and she was struggling to sit up. Putting a hand under her friend's elbow, Cecily asked, "Did Clive tell you what made him run from the woods?"

"No, m'm. We were too busy worrying about James."

"I think we need to speak with Clive. Please find him,

Gertie. He should still be on the grounds somewhere. Have the footmen help you look for him, and while they are about it, have them look for the colonel, too."

"Yes, m'm, though if you ask me, Colonel Fortescue is somewhere out there in the woods."

Phoebe moaned again and slumped back, eyes closed once more.

Gertie stomped off, leaving Pansy to tremble alone. Cecily was about to order the child to the kitchen when the front door opened, and Kevin Prestwick strode into the foyer.

Doffing his hat, he took one look at Phoebe and rushed over to her. "What happened here?"

"Phoebe just heard about the Christmas Angel. The shock made her faint." Cecily watched anxiously as the doctor lifted one of Phoebe's limp arms and took out his pocket watch.

"Pulse is normal," he announced, after a tense moment or two of silence. "I wish I had smelling salts with me." His glance fell on the glass. "Is that brandy?"

Cecily handed it to him. "I thought it might revive her."

The doctor tilted Phoebe's head back. Holding her nose, he tipped the glass to let the liquid run into her open mouth.

Phoebe coughed, spluttered, and sat up. "What are you doing?" She glared at the doctor. "Are you trying to choke me?"

Kevin handed the glass back to Cecily. "She'll be all right. Now, where's my wife? She said she'd be ready to come home by now."

"I'm right here." Madeline appeared as if by magic in the hallway entrance. "What's this I hear about Colonel Fortescue missing?"

Cecily sighed. Apparently Pansy had not been discreet in

her search. "We're a little concerned, since no one has seen him all afternoon. Gertie found his walking stick in the woods on Putney Downs."

Phoebe moaned again, but this time managed to hold on to her senses. "Poor, poor Freddie. Whatever am I going to do without him?"

"I'm sure nothing dreadful has happened to him," Cecily assured her, being sure of no such thing. "Perhaps he got tired of waiting for you and went home?"

Phoebe's face turned red with indignation. "Frederick would *never* go home without me. Even if he had, which is ridiculous to even imagine, he certainly wouldn't walk through the woods to get there. What on earth was he doing in the woods, anyway?"

"We don't know that he was in the woods. We only know his walking stick was found there." Cecily looked at Madeline for help. "Someone could have stolen it and taken it there."

"He had it with him when we got here this afternoon." Phoebe started crying. "I know he's dead. That dreadful murderer has killed him."

"He's not dead." Madeline's voice echoed clearly across the foyer.

Everyone turned to look at her. Cecily caught her breath at the sight of Madeline's face, eyes wide and glazed over, her expression completely blank.

Cecily stole a look at Kevin. He was staring at his wife as if he didn't recognize her. Undoubtedly this was the first time he'd seen her in a trance. Up until now, Madeline had always been careful to conceal that element of her powers from him.

Cecily felt a warm rush of gratitude for her friend. Phoebe would never know the sacrifice Madeline had made to help her.

Madeline spoke again, her voice flat and unemotional. "He's cold. Very cold. He's frightened. All alone in the dark. Trees all around, bushes . . . cold and damp. He's in the woods."

"I told you so." Gertie spoke from the hallway, startling them all.

Madeline blinked, and glanced at her husband.

Phoebe stopped crying and reached for the doctor's hand. "Please, find him for me?"

Kevin seemed not to hear her. He was still staring at Madeline with a strange look on his face that made Cecily nervous. This latest revelation concerning his wife would not sit well with him.

Cecily had not seen Clive standing behind Gertie until he stepped forward. "I'll be happy to search for the colonel, m'm."

Kevin jumped, as if suddenly gathering his senses. "Good man. I have a carriage outside. We'll take that."

"On your way out, Clive, tell Samuel to take the footmen out to help." Cecily held out her hand to Madeline. "Thank you," she said quietly, hoping her friend understood how much she meant it.

Madeline grasped her hand and gave it a little shake. "I know they will find him," she said to Phoebe, who sat rocking back and forth on her chair.

For once Phoebe didn't retaliate with a scornful dismissal of Madeline's powers. Instead, she looked up at her, tears once more trickling down her cheeks. "I hope so," she whispered.

"I'll talk to you later," Kevin said, giving his wife a penetrating look before striding out the door with Clive right behind him.

Cecily watched them leave, praying they'd return with the colonel, safe and sound.

"Clive feels really awful," Gertie said, when Cecily turned to face her. "He heard someone crashing around in the woods while we were out there. He said he thought it was the Christmas Angel and that's why he rushed us out of there, but now he thinks it might have been the colonel. He'll know where to look, so I'm sure he'll find him."

"Oh, my poor Freddie." Phoebe sought for a handkerchief in her sleeve, produced a dainty lace-edged one, and dabbed at her nose.

Gertie dragged a man's white handkerchief from her apron pocket and flapped it at Phoebe. "Here, you can't blow your nose on that flipping thing. Use this and have a bloody good snort."

Cecily winced, expecting the distraught woman to scream in outrage.

Phoebe surprised her, however. She took the handkerchief without a word, dangling it from the tips of her fingers to inspect it thoroughly. Having apparently deemed it suitable to use, she heartily blew her nose.

Gertie beamed. "There, now. Doesn't that feel better?"

"Thank you," Phoebe answered stiffly, and handed the handkerchief back to her.

Stuffing it back in her pocket, Gertie looked at Pansy.

"Come on, mate. We've got to get back to the kitchen before Chubby starts bellowing for us."

She stomped off with Pansy following meekly behind.

"We'll go up to the suite to wait," Cecily said, helping Phoebe up from her chair. She turned to Madeline. "Would you like to wait with us?"

"I might as well." Madeline glanced at the grandfather clock in the corner. "I could walk home, I suppose, but by the time I arrived there, Kevin will probably be back here with the carriage."

"Oh, I hope so." Phoebe clung to Cecily's arm and looked down her nose at Madeline. "I hope for once your ridiculous hocus-pocus works."

Madeline seemed not to take offense. "So do I." She started climbing the stairs, saying over her shoulder, "The colonel may be as daffy as a duck but he turned you into an almost normal, decent human being. I dread to think what you'd become without him."

Phoebe sniffed. "How in heaven's name would you know what constitutes a normal human being?"

Cecily smiled. Phoebe was once more feuding with Madeline. Her friend was feeling better. Now, if only the colonel were to return with Kevin and Clive, everything would be almost normal again. Almost.

"What?" Mrs. Chubb dropped her rolling pin onto the table and slapped a floury hand across her mouth. "Why didn't anyone tell me about all these killings?"

"Because no one was supposed to know," Pansy said in a small voice.

Across the room, Michel slammed a saucepan down with a mighty crash. "*Sacre bleu!* What ees this world coming to, eh? Murderers running around willy-nilly, chopping off ze heads like chickens?"

Gertie gave him a scathing look. "Well, you needn't worry. He only kills men."

The chef's tall hat wobbled back and forth as he shook a finger at her. "None of your sauce, *cochon*. I will not stand for it."

"Who cares where you bloody stand, as long as it's not next to me."

"Gertie!" Mrs. Chubb removed her hand, leaving a white mustache and beard of flour on her face. "That's *enough!*"

"All right, all right, keep your bloody socks on." Gertie walked over to the sink and picked up a potato from the pile on the draining board.

"So how long ago did Clive and Dr. Prestwick leave to look for the colonel?" Mrs. Chubb demanded. "How will they know where to look? He could be anywhere."

"The man is an idiot." Michel slapped a lid on the saucepan so hard it bounced off and clattered to the floor. Cursing, he bent to retrieve it. "If you ask me, he should be locked up where he does no harm, *oui?*"

"Well, you should know," Gertie muttered.

The housekeeper banged her rolling pin on the table, making Gertie jump. "Stop this bickering at once. Answer my question, Gertie."

Opening the drawer next to the sink, Gertie hunted for a sharp knife. Finding one, she pulled it out and began peeling the potato. "Clive thinks he heard the colonel crashing around in the woods this afternoon while we were out there."

"Why didn't you stop to look for him, then?"

"Because at the time Clive thought it was the bloody Christmas Angel, didn't he." Gertie sliced one end off the potato.

"It might have been him," Pansy said, her voice shaking. "The colonel could be dead, and Clive and Dr. Prestwick might run into him in the woods. They could be killed, too!"

Gertie turned on her swiftly. "Don't say that. Don't *ever* say that!"

"Ooh, la la!" Michel swayed his hips from side to side. "Our Gertie has ze *amoureux, non?*"

"No! So shut your bleeding mouth!" Gertie slung the potato across the room at Michel, who ducked. The potato hit a cupboard door and fell with a thud to the floor.

Pansy giggled, then pinched her lips together when Mrs. Chubb glared at her.

The housekeeper turned on her chief housemaid. "Whatever's the matter with you?"

Gertie shrugged. "I'm just worried, that's all. About the colonel," she added, as Michel snickered. "He's an old man. He must be so cold and lost out there all alone."

"Especially with a murderer running around out there," Pansy said, joining her at the sink.

Mrs. Chubb slapped a slab of pastry with her rolling pin. "That's quite enough talk about a murderer. What I want to know is how all those women in the pantomime heard about it. I could hear them screaming from down here. I thought it was part of the presentation, until Pansy told me what it was all about."

Pansy looked at Gertie for help.

"Lizzie told them," Gertie said, splashing her knife into

the cold water in the sink. "At least, one of the performers heard Lizzie telling another maid and she told the rest of them."

"Who told Lizzie, then?"

Pansy swallowed. Still with her back to the housekeeper, she muttered, "It was my fault. I was telling Gertie about it and Lizzie heard me."

Mrs. Chubb paused, both hands still on the rolling pin. "And who was it told you?"

"Samuel did."

"Ah." Mrs. Chubb wiped her mouth with her sleeve. "So what about the Pennyfoot rules that say not to repeat gossip to anyone? Did you all forget that?"

Gertie put down her knife. "It wasn't gossip. It was news, and we didn't tell anyone except ourselves and it wasn't our fault that some people have bloody big ears and were flipping listening to what they shouldn't have been."

For a long moment Mrs. Chubb's fierce gaze bored into Gertie, then she sighed. "Well, all right. I'll let it go this time."

"Speaking of gossip," Gertie said, wiping her hands on a tea towel, "who are the special guests what's supposed to be coming for Christmas? And why didn't you tell me about them?"

"You don't have to know everything, *non*?" Michel muttered.

Gertie ignored him. "Who are they, Chubby?"

"I'm not at liberty to say." Mrs. Chubb waved her rolling pin at her. "And don't call me Chubby! I'll take your afternoon off away if you don't stop calling me that."

"Aw, go on with you. You like it, really." Gertie dug in

her pocket for a handkerchief and blew her nose. "Anyhow, we'll know soon enough when they get here. So you might as well tell us now."

"My lips are sealed." Mrs. Chubb drew a finger across her mouth. "And in future, you both better be extra careful of who might be listening when you're having a private conversation. It can cause all sorts of trouble, like today. Are you hearing me?"

Gertie and Pansy answered together. "Yes, Mrs. Chubb."

Michel echoed with a high-pitched mimic, *"Yes, Mrs. Chubb."*

The housekeeper glared at him, then picked up a lump of pastry and threw it at his head. He didn't duck quite fast enough and the lump of dough knocked off his hat.

In spite of her worry, Gertie laughed. It wasn't often anyone got the best of Michel, but oh, how she loved it when someone did.

"So can I help Doris with her costumes?" Pansy asked, her voice full of hope.

Mrs. Chubb frowned. "I don't know that we can spare the time. We have only two more days left before the Christmas guests arrive."

"I can manage without her," Gertie said, giving her friend a nudge. "She can help me later when she's done with rehearsals."

"Yes, I can do that!" Pansy was practically jumping up and down with anticipation.

Mrs. Chubb looked doubtful. "Well, I don't know. . . ."

"Oh, come on, Chubby. What will it hurt?" Gertie wiped her hands on her apron. "Doris needs someone to help her and she doesn't trust no one else. You don't want to make

Doris look like a fool up there because she doesn't have the right costume on, do you?"

"Well, no, of course not, but—"

"I'll work twice as hard afterward." Pansy held out her hands. "Please?"

Mrs. Chubb shook her head. "Oh, all right. But you'll have to make up for it later, young lady."

"Oh, I will! I will!" Pansy threw her arms around Gertie's waist. "Thank you, thank you! You're the best friend anyone could have. You really are."

Gertie cleared her throat. "Go on with you. Get off me before I choke."

Pansy grinned. "I'm going to get you the best present you ever saw for Christmas. You'll see."

"You don't have to get me nothing." Gertie turned back to the sink. *Just get Clive back alive,* she silently prayed. *Oh, and Dr. Prestwick and the colonel.* That was all she asked. All she wanted.

Baxter's expression spoke volumes as Cecily led Phoebe and Madeline into the sitting room. Only then did she remember his last words. *Just don't bring her up to the suite.* Ah well, it was too late now.

Smiling brightly at him, she said, "Clive and Dr. Prestwick have gone to look for the colonel. We are going to wait here until they all return."

Baxter raised an eyebrow. "I don't suppose they happened to look in the bar, by any chance?"

Cecily gave him what she hoped was a meaningful look. "The colonel is not in the bar, or anywhere else in the Pennyfoot. The men are looking for him in the woods on Putney Downs."

At her words, Phoebe uttered a little moan.

Baxter raised both eyebrows. "In the *woods*? What in blazes is he doing up there?"

"We don't exactly know, darling." Cecily seated Phoebe next to the fireplace and motioned Madeline to sit across from her. "All we know is that Gertie found his walking stick up there and Madeline thinks he's still there somewhere."

"Good Lord." Baxter rubbed his brow. "I hope the poor blighter is all right."

Phoebe whimpered and dug out her handkerchief again.

"I'm quite sure he is," Madeline said firmly.

"Darling, why don't you go down to the library and take your newspaper with you." Cecily smiled sweetly at her husband. "I'm sure you will be more comfortable down there."

To her relief, Baxter picked up his newspaper, nodded at the ladies, and strode to the door. "Please inform me of any news," he said, and closed the door with a firm snap behind him.

"I think he's upset about something," Phoebe said, tucking her handkerchief back in her sleeve. "Sometimes it's hard to know what Mr. Baxter is thinking."

Madeline smiled. "I always know what he's thinking. Right now he's very happy to escape a room that contains three ladies, all of whom are quite capable of taking him down a peg or two."

Cecily laughed. "You may be right. As long as we have this time for ourselves, let's discuss the pantomime." Hoping to take Phoebe's mind off the missing colonel, she turned to her. "How are things with your presentation, Phoebe?"

Phoebe drew a shuddering breath. "As well as can be expected. Doris is an absolute gem, of course. We are so lucky to have her in the pantomime. She is wonderful as Wendy, and the children adore her. She has a way with them, you know."

Cecily nodded. "Yes, I can imagine that. How are my godchildren doing? Are they enjoying their first experience as performers?"

Phoebe actually smiled. "They are wonderful, Cecily. Wait until you see them! James is quite masterful onstage, and little Lillian follows directions beautifully. In fact, all the children are doing extremely well."

Cecily hesitated, then decided she might as well break the news. "Speaking of the children, I don't know if you heard Gertie mention that James has broken his arm?"

Phoebe uttered a cry of dismay. "Oh, no! Does that mean he won't be in the pantomime?"

Madeline uttered a scornful laugh. "Dear Phoebe, always putting her own concerns in front of everything else."

Phoebe scowled. "What exactly does that mean?"

Madeline shrugged. "You could have asked how the child was feeling."

Phoebe looked offended. "I was coming to that." She turned back to Cecily. "I do hope he is feeling well enough to participate in the pantomime."

Madeline rolled her eyes but mercifully said nothing.

"I think that will be up to Gertie to decide," Cecily said.

Phoebe sighed. "It's always something. If we have to do without him, then so be it. We'll manage. I really think this will be the very best event I have ever produced."

"That shouldn't be so hard to do," Madeline murmured.

191

Cecily spoke quickly, before Phoebe had time to realize the sting in that remark. "Splendid! I am really looking forward to seeing the production. I understand Clive put up the wiring for you."

"Yes, he did. He really is a remarkable man. He built the most amazing pirate ship and it's on wheels and actually moves." Phoebe shook her head. "I don't know how he does it. I—" She broke off, her eyes wide as she stared at Madeline's face.

Cecily followed her gaze, and caught her breath. Madeline was in one of her trances, her eyes glazed and staring, her body stiff and motionless.

Phoebe hunched closer to the fire. "I wish she wouldn't do that," she whispered. "It's so unsettling."

Cecily hushed her with a finger over her lips.

Madeline sat like a stone. Her lips moved, though no sound emerged.

Phoebe gulped and drew back on her chair.

The silence in the room was almost painful. Cecily waited, heart pounding, for what seemed like minutes until Madeline stirred.

She opened her eyes and looked straight at Phoebe. Her next words sent a cold chill through Cecily's bones.

"They have found the colonel."

CHAPTER
❈ 14 ❈

"He's not dead, is he? Oh, please tell me he's not dead!" Phoebe leaned forward, one hand pressed to her throat. "I can't bear to think of it."

Madeline blinked. "I'm sorry, Phoebe, truly. I just don't know."

Phoebe sank back, her handkerchief pressed to her mouth. "What am I going to do? What *am* I going to do?"

"Now, now." Cecily reached out to pat her arm. "I'm sure the colonel is perfectly fine." She looked at Madeline, willing her to give them some good news.

Madeline hesitated, then said firmly, "Phoebe, I can tell you that Kevin and Clive are with your husband, and I saw nothing to indicate that he is dead."

Phoebe shuddered. "Just hearing those words makes me

ill. How long do you think it will be before the doctor and Clive return?"

Madeline glanced at the mantelpiece, where an ornate clock sat steadily ticking the seconds away. "Not long, I promise you." Again she paused, then added quickly, "The colonel might not be with them. They might have taken him home first before coming back for you."

"In which case," Cecily put in, "Samuel will take you home immediately."

"We can take Phoebe home," Madeline said, getting up from her chair. She walked over to the window and drew back the heavy velvet curtain to peer outside. "They should be back soon."

"Oh, poor Frederick." Phoebe started rocking again. "He will be so cold and wet. I hope he doesn't get pneumonia or something awful like that."

The thought crossed Cecily's mind that being able to catch pneumonia was better than the alternative. All she could do was pray they'd found the colonel alive and that he hadn't fallen prey to the murderous Christmas Angel.

In spite of Madeline's prediction, it was a long, agonizing wait, during which Phoebe fluctuated between bouts of deep depression, when she was certain her life with the colonel was over, to moments of hope and optimism, where she intended to scold him for straying so far.

At long last, they heard the welcome tap on the door. Madeline's face was inscrutable as Cecily got up from her chair. "Come in!" she called out and reached for Phoebe's hand.

The door opened and Dr. Prestwick strode in, his face a grim mask. He carried his hat in his hand, and it dripped water all across the carpet as he walked toward the fire.

Cecily ignored him, her gaze pinned on the door. For a dreadful moment she thought the colonel wasn't with him, but then a familiar voice bellowed from the other side of the door.

"I say, old chap, unhand me at once. I'm not a blasted invalid!"

Phoebe let out a cry of pure joy and raced across the room to the door, just as a disheveled colonel stepped through it. "Freddie! Are you all right? Are you hurt?"

Cecily hurried over to him and saw Clive standing in the hallway outside, twisting his cap in his hands. "Thank you, Clive." She smiled at him. "Would you please go down to the kitchen and tell Mrs. Chubb to send up a bottle of brandy and glasses."

"Yes, m'm." He touched his forehead, grinned at her, and ambled off down the hallway.

"I say, that sounds like a jolly good idea!" Colonel Fortescue disengaged himself from his wife's suffocating hug. "I could use a brandy, old bean."

"It's on its way, Colonel." She looked at Kevin, who stood with his back to the fire, hands clasped behind him. "I imagine you would like some, too."

"Thank you, Cecily, but we must leave." He reached out a hand to Madeline, who, after a moment's hesitation, took it and rose to her feet. "We have a baby waiting for us at home."

"Yes, thank you, Cecily." Madeline walked to the door, followed closely by her husband. "I shall return tomorrow to finish the decorating."

Troubled by her friend's somber expression, Cecily closed the door behind them and returned to the fire. Phoebe had sat down again, while the colonel had taken up residence with his back to the smoldering coals. Mud stained his heavy coat, his beard was matted with pine needles, and a deep scratch adorned his nose. Otherwise he seemed in good health.

Having apparently assured herself that her husband wasn't seriously hurt, Phoebe demanded, "What on earth were you doing in those woods? Why didn't you tell me you were leaving the Pennyfoot? You know very well you don't go anywhere without me."

The colonel raised his chin. "I was going to buy you a Christmas present."

"In the *woods*?"

"No, of course not." A puzzled look crossed his face, as if he was trying to remember. "I . . . er . . . got waylaid."

Phoebe sounded exasperated. "Waylaid?"

"Yes." He stared into the fire for a moment, then startled them all by raising his hand and shouting, "I was ordered into battle!"

"Oh, dear," Cecily murmured.

Phoebe merely looked exasperated. "Frederick, I don't think—"

"There I was," the colonel bellowed, "surrounded on all sides by the enemy. I took my trusty sword and I had at them."

Phoebe uttered a little scream as her husband lunged forward with an imaginary sword, narrowly missing her head with his fist.

"Colonel—" Cecily began, but now the colonel was at

full throttle and cut her off with an expansive flourish of his hand.

"I caught up with one of them and *charged*!" Once more he dove forward, and this time Phoebe managed to lean back out of harm's way.

"*Frederick!*" She sat up, tugging on her hat to straighten it. "Stop this nonsense at once!"

"I stabbed at the blighter and . . ." The colonel paused, his face going blank. "And then . . ."

Both Cecily and Phoebe stared at him in expectation. After a moment, Phoebe prompted, "And then?"

"He flew off."

Phoebe rolled her eyes. "Flew off?"

The colonel gave her a sheepish smile. "Must have been a blasted pheasant."

Cecily hid a smile, while Phoebe uttered a guttural sound of disgust. "I don't know why I humor him so." She glared at her husband and stood up. "Come, Frederick, it is time we went home. We have inconvenienced these good people quite enough for one day."

"But what about my brandy?" Colonel Fortescue appealed to Cecily. "You did send for brandy, didn't you, old girl?"

"I did, and you are most welcome to it." Cecily glanced at Phoebe, who gave her a fierce shake of her head. "I think, however, that it will have to wait for now." She rose. "I will make sure there is a snifter waiting for you when you bring Phoebe back for rehearsal tomorrow."

The colonel sighed. "Oh, very well. Much obliged, old bean." He took hold of Phoebe's arm. "Come along, then, ducky."

Phoebe looked as if she would like to resist but allowed him to escort her to the door. "Until tomorrow, then, Cecily!" She waved, then disappeared as the colonel tugged her out into the hallway.

A few minutes later Cecily opened the door to find her husband standing outside with a tray of glasses and a bottle of brandy.

"I passed Gertie on the way up," he said, as she stood back to let him in. "Thought I'd save her a trip."

"That's very accommodating of you, my love."

Baxter looked around the room. "Everyone gone home?"

"Yes." Cecily walked back to the fireplace and sank onto her chair. "It's been rather a long day."

"Aren't they all?" Baxter placed the tray on the side table. "Since we have a bottle of excellent brandy right here, we might as well enjoy a sip, don't you think?"

She smiled, feeling suddenly weary. "Excellent idea."

He gave her a hard look as he handed her a glass. "Investigation not going well?"

Deciding there was no point in keeping everything from him, she told him all that had transpired that day. "I don't seem to be getting any closer to solving this one," she said, while Baxter sat stern-faced and silent. "If only I could understand the reason behind the killings, and by what criteria the Christmas Angel selects his victims, perhaps I could pinpoint the culprit. He is clever. Except for the angel stamp and the missing lock of hair, he is meticulously careful to leave no clues."

"You don't have any suspects?"

Cecily took a sip of the brandy, wincing as usual as it

burned her throat. "Oh, I have suspects. I just can't seem to connect them to all of the crimes. Each suspect has a motive for killing one of the victims, and none of the others."

"Maybe they're all copying the first one."

"I thought of that." Cecily sighed and put down her glass. "But that would mean there are four killers running around out there. I find that hard to believe."

"It does seem improbable." Baxter tipped his head back to savor a mouthful of brandy before swallowing it. "So, what's the answer?"

"I don't have one." Cecily fought a wave of depression as she gazed at her husband's troubled face. "For the first time since I began this questionable pastime, I really believe I am out of my depth. This killer might be just too clever for any of us. If that's so, we are all in terrible danger."

The following morning, Cecily woke up early, determined anew to attempt to track down the Christmas Angel. Her destination, she told Samuel, was to the paper factory in Wellercombe.

She had to wait more than half an hour for Basil Baker to join them in the drafty entrance. He seemed ill at ease and refused to look Cecily in the eye when she greeted him. Instead, he pretended to have an intense interest in a printed advertisement for soap that hung on the wall.

"I spoke to your manager the other day," Cecily said, coming straight to the point. "He tells me you have Sundays off. Is that right?"

Basil shrugged. "Yeah? So what?"

Samuel made a movement, and Cecily held up her hand before he could say what was on his mind. "Jimmy Taylor died on a Sunday."

Basil didn't answer, but his mouth started twitching at one corner.

"You were not working that day, Basil. I want to know why you lied."

For a moment she thought he was not going to answer her, but then he turned so suddenly he made her jump. "I lied because I knew you wouldn't believe me when I said I didn't kill Jimmy. I knew you'd find out we had that fight, and I thought you'd blame me for his death. I wasn't anywhere near him that day. It wasn't me what threw that rock, I swear it."

"Very well, but there's something else I need to know." Cecily watched him carefully. "What I want to know is if you paid Colin Mackerbee a visit this week."

Pure amazement crossed his face. "Mackerbee? Why would I go over there?"

"You used to work for him, I believe."

"Yes, I did, but—"

"I understand that he considered you unsuitable for farmwork."

Basil's face darkened. "He had no right to tell me that. I worked hard, I did, and that man got rid of me even though I was taking good care of his animals. He should have been grateful, but instead he threw me out like I was a criminal or something."

"And you were angry with him about that."

"Not only that." Basil swiped at the advertisement with his hand, knocking it to the ground. "He told every other farmer I went to that I wasn't cut out for farmwork. He cost me a lot of jobs, and I have him to thank for me ending up in this rotten hole."

"So you decided to punish him."

"What?" Basil looked straight at her for the first time since the conversation began. "I've never punished no one. I haven't seen that miserable bugger since the day I left the Mackerbee farm." His eyes narrowed. "Why are you asking me all these questions about him, anyway? What's it to you?"

"Colin Mackerbee was killed the other day. Someone took a knife into the barn where he was working and stabbed him."

Basil's jaw dropped. "Blimey, not another one."

"So you're saying you didn't know?"

"No, I didn't know." Basil thrust out his jaw. "And don't you go putting this on me, neither. I ain't been near that farm since the day I left, and that's the truth. Now I've got to get back to work or I'll be losing this flipping job as well."

Cecily let him go, knowing there was nothing else she could get out of him. Disgruntled, she said little to Samuel as they made their way back to the carriage.

She was getting tired of spinning her wheels with nothing to show for it. She could neither pin down a suspect nor eliminate one entirely. The only logical conclusion was the theory that the killer was totally unrelated to his victims and therefore an unknown factor in the investigation.

She would be more inclined to believe that if it wasn't for the annoying niggling feeling in the back of her mind that she already knew what she needed to know and just couldn't recognize it.

This had happened so often in the past now that she clung to it like a life raft. Sooner or later, she was sure, the solution to the puzzle would reveal itself. She could only hope that happened before someone else lost his life.

Pansy was in a fever of impatience as she cleared the tables after the midday meal in the dining room. Her first rehearsal was starting in a few minutes, and she wanted to get there before Doris to show her eagerness to do her part.

She was placing the last of the dishes on the tray when two arms snaked around her waist, making her squeal.

Her face warming, she turned to greet Samuel. "Whatcha doing here?"

"I just got back from taking madam into Weller-combe." Samuel unbuttoned his coat. "It's getting warmer outside."

"Yeah, I know." Pansy went to lift the tray but Samuel took it from her. "I don't suppose she's caught the Christmas Angel?"

"Not yet." He pulled a face at her. "She wasn't happy that everyone found out about it. I told you not to tell anyone."

"Sorry." Pansy walked ahead of him to open the door. "It just sort of slipped out while I was talking to Gertie and dopey Lizzie heard me and went around telling everyone that a killer was chopping off people's heads."

"Yeah, so I heard." The glasses rattled on the tray as Samuel carried them to the dumbwaiter. "This is a bad one. I can tell madam's worried about it. She's afraid if she doesn't find him soon someone else will get bumped off."

"What are the constables doing about it, then? Isn't it their job to find him?"

Samuel snorted. "Supposed to be, isn't it. Those twerps couldn't find a murderer if he danced in front of them. Though I must say, this one is clever. He doesn't make mistakes or leave clues behind. Unless P.C. Northcott isn't telling us everything."

"You think he's hiding something from madam?"

"I don't know what to think. I just know that madam is having a lot of trouble with this one." He placed the tray on the dumbwaiter and tugged on the rope. "Come on, I'll walk down to the kitchen with you. I want a word with Mrs. Chubb."

"I'm not going to the kitchen." Pansy pulled off her apron and shoved it in on top of the dishes.

Samuel raised his eyebrows. "Where are you going, then? It's not your afternoon off."

"I know." She took a deep breath, then added in a rush, "I'm going to help Doris with her costumes in the pantomime. I'm going to rehearsal now."

Samuel's eyebrows twitched even higher. *"Doris?"*

His voice had come out all squeaky, and Pansy glared at him. "Yes, Doris. The big love of your life. She asked me to help her and I'm going to do it."

For a moment Samuel looked as if he might be cross, but then he smiled. "That's exciting, Pansy! I'm happy for you. Really I am. You'll have a great time. Doris is a lovely person, and you'll enjoy working with her."

"Yeah, I know I will." She studied his face, trying to read what he was thinking behind that smile. Was he still in love with Doris? If only she knew for sure. If only he would say he loved *her*, then she could stop worrying about the songstress.

"Well, I'd better let you go, then," Samuel said, giving her a quick hug. "You'd better scram or you'll be late."

He walked off, leaving her staring after him, unsure now if she really wanted to help Doris after all.

CHAPTER
❈ 15 ❈

Gertie smiled at the young woman hurrying toward her across the foyer. "Doris! I haven't seen you since you bloody got here. Where have you been hiding?"

Doris paused, brushing a strand of hair out of her eyes. "I've been busy with rehearsals and trying to spend time with my husband and daughter. Mrs. Fortescue keeps us all on our toes."

"Yeah, she's a bloody slave driver, that woman. I'm glad I don't have to work for her." Gertie looked around. "Where is Essie, then? Is she with Daisy and the twins?"

An odd look crossed Doris's face, giving Gertie a stab of uneasiness. "No, actually Daisy went into town to do some Christmas shopping."

Gertie felt even more anxious. "She didn't take the twins

with her, did she? They're supposed to be at rehearsal this afternoon."

Now Doris looked really uncomfortable. "No, I thought you knew. The twins are with Clive. He's taking care of them for Daisy."

Gertie's annoyance was tempered with relief. "Well, she might have bloody told me she was going to dump them on Clive. She should have asked me first."

"I believe she did look for you but couldn't find you. One of the footmen was going into town this morning and offered her a ride in the carriage. She thought about taking the twins, but Clive was there at the time and he suggested the children would be happier building a snowman with him. He said the snow would all be gone by tomorrow and this was their last chance."

Gertie had to smile. "That sounds like Clive. He's good with the kiddies. I heard he used to be a schoolteacher."

"He was? I wonder why he stopped teaching."

"Yeah, there's a lot I don't know about him." Gertie peered at the grandfather clock, wondering if the twins had made it to rehearsal on time. If not, Phoebe would be having a fit by now. "I keep meaning to ask him about his past, but there never seems to be a good time."

"He'd make a wonderful father." Doris followed her gaze. "I'd better get down to the ballroom. Mrs. Fortescue will be screaming for me any moment. Clive took the twins down there a while ago."

Relieved, Gertie waved a hand. "Oh, thank goodness. Good luck with the pantomime!"

She was about to head for the stairs when Doris called out, "He's in love with you, you know."

Gertie stopped dead, her heart skipping a beat. "Who is?"

"Clive, of course. You must know that. It's obvious by the way he talks about you."

Gertie laughed, though it sounded hollow, even to her. "Clive talks that way about everybody. He loves people, that's all."

Standing in the entrance to the hallway, Doris looked back at her. "No," she said, shaking her head. "He's in love with *you*, Gertie. He's a good man. Don't keep him dangling too long or you'll lose him."

With a quick wave of her hand she was gone, leaving Gertie staring after her, speechless and dumbfounded.

"Doris isn't here yet," Phoebe said, waving an irritated hand at Pansy. "When you find her, tell her we're waiting for her."

Pansy started to speak, but Phoebe shot up her hand again. "I don't have time for anything else. Go, child! Find my star!"

"I thought I was your star," Deirdre whined from the stage. "The pantomime is called *Peter Pan*, isn't it? I'm Peter Pan, aren't I? I should be the star."

A chorus of voices echoed her.

"Yeah, she's Peter Pan!"

"Yeah, she's the star!"

"Deirdre's Peter Pan!"

"Yeah, she's just as good as Doris!"

"*Quiet!*" Phoebe clapped her hands. "I will not have this insubordination on my stage."

"There's that word again." Deirdre advanced to the front

of the stage. "Why don't you speak bloody English?" The titters behind her grew louder.

Phoebe's face turned scarlet.

Pansy held her breath, waiting for the onslaught.

Phoebe marched up to the front of the stage and shook her fist at the grinning Deirdre. "If I have to speak to you again," she roared, in a surprisingly strong voice for a woman of such petite stature, "it will be to tell you to get off my stage. You're not the only one who can play Peter Pan. Everyone knows your lines by now. It won't be that difficult to replace you. If I do that, make no mistake, you will never appear on this stage again. Do I make myself perfectly clear?"

Deirdre stopped grinning and, mumbling something under her breath, backed away.

"Good." Phoebe folded her arms. "Now you listen to me, all of you, just in case someone else has delusions of grandeur. Mrs. Lansfield is far and above you pathetic amateurs. She is a star in every sense of the word. She is a professional, and as such she will be treated with the respect she deserves. Anyone of you can be replaced. Doris cannot. Do you understand?"

Mumbles and grumbles drifted down from the stage.

Phoebe raised her voice again. "I repeat, *do you understand?*"

A few voices muttered, "Yes, Mrs. Fortescue."

"I'm not a professional. Not anymore."

Pansy swung around as the new voice spoke from behind her. Doris smiled at her. "Hello, Pansy. Thank you for coming."

Phoebe frowned. "Do you need her to fetch you something?"

"No." Doris linked her arm in Pansy's, making the younger girl's knees go weak. "Pansy has kindly offered to be my dresser for the pantomime."

Phoebe's charcoaled eyebrows disappeared under her hat. "Your *dresser*? But . . . but she's one of the *maids*!"

"So was I, once." Doris started walking toward the back-stage door, pulling Pansy along with her. "And look at me now." With that, she tugged Pansy through the door and closed it behind them.

Cecily was enjoying a quiet meal with her husband in their sitting room that evening when Pansy disturbed them with the news that P.C. Northcott was waiting in the library to see her.

Baxter exploded as usual. "Who the devil does that blasted man think he is, invading our privacy at this hour?" He turned on Pansy, who was hovering in the doorway, fingers nervously plucking her apron. "Tell him madam is indisposed, and he will have to wait until she is ready to receive him."

"Yes, sir." Pansy hesitated, biting her lip.

"Well, what is it, child? Speak up!"

"Hugh," Cecily warned, feeling sorry for Pansy.

"It's the constable, sir," Pansy said, stumbling over her words in her haste to get them out. "He said as how it was very important he speak with madam. Urgent, he said."

"Oh, dear." Her appetite gone, Cecily laid down her dessert spoon. "That can only mean one thing." She stood. "Thank you, Pansy. Please tell the constable I will join him directly."

"Yes, m'm." Pansy ducked a curtsey and fled.

"You don't have to drop everything at the beck and call of that imbecile," Baxter said, with a disgruntled sigh. "He probably just wants to know how the investigation is going. He could have waited until tomorrow for that."

"Exactly." Cecily crossed the room to the door. "In which case, I'm very much afraid that he is here to tell me about another victim of the Christmas Angel."

"If that's so, then I'm coming with you." Baxter threw down his serviette in disgust. "Much as I hate talking to that fool, if he is going to involve you in yet another dastardly murder, I want to hear about it."

Worried now, Cecily tried to dissuade him. "You know how he always irritates you so. Why don't you allow me to talk to him alone, and then I'll tell you everything when I return."

"Because, my dear, much as I adore you, I cannot trust you to tell me everything. You have a tendency to omit certain information under the mistaken impression it will ease my concerns about your safety."

"I always tell you everything eventually, Bax. You know that."

"True, you do tell me. Usually, however, after you have escaped from the jaws of some frightful danger. Except, of course, for the rare occasion when I have had to rescue you myself."

Cecily smiled. "Look how noble it makes you feel to have rescued me."

Baxter's stern features softened. "I'd vastly prefer it if you avoided danger altogether."

"Yes, I know." Resigned to having him listen in on her

conversation with Sam Northcott, Cecily opened the door. "We have had that conversation numerous times, darling. There's no point in rehashing it now. Come along, then. Let's hear what awful news Sam has brought us this time."

The constable stood in his usual spot with his back to the fireplace when Cecily entered. Following closely behind her, Baxter closed the door and ushered his wife to a maroon velvet armchair.

Sam Northcott seemed shocked at Baxter's presence. He hummed and ah'd quite a bit before coming to the point. "I'm sorry to h'inform you, Mrs. B., that there's been h'another unfortunate incident concerning our . . . mutual acquaintance." He shot a look at Baxter, obviously hoping that he would not understand the meaning behind his words.

"It's all right, Sam. Baxter knows all about the Christmas Angel and my participation in the investigation." Cecily sat down on the armchair, feeling the familiar sense of hopelessness that grew stronger with each new murder. "Who is it this time?" She clasped her hands in her lap, praying it wasn't someone she knew.

Sam still seemed uncomfortable. He kept sliding his gaze sideways at Baxter, as if expecting him to erupt in a torrent of abuse at any moment. "He's outdone himself this time, m'm. The Angel, I mean. He didn't just go after one person; he tried to take out the entire membership of the Fox Hunters Club."

Baxter swore, something he rarely did in public, while Cecily fought hard to regain her breath. "Dear God. What happened?"

"They were all at their annual Christmas meeting earlier this evening. Fifty-four members in all. The Angel set fire to

211

the place. Burned to the ground, it did, before the fire engines could get there from Wellercombe."

Cecily felt her throat tighten up and swallowed. "How many, Sam?"

"By good fortune, they managed to get all but one out of there before the roof caved in. The firemen found his body when they went in."

Her mouth was so dry she had trouble forming the words. "Was the lock of hair missing?"

"Not that I heard. The doctor was still down there when I left, so I don't know all the details yet."

"Then how can you be sure it was the work of the Christmas Angel and not simply an accidental fire?"

Northcott puffed out his chest. "They were those little golden angels scattered all around on the ground outside the meeting hall."

Baxter swore again. "For heaven's sake, man, when are you going to catch this madman? He's got to be stopped."

Northcott scowled. "We are doing the best we can, under the circumstances. We've never had a case like this one before."

Baxter waved his hand in irritation. "Isn't it time you brought in Scotland Yard?"

The constable winced. "We're considering it."

Cecily felt sorry for him. Failing to solve this case would mean much more for him than a missed Christmas visit to London. He had let things get too far along without involving Inspector Cranshaw. If the inspector got word of the murders now, he would be down on Sam Northcott's head like a herd of raging bulls. It could even cost Sam his job. His only salvation was to solve the case and quickly.

That didn't seem likely at this point, and Cecily was inclined to agree with her husband. They needed the full force of Scotland Yard if they were to capture the Christmas Angel and put an end to this deadly onslaught of terror.

She was about to say as much when a familiar sensation filled her head. She knew the answer. It kept tantalizing her, only to disappear like a mischievous sprite when she reached out to grasp it.

Often, when the feeling was this strong, it meant she was close to solving the puzzle. She leaned forward, looking earnestly into the constable's face. "Give me two more days," she said, aware of Baxter's disapproving gaze on her face. "If I don't have the answer by then, we will call in Scotland Yard."

Sam's nod was skeptical, and he frowned as he reached for his helmet. "If we have to do that," he muttered, as he made his way to the door, "it will be a miserable Christmas for everyone."

"He's right," Baxter said gruffly, as the door closed behind him. "I wasn't going to tell you this, but we received another telegram this morning."

Cecily looked up at him. "Who from? Not . . . ?"

"No. As far as I know, our important guest is still coming. It's unlikely he's heard the news, or Badgers End would be swarming with bobbies from the Yard."

"Then who?"

"It was from the Windermeres. They must be friends of Lord Chattenham."

"Canceling their reservation?"

"I'm sorry, m'dear. It looks as if news of our infamous murderer is spreading."

Cecily got up from her chair. "Two days. That's all I have. Let us pray it's enough."

"Amen." Baxter opened the door for her and followed her outside into the dimly lit hallway.

Cecily slept badly that night, haunted by dreams of golden angels buzzing around her head while she followed a shadowy figure through a dark forest of trees.

She awoke with a start to find her husband gone and daylight streaming through the window. Annoyed at herself for sleeping late, she hurriedly dressed and went in search of Baxter.

She found him in her office, working on the stack of papers he'd brought home from the city. He looked up when she opened the door.

"Ah there you are." He shuffled the papers and piled them on the side of the desk. "I let you sleep. You had a restless night."

"Yes, I did. Have you had breakfast?"

"An hour ago." He got up and walked around the desk to plant a kiss on her cheek. "Would you like something sent up to the suite?"

"No." She patted him on the arm. "I should look in on the kitchen, so I'll find something there to eat. I was going shopping this morning but I think I'll wait until tomorrow. Go back to work."

He tilted his head to one side and regarded her with a frown. "You look tired, Cecily. This Angel business is getting you down."

"I'm all right." She managed a smile. "One way or another, this will all be over in two days. Once Inspector Cranshaw takes over I shall leave him to it."

Baxter raised an eyebrow. "It isn't like you to give up."

"Maybe I'm just getting too old to do this anymore."

"Now I am worried." He raised her chin with his finger. "You will never be too old for anything, my love. You have a young heart and soul, and age can't take that away from you."

Touched, she went up on her toes to kiss him. "It is you who keeps me young. But thank you. Now go back to work. I've distracted you enough."

Feeling a little less downhearted, she left him and made her way down to the kitchen. The wonderful spicy aroma of steamed puddings greeted her when she pushed open the door.

Michel caught sight of her first and called out a greeting. Mrs. Chubb looked up from the bowl of eggs she was beating and waved the whisk at her.

"Madam! We were wondering what happened to you. You haven't had any breakfast. What can we get for you?"

"Just two scones and a cup of tea, Althea." Cecily glanced at the two maids washing dishes at the sink. "How are things coming along?"

"We're catching up." The housekeeper nodded at Michel. "The last of the Christmas puddings are boiling on the stove, and the mince pies are in the pantry. I'll start icing the Christmas cakes this afternoon."

"Wonderful." Cecily sat at the table to wait for her tea and scones. "The guests will be arriving the day after tomorrow. We should be ready for them by then."

"We'll be ready." Mrs. Chubb drew closer and lowered her voice. "I don't suppose there's any word about this Christmas Angel, m'm?"

Cecily hesitated, wondering how much they all knew. "Not yet, but there's really no need to worry, Althea. It won't affect anyone here in the Pennyfoot."

Mrs. Chubb nodded. "I only asked because of all the rumors floating around. Lizzie was convinced he was running around chopping off people's heads."

"I can assure you, that's not happening." Cecily smiled as one of the maids brought her a steaming cup with saucer and a plate of scones. "We must stop these ridiculous rumors from making the rounds. We don't want to frighten the guests when they arrive."

"Yes, m'm. We'll do our best. Though, I'll be surprised if they haven't heard about it. Such terrible things going on out there."

"Yes, well, hopefully it will all end soon and we can all stop worrying about it." Determined to change the subject, she asked the housekeeper about her daughter and managed to enjoy her breakfast while Mrs. Chubb happily gave her the latest news.

After leaving the kitchen, Cecily headed for the library. Madeline had planned to decorate the tree in there that morning and Cecily wanted some time alone to talk to her.

Madeline was over by the window, putting the finishing touches on the magnificent fir that had taken three footmen to set up in the corner.

Cecily took a moment to drink in and enjoy the sight. As always, Madeline had created a breathtaking vision of color and design. Balls of frosted glass spun slowly on silver strings, pomander spice balls dangled from red ribbons, and a cascade of crocheted snowflakes clung to every branch.

In between hung tiny bags of bright green and red cotton, filled with candied fruit and almond sticks for the children. There were even glistening sugar fondants nestled among the branches in various shapes and sizes.

"Madeline! It looks absolutely beautiful! I don't know how you do it."

Madeline stood back to inspect her work. "Really? I was thinking it looked a little insipid. It needs more color, don't you think?" She dug into a box and pulled out a handful of bright red velvet birds. "How about these scattered about? Like so." She perched one of the birds on a branch and stood back again, her head tilted so that her shiny black hair swung about her hip.

"They are adorable!" Cecily moved closer to examine the colorful ornament. "Wherever did you find them?"

"In a curiosity shop in Wellercombe." She darted about the tree, poking the birds in between the branches. "They had all kinds of new ornaments there. Most of them are made by the villagers. You should go with me next time. We'd have fun picking out pieces we like."

"I'd love that." Cecily walked over to the window. "The snow has almost all gone now. At least I don't have that to worry about now."

"You have nothing new on the murders?"

Cecily wandered back to the tree. "Nothing, unless news of the fire at the Fox Hunters Club didn't reach you yet."

Madeline looked at her, her eyes troubled. "Kevin was called out to the scene yesterday. That was the work of the Christmas Angel?"

"We think so. Though the only clue they found were the gold angels scattered about. Those stamps are easy enough to come by and could have been left by anyone. It was fortunate that all but one survived, though that won't be any comfort to the family of the victim."

Madeline placed another bird on a branch. "Well, this might sound uncharitable, but that's at least one hunter who won't be chasing an innocent fox."

Knowing how her friend felt about hunting, Cecily merely nodded.

"Not that I wish death on any of them," Madeline added, "but I do wish the destruction of their clubhouse and the loss of a member would put an end to their diabolical practices. Foxhunting is particularly cruel and inhumane. It should be banned."

Something inside Cecily's mind ticked over. "I wonder if that could be a motive for the fire," she murmured. "Maybe someone else feels as strongly as you do about foxhunting and decided to take advantage of the search for the killer to get rid of a few hunters and put the blame on the Christmas Angel."

She had been more or less making light of her suggestion, but Madeline immediately raised her head. "It's certainly a possibility. I'm sorry, Cecily. I don't have anything that would help you. When I think about the Christmas Angel all I see is darkness and confusion. If that is the mind of the killer, then he is in a very dark place indeed."

"He would have to be to destroy the lives of so many people—none of whom seem deserving."

"Obviously the killer thinks they're deserving."

"Exactly." Cecily uttered a sigh of frustration. "If I only knew why he thinks so, I might be able to find him."

Madeline started packing up the box. "Just be sure he doesn't find you first. By now he must know you're looking

218

for him. Be on your very best guard, Cecily. I have a feeling the time is near when you will meet."

Startled, Cecily was about to ask what she meant by that when a tap on the door interrupted her. Pansy sidled into the room and curtsied. "Dr. Prestwick is here, m'm. He's waiting for Mrs. Prestwick in the lobby."

Madeline picked up the box. "I'm coming right now." She smiled at Cecily. "Don't worry, my friend. It will all turn out all right in the end."

She sailed through the door, leaving Cecily to stare after her.

CHAPTER
❀ 16 ❀

The dress rehearsal for the pantomime had already started by the time Pansy was through with her chores. Even though it was forbidden, she picked up her skirts and tore down the corridor to the ballroom.

Arriving breathless, her cap askew on her head, she darted past a disapproving Phoebe and barged through the door to backstage.

Seated at the mirror in the dressing room, Doris was already in her first costume. She was doing something to her eyes as Pansy rushed over to her, scattering the group of children waiting for their cue.

"I'm sorry, Mrs. Lansfield, really I am." Pansy fought back tears. "I had to clear all the tables and set them up again and—"

Doris laid a slender hand on her arm. "It's all right, Pansy.

Really. I was a maid here once, and I know what it's like. I'm just happy you are here now, and please, call me Doris."

Pansy could have hugged her. "Thank you so much, Mrs. . . . Doris. I'll get the next costume ready right away."

A loud rapping on the door turned both their heads. "You're on, Wendy," a male voice announced.

Pansy recognized him as one of the footmen working backstage. "She's coming," she called out.

Doris got up and hurried over to the door. "Thanks, Pansy." She flashed a smile that dazzled Pansy so much it made her blink.

The door closed behind the songstress, and Pansy turned her attention to the row of costumes. Behind her, the children chattered with excitement, and Phoebe's dance group huddled together in a corner discussing something that caused eruptions of giggles.

Pansy felt a warm glow of immense satisfaction. She loved being part of it all, being backstage to see the performers getting ready and then coming back to talk about how it was out there onstage.

What a thrilling life it must be for people like Doris, who had performed in front of huge crowds in the West End. It had to be the most exciting thing in the whole world.

Caught up in her thoughts, she didn't hear her name called until one of the dancers poked her in the ribs. Turning, she was surprised to see Phoebe standing in the doorway, flapping her hands, the wide brim of her hat flopping up and down in her agitation.

"Pansy, for heaven's sake, child. I need you onstage. Tinker Bell is sick, and I need someone to take her place."

Pansy's jaw dropped. "What?"

"Now, child, *now*. Get into the costume and be out there in five minutes."

She started to turn away but paused when Pansy cried out, "I can't be Tinker Bell."

Phoebe turned back, hands on her hips. "Why not?"

"I've never been onstage before."

"Well, there's always a first time."

Again she turned away, only to be brought up short by Pansy's agonized protest. "But I don't know the *part*."

Once more Phoebe faced her. "You don't have to know the part. Tinker Bell doesn't have any lines. I'll talk you through the dress rehearsals and the other actors will prompt you for the performance. Don't worry, child. You'll manage beautifully. Now get into costume."

"But what about Doris? I'm supposed to be her dresser."

"You can dress each other."

"But—"

Phoebe turned back again, her voice rising to yell, "That's enough buts! You are the only one scrawny enough to fly on those wires. Now, either you take the part or we cancel the entire production!"

Howls of protest filled the room, and dozens of eyes glared at Pansy. She opened her mouth to say something but Phoebe had already disappeared.

"Come on, I'll help you." One of the dancers rushed over to her and grabbed the glittering costume from its hanger.

As if in a dream, Pansy felt the smooth white satin slipping over her head. The costume left more of her arms and legs exposed than she'd ever allowed before, but somehow it didn't seem to matter.

One of the dancers painted her face while another placed a sparkling tiara on her head and attached wings to her back with a heavy brace. Someone else helped her into the harness that would take her flying across the stage.

Looking at her reflection in the mirror, Pansy couldn't recognize herself. Surely this radiant creature couldn't possibly be her. This was all a dream, and any minute now she was going to wake up and find herself lying on her cot in the maids' quarters.

Oh, if only Samuel could see her now! It might just be enough to make him forget about Doris. Maybe he'd even be so impressed he'd finally tell her he loved her.

Another loud rapping on the door shattered her thoughts. "Tinker Bell! You're on!"

One of the dancers gave her a little push. "Go on, luv. Break a leg!"

Pansy gave her a horrified look. "That's a nasty thing to say!"

The other dancers laughed, and one of the children piped up, "It's what actors say for good luck."

"Oh. All right, then. Thank you." Stumbling out the door, Pansy felt a momentous wave of panic. What did she know about performing onstage? She was going to make a complete and utter fool of herself up there.

She had to fly, for goodness' sake! What if she fell off and really did break a leg? Her Christmas would be ruined, and the pantomime would have to be canceled, and everyone would blame her for being such a clumsy twerp.

She reached the edge of the stage and heard Peter and Wendy speaking their lines.

"She's hiding in here somewhere," Peter said, bounding toward the fake sideboard.

Frozen to the spot, Pansy watched helplessly as Peter opened a drawer and peered inside. Someone behind her fiddled with her harness, but she paid no attention, her mind a complete blank. Then she felt a sharp shove in the back and all of a sudden she was lifted off the floor.

Letting out a yell, she flailed her arms and legs, which tipped her upside down. Her tiara fell off as she swooped across the stage, her screams echoing up to the rafters.

"Let her down!" Phoebe yelled from somewhere out front. "Get her down, *now*!"

Pansy shut her eyes as the floor came up to meet her. Someone caught her and held her tight until her feet touched the floor. Opening her eyes, Pansy saw Doris's anxious face.

"Goodness, are you all right?"

Pansy grinned. "I'm fine." With that she closed her eyes again and gave up to the darkness sweeping over her.

Still mulling over her conversation with Madeline that morning, Cecily decided to go down to the ballroom to see how the rehearsals were coming along. Perhaps if she gave her mind a rest she could eventually understand what her instincts were telling her.

Besides, she was anxious to see her godchildren performing onstage, and this would be a good excuse to peek in on them.

Crossing the foyer, she was too late to avoid the colonel, who was apparently on his way to the bar, as usual.

"Hello, there, old girl!" He put a hand up to his head, apparently forgetting he had already removed his hat. "Looks like the snow's disappearing, what?"

"It does, indeed, Colonel. The weather is warming up at last."

"Jolly good show. It was dashed cold out there in the woods, I can tell you. All that snow about."

"I'm sure it was." Cecily edged closer to the hallway. "I'm just on my way to the dress rehearsal, so if you will excuse me . . ."

"I just hope I don't run into any more pheasants out there. I should have had my shotgun with me. A blasted sword is no good for killing pheasants, you know. They move too fast."

Nodding, Cecily backed away. "I believe they have a new delivery of scotch in the bar. I'm sure you would enjoy—"

The colonel didn't even bother to answer her. With a brief salute he was off and running, leaving her free to continue on to the ballroom.

She reached there just in time to see Tinker Bell buckle at the knees and fall to the floor.

"I *told* them not to hook her up to the wires yet," Phoebe exclaimed, as Doris knelt by the prone figure. "She needs to be taught how to fly. I was going to have Clive show her after rehearsal." She clasped her hands together. "This is all the fault of those incompetent footmen."

Recognizing her maid, Cecily gestured at the stage. "What on earth is Pansy doing up there, anyway?"

"She's taking Becky's place." Phoebe threw up her hands in despair. "Poor child is in bed with a nasty case of ague, and Pansy is the only one I know who isn't too heavy for the wires. Clive made it very clear that only lightweight people should fly. I didn't know what else to do."

"She's all right," Doris called down from the stage, before Cecily could answer. "She's waking up."

Cecily walked up to the stage, where a white-faced Tinker Bell was sitting up. "Are you hurt, Pansy?"

The maid shook her head. "No, m'm. I just feel stupid, that's all."

Phoebe appeared by Cecily's side. "Well, you could hardly know how to fly on those wires without someone showing you how to do it. I'll have Clive come by and teach you. If he can teach Deidre how to do it he can teach anyone."

"Here!" Deirdre complained, but Phoebe took no notice of her.

"Stand up, child," she ordered. "Let's make sure you didn't break anything."

Pansy stood, holding on to Doris's shoulder for support. "I'd like to try it again, Mrs. Fortescue. I think I can do it."

"Not until Clive has shown you how to fly." Phoebe straightened her hat. "We'll do the rest of the rehearsal without Tinker Bell on the wires." She clapped her hands. "Places, everyone!"

Reassured, Cecily drew back from the stage and waited by the windows for the twins to appear. Staring out at the gathering dusk, she was happy to see that almost all of the snow had melted from the lawns. That meant the roads would be clear for travel.

Thinking of the snow reminded her of her conversation

with the colonel. The poor man must have been freezing. It was a miracle Clive and Kevin had found him. He really wasn't safe to be outside on his own.

It was just as well he hadn't had a sword out there, slicing at a poor pheasant. He could have injured himself quite badly. Both he and the pheasant had had a lucky escape. She could only hope the colonel didn't take a shotgun into the woods. Goodness knows what he would shoot at out there.

Cecily stared at the grassy slopes leading down to the trees. Imagining the colonel shooting at pheasants had brought another image to mind. Henry Farnsworth had been shooting pheasants when he was killed.

She frowned, wondering why that seemed significant. Was it something that was said during her conversation with Lady Marion? Behind her, the children were singing a ragged chorus, and she tried to shut them out in order to focus on whatever her muddled brain was trying to tell her.

Apart from heaping praise, Lady Marion hadn't said much about her gamekeeper. Most of the conversation had been about Thomas Willow and the shoe shop.

The noise from the stage had become distracting. The twins were front and center, singing their hearts out. She waited long enough for the song to end, then hurried out of the ballroom and headed once more for the library. She needed silence and time alone to think.

To her relief, the library was empty when she entered. The Christmas tree caught her eye, and she wandered over to admire the purple glass grapes and gold-edged pears her talented friend had added to the branches.

The absence of angels disturbed her, reminding her of the

formidable problems facing her. Madeline had been careful to omit candles from the tree as well. Another bad omen to haunt her.

She could still remember the Christmas when the candles had caught the tree alight, filling the room with smoke. The locked door preventing her escape. The awful smell of burning, the heat overcoming her . . .

Once more the feeling of recognition nudged her. She shook her head, forcing out the memory. That had nothing to do with Thomas Willow and the shoe shop.

She moved closer to the fire, holding her hands out to the warmth. Lady Marion had said she felt sorry for Lester. It must have been a shock for the assistant to find out the shoe shop was in debt. Especially since he must have been hoping to repay his gambling debts.

Cecily caught her breath. She could see in her mind the musty little parlor in the back of the shop. What if . . . ? Her thoughts raced on, piecing everything together.

She had more shopping to do and a gown to fetch from Caroline Blanchard. Tomorrow she would pay a visit to Willow's shoe shop. She had an idea that she would find the answers there that had so far eluded her.

Gertie was piling serving dishes onto the dumbwaiter when Pansy rushed into the kitchen.

"You're late." Mrs. Chubb threw a clean apron and cap at her. "Get these on and get up to the dining room. Lizzie is already serving supper up there."

"Yes, Mrs. Chubb." Pansy fastened the apron around her waist and tugged the cap on her head. Fishing in her frock pocket she found two hairpins and stuck them into the cap to hold it in place.

She kept signaling Gertie with her eyebrows, trying to let her know she had something terribly important to tell her.

Gertie merely flipped her eyebrows up and down in answer, and Pansy had to hold in her excitement until after supper had been served and she could finally get back to the kitchen.

Mrs. Chubb and Gertie were alone when Pansy burst out with her news. "Guess what!" she said, as both women stared at her in expectation. "I'm going to be in the pantomime!"

Gertie frowned. "I know, you already told us you were going to help Doris with her costumes."

"No, no." Pansy danced over to her and grasped her arm with both hands. "I'm going to be *in* the pantomime. I'm playing Tinker Bell!"

There was a moment of shocked silence, then both Gertie and Mrs. Chubb burst out laughing.

"Yeah," Gertie said, "and I'm going to be Peter Pan."

Pansy shook her arm. "No, really I am. Ask Mrs. Fortescue. She'll tell you. No, ask Clive. He's going to teach me how to fly on the wires tonight."

Gertie's face was rigid with disbelief. "Go *on*!"

Pansy jumped up and down in her excitement. "I'm wearing this lovely filmy costume with wings and everything, and I don't have to learn any lines so it wasn't hard at all to know what to do, and I'm going to be flying all over the stage, so you'll have to come and see me." She looked at Mrs. Chubb. "Both of you!"

Mrs. Chubb looked worried. "You're going to fly?"

"Yes, it's all right, Clive will teach me how." Pansy

skipped around the kitchen table. "I tried it this afternoon, but I turned upside down so now I have to learn how to stay upright. Deirdre said it's easy so—"

Mrs. Chubb interrupted her. "Isn't that a bit dangerous?"

"Not if you know what you're doing." Pansy skipped up to her. "I'm going to perform on the *stage*. I can't wait to tell Samuel." She glanced at the clock on the mantel. "I have to go now. Clive is waiting for me in the ballroom."

"What about the dishes?" Gertie gestured at the sink. "They all have to be washed and dried."

"I'll do it after I learn how to fly." She rushed to the door, looked back at their doubtful faces, and added, "I'm going to be a *star*!"

"Oh, gawd," Gertie muttered. "That's all we bloody need."

Pansy paid no attention. Her mind was fully focused on the lesson ahead, and she could think of nothing else.

Clive hadn't arrived yet when she got to the ballroom. Alone in the vast room, she climbed up onto the stage and surveyed the expanse of floor in front of her.

On the night of the performance the chairs would be lined up in neat rows in front of the stage and all the toffs would be watching her. Maybe even Samuel would come and watch her.

The thought made her nervous. Maybe she should rehearse her curtsies, just so she didn't fall over and look silly in front of everyone. She was perfecting her fourth curtsey when Clive spoke from in front of the stage.

"Very nice. You look like a professional up there."

She beamed at him. "Really? You really think so?"

"Yes, I really think so." He disappeared, only to appear a

moment later in the wings. "Come over here. I have to hook you up to the wires."

She walked over to him, tingling with nervous excitement. He turned her around with gentle hands and fitted the harness she'd worn earlier over her shoulders and around her midriff.

"Now," he said, when he was done, "the trick is to arch your back and keep your head up. Like this." He curved his back, stretched out his arms, and swooped them around as if he were flying. "Now let me see you do it."

Pansy copied him as best she could.

"More," Clive said, putting a hand against the middle of her back. "Stretch it out, right here."

He applied pressure, and she pushed her hips forward. "Like this?"

"That's it. Now I want you to run back and forth across the stage, feeling the pull of the wires. Don't try to fly just yet, just get the feel of it."

She did as he asked, running back and forth while he called out, "Arch that back! Head up! Shoulders back!"

Just as she was getting tired of it all, halfway across the stage she felt the wires tugging and her feet left the floor. She uttered a little shriek of surprise, and lost her posture for a moment.

Clive called out to her, urging her to keep her head up, and then she was flying, swooping across the stage like a bird. At first she was scared, but gradually her fear melted away and she was having fun. No, it was more than that. It was the most thrilling experience of her life. She wanted it to go on forever.

She felt a deep regret when Clive called out, "That's

enough!" Her feet touched the floor and she managed to land gracefully, though her body felt heavy and clumsy when she walked over to him.

"That was so . . . so . . ." She couldn't think of a word good enough to describe the sensation.

Clive grinned. "You're a natural," he said, unhooking the wires from her back. "You'll be a splendid Tinker Bell."

"Thanks to you." She smiled up at him. She'd never noticed before, but he had a really nice smile. In fact, he was almost handsome in a rough sort of way. A big man, too. Big enough to tower over Gertie.

Remembering her Christmas wish for her friend, Pansy decided to seize the chance to make it come true. "I was wondering what to give Gertie for a Christmas present," she said, struggling to take off the harness. "Do you have any ideas?"

Clive raised his eyebrows. "Me? I don't really know what she likes."

Pansy pretended to think. "Well, I know what she wants, but I don't think I can get it for her."

To her relief, Clive took the bait. "What does she want, then?"

Pansy leaned closer. "Well, don't tell her I told you, but she's lonely. She wants to meet someone nice who will love her and take care of her and the twins."

Clive got a really strange expression on his face. "Oh, she does, does she? That's a bit of a tall order for a Christmas present."

Pansy heaved a loud sigh. "Yeah, I know. I would love to get it for her, but I suppose I'll have to make do with handkerchiefs or something."

"Probably." Clive's voice sounded funny and he cleared his throat. "Well, I have to be off. I have to make my rounds before turning off all the lamps."

"Oh, all right." Pansy smoothed down the ruffles in her frock caused by the harness. "Thank you so much, Clive. That was really nice of you to teach me to fly."

"The pleasure is all mine." Clive touched his forehead with his fingers. "Give my regards to Gertie."

"Oh, I will!" Pansy tore off the stage and across the ballroom. Now to put into motion the second part of her plan. One way or another, she'd get Gertie and Clive together for Christmas. It was the very least she could do for her friend.

CHAPTER

❋ 17 ❋

"I had a lovely talk with Clive," Pansy said, as she dragged a large china tureen from the soapy water.

Gertie took it from her and stood it on the draining board. "Did he teach you how to fly?"

"Yes, he did." Pansy felt her face growing warm as she told Gertie about the lesson. "It was the most fantastic feeling, flying across that stage like I was a bird. I wish I could fly like that without wires. It must be so wonderful to be a bird, flying up into the sky and over the chimney tops without having to worry about falling down."

"There's a machine you can fly in," Gertie said. "I read about it in the newspaper. It said that one day people will be able to fly in it from one town to another without ever touching the ground."

"Go on!" Pansy stared at her, feeling a longing so strong it took her breath away. "Oo, how I'd love to do that!"

"Well, maybe you will, one day." Gertie held out her hand for the next dish. "But for now you'll have to make do with wires, and if we don't get these dishes done soon, all the lamps will be out in the hallways and we'll be feeling our way along in the dark."

Speaking of the lamps reminded Pansy of her plan. "Oh, I forgot to tell you. Clive said he needed new wicks in the main hallway lamps. I told him I'd take some up for him, save him coming all the way down here to the supply room. He's late making his rounds tonight because of all the time he spent teaching me to fly."

"That was good of you."

"Yeah." Pansy leaned down and rubbed her knee, screwing her face up as if in pain. "Only I hurt my knee when I landed wrong. I was wondering if you'd mind taking them up for me."

Gertie stacked two plates on the draining board and picked up the tureen. "Daisy's going to kill me if I don't get back there soon."

"I know, I'm really sorry, but Clive will be waiting for me and with this bad knee and all . . ."

Vigorously polishing the tureen with a dry tea towel, Gertie rolled her eyes. "All right, I'll go. But you'll have to put this lot away before you go to bed." She gestured at the dishes.

"I will, I promise." Pansy glanced at the kitchen clock. "You'd better go now, though. Clive will be wondering where I am."

Gertie threw down the towel and dragged off her apron. "I'm going. I'm going." She waved a hand as she headed for the door. "G'night."

Pansy grinned and waved back. "Good night. Good luck!"

Gertie gave her a puzzled look and disappeared.

Pansy smiled as she lifted the last dish from the sink. She'd done her best to set the scene. Now it was up to Clive. She just hoped Gertie would appreciate her efforts when Clive invited her to go out with him.

Humming to herself, she carefully piled the dishes into the cupboard. Now she could go to bed and dream she was flying. All by herself over the ocean and on to foreign lands. What an adventure that would be.

Gertie stomped up the stairs, none too pleased at being cajoled into an errand that would make her late to relieve Daisy of her duties. Although, since Daisy had time off to go shopping earlier, it wouldn't hurt her to stay up a bit longer.

That wasn't what was bothering her now, though. After what Doris had said about Clive being in love with her, she was feeling awkward about seeing him again. Especially being alone with him in the darkness of the halls, late at night. Just thinking about it gave her goose pimples.

She was relieved to see that some of the lamps were still lit as she reached the foyer and crossed to the hallway. The long corridor leading to the ballroom was in darkness, however, and so far she'd seen no sign of Clive.

Just as she was about to find her way down there, she

heard a scuffling sound from close to the ballroom doors. Squinting, she peered into the black shadows, but couldn't see anything moving.

"Clive?" Her voice sounded loud, and a little shaky. She cleared her throat. "Are you there?"

From inside the ballroom came the shuffling noise again. She tried not to think of golden angels and missing locks of hair. The Christmas Angel couldn't possibly be in the Pennyfoot, could he? She remembered Lizzie's words, saying as how the killer went around chopping off people's heads.

Little rivers of fear trickled down her back. *Don't be bloody daft. It's not the killer.* She called out again. "Clive?"

The scuffling stopped. The silence that followed was even more terrifying. Panic swept over her so suddenly she had no way to fight it. Uttering a yelp of fright, she dropped the box of wicks and spun around, intent on making it back to the foyer and the light. She charged forward and ran full tilt into a large, warm body.

"Oof!" Clive's voice spoke in her ear as his arms wrapped around her. "What the devil?"

Warm with embarrassment, she shoved him away and backed off a few steps. "You bloody scared me to death," she said, holding a hand over her heart. She could actually feel it pounding beneath her fingers.

"What are you doing up here this time of night?"

She peered up at him. He looked different against the flickering glow from the gas lamps behind him. Sort of dark and mysterious.

She felt awkward again, and wished he would go back to being the familiar friend who'd always made her feel comfortable. "I brought you some wicks." Remembering that she dropped them, she looked back behind her. "They're down there somewhere."

"Wicks?"

His voice sounded funny, and she frowned. "Yeah, wicks. Pansy said you needed some new ones and she hurt her knee so I brought them up instead."

"I see."

He still sounded strange. She turned back to look for the box, mumbling, "I wish I did."

"Never mind, Gertie. I'll find them." He came up behind her, and she flattened herself against the wall to let him pass.

"Wait!" Suddenly remembering what had scared her in the first place, she grabbed hold of his sleeve. "I think there's someone in the ballroom. I could hear him moving around. I thought it was you."

"In the ballroom? I'll take a look. Wait here."

"Not on your bloody life. I'm coming with you." She took a tighter hold of his arm. "I don't want to be alone out here."

"All right, but stay behind me. Just in case."

In case of what? She decided she didn't want the answer to that. Creeping along behind his bulky body, she felt both scared and strangely exhilarated. Clive could take care of anyone, she told herself. Even the Christmas Angel. He would protect her. She liked the idea of that.

Clive halted, making her bump her nose on his back. "Sorry," she muttered, then shut her mouth when he sharply lifted his hand.

She could just make out the outline of the doors to the

ballroom. Very carefully, Clive pushed one open and stepped forward.

Gertie had a desperate urge to wrap her arms around his waist, but managed to restrain herself. She realized she'd been holding her breath too long and let it out on a puff of anxiety.

She heard the sound of rustling from across the room and ducked behind her protector, closing her eyes, though it was too dark to see anything anyway.

Clive stood so still she wondered if he was paralyzed with fright. Then, without warning, he uttered what sounded like a low curse and strode forward into the shadows, leaving her shivering alone by the door.

Her first instinct was to turn and run for her life, but the thought of Clive at the mercy of a deranged killer was too terrible to bear.

Flinging herself forward, she yelled, "You leave him alone, you murdering sod, or I'll tear out your bleeding liver with my bare hands!"

Clive was over by the window. She could see his outline as she belted toward him.

He called out, "Gertie! Wait!" but she was on him, trying to drag him back toward the door.

"Come on, come *on*," she said, over and over when he refused to move.

"Gertie." His voice was gentle and not at all scared, like she would have expected him to be when facing a murderer.

It dawned on her then that maybe it wasn't the Christmas Angel threatening him after all. In fact, she realized several things at once. That the window behind Clive was partly opened and the rustling sound was coming from the garlands hanging above them. That Clive smelled like the woods after a rainstorm—clean, fresh, and earthy. That he had his arms around her. That she liked it.

Coming to her senses and feeling foolish now, she backed away from him. "I thought . . ." She couldn't finish what she'd thought.

"I know what you thought."

Anyone else would have made fun of her, but he didn't sound in the least bit amused. In fact, his voice sounded strange again, as if he was having trouble getting the words out.

She felt all shivery herself, hot and cold all at the same time. "So it was the wind making the decorations move," she said, striving to sound normal.

"Yes." He took a step toward her and she wished she could see his face. "Look, I don't blame you for thinking it was . . . an intruder. I thought the same thing myself when I first came in here."

"You did?"

"Yes, I did. And, Gertie . . ."

"Yes?"

"That was very brave, and extremely good of you to come to my aid, considering what you thought was out there."

She couldn't seem to find the words she wanted. All she could manage was a mumbled, "That's all right."

"I won't forget it, Gertie." He took another step forward. "It meant a great deal to me."

Warning bells started going off in her head. She didn't want to feel this way. This was how it had started with Dan, and look at what had happened there. He'd broken her heart.

She couldn't go through that again. She didn't ever want to hurt like that again.

"It's nothing," she said, backing away. "I would have done it for anyone." With that, she turned and fled from the ballroom and didn't stop running until she was safely inside her room with the door shut firmly behind her.

CHAPTER

❈ 18 ❈

"We will be going to Caroline's Blanchard house," Cecily told Samuel the next morning. "My gown should be ready by now."

Holding open the door of the carriage for her, Samuel's face lit up. "I'll be happy to take you there, m'm."

Cecily hauled herself up into the carriage. "Well, I also have to do a little shopping in town, so we'll go there first."

"Yes, m'm. Where to, then?"

"To Willow's shoe shop. But before we go, I need to talk to you about something." Cecily leaned forward and patted the seat opposite her. "Come and sit here for a moment while I explain. We won't be overheard in here."

Samuel's expression grew guarded. "We're not going to do anything dangerous, are we, m'm?"

"No more than usual, Samuel." Cecily patted the seat again. "Come, we have no time to waste."

Samuel took his time climbing onto the seat opposite her. "You know what Mr. Baxter said about me letting you get yourself into trouble again?"

Cecily pulled a face. "No, but I can imagine."

"He said he'd send me packing." Samuel folded his arms. "That's what he said."

"Piffle. You know very well we could not manage without you."

"He was very clear on that, m'm."

"Well, he doesn't do the hiring and firing in this establishment. I do, so don't you worry about it." She smiled at him. "Cheer up, Samuel. This is another adventure and you know you always enjoy our adventures."

"I have a nasty feeling I'm not going to like this one."

Cecily sighed. "Let me tell you what I have in mind. Then, if you decide you don't want to come along, I'll understand."

He gave her a suspicious look. "All right."

Cecily leaned forward and, in spite of the rattle of carriages and clip-clop of horses' hooves passing by, lowered her voice. "I have reason to believe that Lester Salt is the Christmas Angel."

Samuel's eyes widened. "Go on! What makes you think so?"

"Well, Madeline told me that there's a ritual involving the locks of hair belonging to the dead. It's supposed to send their souls to the devil."

"Blimey." Samuel rubbed his arms as if he were cold. "But what makes you think it's Lester Salt?"

"I noticed a book by the fireside when we were there. It

was called *Tales of a Mystic*. I think Mr. Salt is practicing black magic."

Samuel frowned. "But why? Why would he want to kill all those people?"

Cecily leaned back. "Well, I have to admit, I don't think he killed Jimmy Taylor. I do believe, however, that he killed Thomas Willow. Lester was deeply in debt and being threatened. I think he had been trying to think of a way to get his hands on the shop for some time."

"So he killed Thomas to get the shop?"

"Yes, so he'd have the money to pay back Sid Tippens. I think he saw who killed Jimmy Taylor, and saw a chance to kill Thomas and put the blame on Jimmy's killer."

Samuel's frown deepened. "But if he saw who killed Jimmy, wouldn't he have told the bobbies?"

"Not if he thought that Jimmy's killer could prove he didn't kill Thomas, then the constables would be looking for who did kill him."

Samuel shook his head. "I don't know how you worked all that out, m'm, but it's clever. But what about all the other murders? Why did he do that?"

"I'm coming to that." Cecily tightened her scarf about her neck. "Lady Marion mentioned that Thomas Willow was also deeply in debt. Apparently the shoe shop wasn't making any money. When Lester found out, he was desperate. Perhaps the bookmaker threatened him again."

"So he had to find the money from somewhere else to pay Sid back."

"Mrs. Mackerbee told me that the farm had done very well, and they'd had the best year they'd ever had. She also said that her husband had visited the shoe shop. No doubt he told Lester Salt what a great year he'd had."

"So good old Lester decides to take some of it for himself."

Cecily nodded. "That's what I think. I think Lester went to the farm to rob the Mackerbees, Colin Mackerbee caught him, and there was a fight."

Samuel rubbed his chin. "He must not have got any of the money, though."

"Very good, Samuel." Pleased with her stable manager, Cecily beamed at him. "Lester must have come away empty-handed and decided to rob the Bellevue mansion instead. According to Lady Marion, he was well acquainted with both the gamekeeper and Lord Bellevue."

"So you think Henry Farnsworth caught him trying to break into the mansion, and Lester shot him?"

"Precisely."

Samuel stared at her. "But what about the Fox Hunters Club? What happened there?"

Cecily shook her head. "I don't know. Maybe Lester broke in to rob the place and accidentally set it on fire." She turned her gaze to the street outside. "I have to admit, Samuel, this is all guesswork and theory. That's why I have to visit Lester Salt today. I have to somehow make sure I'm right before I set off my plan."

Samuel sat up. "What plan?"

Quickly, Cecily outlined it for him.

Samuel immediately shook his head. "No, it's too dangerous. I can't believe Mrs. Prestwick agreed to help you with this."

"Actually," Cecily said, feeling guilty, "Mrs. Prestwick hasn't agreed. I haven't discussed it with her yet. But once I do, I'm certain she will want to help me stop this madman before he kills anyone else."

"Well, I hope she refuses to help you. If anything happened to you, m'm, I'd never forgive myself. I just can't let you do this."

"You really don't have any choice, Samuel. With or without you, with Madeline's help I intend to trap our killer."

She could see the struggle going on in his head. Finally, he let out his breath on a puff of frustration. "All right. If I can't stop you, then I'm coming with you."

She smiled. "I thought you would, Samuel. Now, let's be on our way. We have a long day ahead of us."

"Yes, m'm." His face creased in worry, he climbed out, closed the door, and jumped up to his seat. With a flick of the reins they were off, and Cecily sat back with a sigh of relief.

She had expected Samuel to put up a fight, but she knew her stable manager. He'd die first before allowing her to face danger without him. She could only hope and pray it wouldn't come to that.

Gertie had spent a fitful night, waking up at intervals with an ache that had nothing to do with the bread and cheese she'd consumed just before retiring.

She kept hearing her own words over and over in her head. *I would have done it for anyone.* How ungracious that sounded now. She'd blurted it out without thinking, anxious to get away from the temptation to take that step that would bring her closer to Clive.

All through the breakfast rush she kept thinking about it, until Pansy declared with more than a hint of impatience, "What is the matter with you this morning? Get out of the wrong side of the bed?"

Gertie scowled at her. "Very funny." She hesitated, her tray of dirty dishes balanced on her hip. Maybe if she talked about it she wouldn't feel so guilty. After all, it wasn't as if she'd said anything nasty.

Pansy was about to turn away when Gertie added, "If you must bloody know, I said something I shouldn't have yesterday and I'm wondering if I should apologize."

Pansy looked over her shoulder at her. "That's nothing new. Who did you say it to?"

Gertie paused again, then said sheepishly, "Clive."

Pansy's cry of dismay took her by surprise. "What? You didn't! What did you say to him?"

Thankful they were alone in the dining room, Gertie wished she'd never said anything. "Oh, it was nothing."

Pansy dug her hands into her hips. "If it was nothing, why are you worrying about apologizing?"

"No, twerp. I mean, that's what I said." Gertie sighed. "I was in the ballroom with Clive and—"

Pansy's gasp interrupted her. "What were you doing in the ballroom with him?"

Gertie could feel her cheeks growing warm. "Nothing we shouldn't be doing. I heard a noise, and thought it was someone breaking in and Clive went to see and I went with him and yelled at the burglar only it wasn't a burglar and Clive thanked me anyway and I said it was nothing."

Kate Kingsbury

Pansy's face had expressed a number of emotions, from shock and concern to puzzlement. "Is that all?"

Gertie had to agree that, told like that without any of the charged emotions she'd felt when it happened, it did seem a bit tame. "Yeah, that's all. Never mind. I'm just tired. I didn't get much flipping sleep last night."

"Well, you'd better get some sleep tonight. The Christmas guests will be here tomorrow." Pansy dragged a white lace-edged cloth from a table and dropped it in the laundry basket. "I can't wait to see who our special guests are, can you?"

Gertie shrugged. "Unless it's the flipping king, I don't suppose we'll even know who they are."

Pansy breathed a sigh. "Oh, wouldn't that be something! To wait on the king!"

"Yeah, well, I did it once and it's not all that much fun. His valet wouldn't let me get near him. Took everything out of my hands before I even got to the door."

Pansy turned away with a grunt of disappointment. "Oh, well, it's probably not him anyway."

Gertie had stopped paying attention. She had just seen Clive pass by the dining room doors. "I've got to go," she said abruptly, causing Pansy to spin back again. "There's something I've got to do." Leaving the tray of dishes on the table, she dashed out of the room and into the corridor.

Clive had disappeared, and she raced for the stairs. She reached the top just in time to see the front door close behind him.

Heedless of the cold wind, she dived through the door and down the steps, calling out, "Clive! Wait!"

Clive had reached the corner of the building. He stopped

248

and looked back, the wind whipping his dark hair back from his face.

He seemed uneasy as she drew nearer, looking around as if worried somebody might see them together. "Is something wrong?"

She almost laughed. Everything was wrong. If she said the wrong words now, she could break up a friendship that meant more to her than she'd realized. Now that she was in danger of losing him, she wanted to hang on to him with both hands and never let go. "I want to talk to you."

He searched her face, then nodded. "Come around here, out of the cold."

She followed him through the gate into the courtyard, where they were sheltered by the kitchen wall. She noticed that he stood between her and the beach, protecting her even more from the brisk ocean wind. That was Clive, always protecting her. Always making her feel safe.

She smiled at him. "I was scared last night."

"I know you were."

"I didn't want you to get hurt."

A frown flicked across his face. "Gertie, it's all right. You don't have to explain. I understand."

She shook her head. "No, you don't." She paused, struggling for the right words. "I like you, Clive. Really I do. You've been a wonderful friend to me and the twins and we all think the world of you."

He started to speak and she held up her hand. "No, wait. If I don't get this out now I'll never bloody say it at all."

His mouth twitched in a smile, then he looked serious again. "All right."

"It's like this." She pulled in a deep breath. "I don't

have much luck with blokes. First there was Ian, and, well, you know about him. He was the father of my twins, and never bothered to tell me he was married to someone else. Then there was Ross McBride. He was a lot older than me but he was good to me and my children. When he died I thought that was the end of it for me. But then I met Dan."

Her voice had wobbled. Cross with herself, she paused to get it under control again.

"Gertie, you don't have to do this—"

"Yes, I do. Let me finish." She struggled on. "I really, really loved Dan, even though I knew he wasn't the right one for me. I kept hoping we—" She took another deep breath. "Anyway, what I'm saying is that after all that hurting, I don't think I can ever do it again."

"Gertie—"

Again she held up her hand. "But if things had been different, if I could have felt that way again, it would have been with you."

Her fingers were clenched so tightly her nails dug into her palms. She didn't know if she'd said it right, or if he'd ever understand what she'd meant. She watched his face, and for a moment felt panic at his grave expression.

Then he smiled. "Gertie, I have never met a woman like you. You have a heart as big as the sky, and I know that one day—maybe not soon, but one day—you'll be able to trust it to someone again. I want to be around when that happens, just in case you decide to give it to me. So I'll wait. For as long as it takes. Until then, I hope we can still remain friends."

She never cried. So that moisture in her eyes had to be

caused by the wind. "You're the best friend anyone could ask for, and my twins would kill me if I didn't stay friends with you."

He laughed, that deep rich sound that always made her feel warm inside. "Then we can't disappoint the twins, can we. By the way, I've finished the rocking horse I made for their Christmas present. Come and see it and tell me what you think."

She grinned at him. "I'd love to, but it'll have to be later. I've left dirty dishes on the table and Chubby will have my guts for flipping garters if I don't get back there."

"Later, then." He lifted his hand at her, then strode off around the corner.

She kept the grin on her face all the way back to the dining room.

People packed the High Street as Samuel guided the chestnut to a stop a few yards from Willow's shoe shop. "I want you to stay here and wait for me," Cecily told him as he helped her alight from the carriage.

"I'm not going to let you go in there by yourself." Samuel took her arm in a firm hold. "I'm here to protect you, and I can't do that sitting out here on the street."

"Nonsense, Samuel." Cecily gently pried his fingers from her arm. "Nothing is going to happen to me in a shop full of customers."

"If this bloke is as evil as you say, anything could happen to you."

"Piffle. I will be quite all right. Just wait here for me. I find that people are more forthcoming when alone with someone. If I'm to trick Mr. Salt into incriminating himself I need his full confidence."

Samuel still looked defiant. "If he's that clever, he's not going to say anything that will give him away."

Cecily smiled. "Quite the contrary, Samuel. People such as Lester Salt are full of their own importance. Sooner or later he will say something that will give me the answers I need."

"Well, if you say so, m'm. I don't have to like it, though."

She patted his shoulder. "I shan't be long."

Fighting down her own doubts, she hurried into the shop, where one of Lester's assistants bounded forward to greet her. Before she could make her request, however, the abrasive voice of Lester Salt silenced her.

"Mrs. Baxter! How good to see you. How can we help you today?"

He stood in front of the curtain that led to the parlor, impeccably dressed as always, though a persistent lock of hair hung over his forehead, and his mustache looked somewhat bedraggled.

"I'm here to purchase slippers for my husband." Cecily looked around at the shelves. "I'd also like a pair for my stable manager."

Lester rubbed his hands together. He seemed in a particularly good mood as he marched forward. "Yes, yes, of course. No need to stand about here, however. Come back into my parlor and I'll show you our incredible selection of slippers. I'm sure we can find exactly what you want."

Now that the moment was at hand, the last thing Cecily wanted was to be alone in the parlor with this man. There didn't seem to be any other way, however, to have the conversation she needed to have with him.

Swallowing her fear, she managed a smile. "Thank you. I appreciate your kindness."

"My pleasure, Mrs. Baxter." He turned to the hovering assistant. "Nathan! Fetch the lady all the slippers you can find and bring them to the parlor." With that, he grasped Cecily's arm with firm fingers and propelled her through the curtain and down the hallway to the parlor.

"Can I offer you some tea?" he asked, as she reluctantly seated herself by the fire.

"Thank you, no." She glanced at the clock over the fireplace. "I have another appointment shortly so I really can't linger too long."

"Ah, I understand." He took the chair opposite her and sat down, leaning forward to ask, "I suppose the Pennyfoot will be filled with guests for Christmas?"

"Yes, indeed. We usually have a full house for the season." She glanced at the table next to her. The book was still there and she picked it up. "*Tales of a Mystic*! I don't think I've heard of this. Is it a good book?"

Lester smiled. "An excellent book. I highly recommend it. It's the story of a poor lad who stowed away on a ship in search of the true meaning of religion. Very enlightening and provocative."

Cecily stared at him. "Religion?"

He seemed puzzled by her reaction. "Ah . . . yes. It's an interest of mine."

She put the book down, her mind in a whirl. Of course. Mysticism. It could mean so many things. She had jumped to the wrong conclusion and her main theory had just flown out the window.

Obviously unsettled by her silence, Lester leaned forward. "Is everything all right, Mrs. Baxter? You're not feeling ill, I trust?"

Shaking her head, she struggled to get her thoughts together. "I'm feeling quite well, thank you." For want of a way to change the subject, she gestured at the empty corner of the room. "I don't see Rex anywhere. I hope he's in good health?"

Lester seemed preoccupied. "Rex? Oh, he was getting to be a nuisance. He was always in the way, wanting to be stroked or to be let out on the street. I took him over to Caroline Blanchard's house. She collects strays, you know."

So that was why the dog in Caroline's home had seemed familiar. "Yes," she murmured, "I know Caroline quite well."

Lester pulled a face. "Well, forgive me for saying so, but that woman is the most unsociable snob I have ever come across. She treats animals like people and people like animals."

If he hadn't been so vehement in his disgust, Cecily would have smiled at the rather apt description of her seamstress.

"Still, she's very good at handling the dogs. Caroline is quite the fanatic when it comes to her animals. She can't bear to see them in pain. It's almost as if she feels their agony herself."

He gazed at the corner with a soulful expression, as if he missed the dog. "Yes, indeed. Rex will be well taken care of there. Funny thing about dogs. Old Thomas was cruel in his treatment of Rex, but Caroline told me the dog refused to leave the old man's side when he died. Just sat there and howled. Sad, really."

Cecily's throat closed up, forcing her to cough. For a moment she fought to get her breath while Lester Salt watched her in concern.

"Would you like a cup of tea?" he asked, dragging a handkerchief out of his pocket to offer her.

She shook her head. "Thank you," she said hoarsely. "It's just a tickle in my throat." She glanced at the door, wishing Nathan would get there with the slippers.

"Well, if you're sure." Lester leaned back. "I don't suppose you have any news of the Christmas Angel? I would dearly love to see the brute who killed dear Thomas brought to justice and punished."

Cecily swallowed hard. "No news yet, but we are getting close."

"Oh? You have a suspect?"

"Perhaps." She shifted on her chair, uncomfortable with the intense look on his face.

"Is it someone in the village?"

"I can't be sure at this point, but I hope to bring the case to a close very soon." To her relief, Nathan appeared just then, his arms clutching what looked like dozens of slippers.

Cecily pretended to study the styles, then hurriedly picked out the pairs she thought would fit and gave them to Nathan to wrap. After paying for her purchases, she bid a hasty farewell to a confused Lester Salt and walked briskly over to the carriage.

Samuel just about leapt on her as she approached. "I was worried," he said, as he helped her into the carriage. "You were gone so long."

She dumped her packages onto the seat. "We have a

change of plan, Samuel. Take me to Mrs. Prestwick's house and please hurry."

Samuel's face creased in worry. "You found out Lester Salt is the Christmas Angel."

"Not exactly. I will explain once we get to Mrs. Prestwick's house. Hurry, Samuel. We don't have much time."

"Yes, m'm."

Samuel hurriedly slammed the door shut before she was properly settled. Her thoughts in a turmoil, she leaned back, her mind working feverishly. How could she have missed it? It was right there in front of her all the time.

There was only one way to resolve this. It would mean putting them all in danger, but if her plan worked out, it should all be well in the end.

Now all she needed was for Madeline to help her. It would be asking a lot of her friend, but with everything that was at stake, she was sure Madeline would agree.

"Where did you go?" Pansy demanded when Gertie dashed into the dining room. "Mrs. Chubb will have a fit if we don't get all these dishes down to the kitchen. We won't have time to get them washed and dried in time for the next meal at this rate."

"Sorry. I had to talk to Clive for a moment."

Pansy immediately brightened. "What for?"

"Never you mind."

"Did you give him the wicks last night?"

"Yes," Gertie said, as she hauled the pile of tablecloths into a basket. "I gave them to him."

Pansy waited in vain for the rest of the story. When

Gertie didn't elaborate, she prompted her with an impatient, "Well?"

"Well, what?"

"And?"

"And, what?" Gertie nodded at the cupboard. "We need those serviettes, too."

Frustrated, Pansy pulled the serviettes down from the shelf. "Didn't he say anything?"

"Who?"

Now she was getting annoyed. "You know who. *Clive*."

"Oh, him. Yeah. He said thank you."

Pansy uttered a sigh of exasperation. "Is that all?"

Gertie frowned. "What was he supposed to say?"

Throwing caution to the wind, Pansy flung the serviettes in the basket. "Don't you even *know* he likes you?"

Gertie picked up the basket and settled it on her hip. "Yeah, I know. I like him, too. So bloody what?"

"No, I mean *like* you. Like he's in love with you."

Gertie uttered a scornful laugh. "You've got your head too bloody full of Samuel, that's what. Clive and I are just friends, that's all. That's all we want to be, so don't go thinking there's anything else to it, all right?"

She barged out of the room, shoving the door open with her elbow. Pansy followed, shaking her head. She knew Gertie. She knew all that blustering was to cover up what she was truly feeling and thinking.

It was going to take a lot longer than she'd thought to get those two together, but if Gertie thought she was going to give up this easily, then her friend was mistaken. Clive and Gertie were perfect for each other, and if it took Pansy Watson to prove it to them, then so be it.

Someday she would think of the right plan. A foolproof plan. Maybe she'd ask Samuel to help her. The thought brightened her considerably, and her step was light as she made her way back to the kitchen.

Cecily was relieved to find Madeline alone with her baby when she and Samuel arrived there. The doctor, it seemed, was on his rounds.

"He won't be home until suppertime," Madeline said, laying Angelina down in her cot. "I'm putting a joint of roast beef in the oven. That man has a voracious appetite for someone so slender."

Cecily offered the baby her thumb, and smiled when Angelina grasped it with tiny fingers. "Kevin works a long day."

"Yes, he does." Madeline walked over to the settee and sat down.

Cecily sat down next to her, and beckoned Samuel to take one of the armchairs. "I'm glad he's not here. There's something I need to talk to you about and . . ."

"It's something he shouldn't hear."

Cecily sighed. "I know he doesn't believe in your powers, or agree with your methods of healing. It must be so hard to keep such an important part of your life separate from him."

Madeline tilted her head on one side. "You came here to talk about my husband?"

"No, of course not." Cecily hesitated, then added, "It was the way he looked at you when you left the other night. After you told us that Colonel Fortescue was in the woods. I worried there might be repercussions from that."

Madeline smiled. "No, Kevin didn't say a word. Would it have made a difference if he had?"

"Perhaps. I sometimes feel that I cause contention between the two of you by relying on your powers so much."

"Oh, bosh!" Madeline flapped a hand at her. "Kevin knew about my interest in healing herbs and potions long before he asked me to marry him. We may not always see eye to eye on matters of medicine, but it's not a huge conflict between us."

"But what about . . . you know . . . the trances and other things like that?"

Madeline pursed her lips. "Ah well, the less he knows about that, the better. So far he has seen only glimpses of what I can do, and that's the way I hope to keep it."

"Well, I certainly shan't enlighten him." Cecily stretched out her feet and studied her boots.

"Is that what you want from me now? I told you I can't see much beyond the darkness when I try to see the Christmas Angel."

"No, it's not that." Cecily looked up. "I think I have found the link between the murders." She paused, then added, "Madeline, you mentioned the other day that there are certain spells associated with locks of hair from the deceased."

Madeline sent a swift look at Samuel before answering. "I did."

"It's all right," Cecily said. "Samuel knows all about this. He's here to help."

"I don't know everything," Samuel said, looking worried.

"I'm coming to that." Cecily turned back to her friend. "Is there, by any chance, a ritual that involves burning the hair?"

The loud tick of a clock was the only sound in the room for several moments. Then Angelina stirred and whimpered, and Madeline got up. She bent over the cot, settling her daughter again before returning to the couch.

"Yes, there is. The hair is burned to ensure that the soul goes to hell."

Cecily drew in a sharp breath. "Ah, I thought it might be something like that. One more thing. I saw a strange carving the other day. It looked like a wagon wheel, with gems at the end of each spoke. The jewels were in the shape of cats. Does that sound significant to you?"

Madeline raised her eyebrows. "Where did you see this?"

"In my suspect's house."

"Then I'd say your suspect is engaged in some kind of occult activity. The wheel, or ring, is the major symbol. It protects everything inside it and can represent many things—woman, the circle of life, the wheel of fortune among others. The cat jewels are also protection, and can also represent prophecy, and the granting of wishes."

"As I expected." Cecily shook her head. "I don't know how I could have been so blind." She leaned forward. "Madeline, I have something to ask of you. I would not involve you unless it were imperative that I do so. We need your help to bring to justice a particularly dangerous adversary. This is what we have to do." Quickly she outlined her plan.

Madeline's gaze probed her face. "You know who is behind the murders."

"I think I do. I hope to know for certain in a short while. Will you help us?"

Madeline's gaze strayed to her baby. "If it were anyone else asking me, I would most likely have to decline. I know, however, that you would not ask if there was any other way. Don't worry, Cecily. Together we will defeat the Christmas Angel."

"It is a risky venture," Cecily admitted, "but if we are all alert and on our toes I think we can bring this to a satisfactory conclusion."

"It would seem so." Again Madeline glanced at the cot. "I will have her nanny take Angelina over to her mother's house until it is safe to bring her home."

"That's a good idea." Cecily rose, prompting Samuel to jump to his feet. "Let us hope that this will soon be over."

"I certainly hope so." Madeline led them to the door. "We must be very careful, Cecily. This is a devious killer and a desperate one. There is nothing more dangerous."

Cecily hugged her friend. "If all goes well, if we do this right, the villagers will sleep easier in their beds tonight."

"Then let's pray all goes well."

That was all she was praying for, Cecily thought, as she stepped out into cold wind. For if things went badly, who knew what might happen.

Samuel followed her to the carriage, saying nothing until he handed her up onto her seat. "You think Caroline Blanchard is the Christmas Angel?"

Watching his face, Cecily felt sorry for him. "I'm afraid I do, Samuel. We will know for certain later this afternoon, but first we have to set the trap. Fetching my gown will give me the perfect excuse."

"But how . . . why . . . I don't understand."

Cecily nodded. "Neither did I until this morning. Let's hurry, Samuel. If this is going to work, we have to time it just right."

"Yes, m'm." Looking shaken, Samuel slammed the door shut and climbed up onto his seat.

Cecily leaned back, feeling worried. Everything depended on Samuel behaving as naturally as possible. Knowing how her manager had felt about Caroline, she hoped he was able to control his emotions.

Caroline seemed flustered when she opened the door. "Oh, Mrs. Baxter! Your gown is not quite ready! I have been quite busy lately. I was hoping to bring it over to you tomorrow."

"Oh, dear." Cecily stepped over the threshold, forcing the other woman to back away. "I was under the impression it would be ready today. Since I was passing by, I thought I would save you a journey to the Pennyfoot and pick it up myself."

"That's very kind of you, I'm sure, but—"

Cecily motioned to Samuel to follow her, though it was hardly necessary since her stable manager was practically falling over himself to get inside the door. "I'm sure there can't be much more to do with the gown. We don't mind waiting while you finish up on it, do we, Samuel."

Samuel cleared his throat and in an unnaturally loud voice, said, "No, no, not at all."

Caroline shot a look over her shoulder. "Well, I really wasn't expecting company. The animals, you know. They're all in the sitting room and I haven't really had time to look in on them and make sure they've been behaving themselves, if you know what I mean."

Cecily did know, and didn't relish the prospect of walking in on a room reeking of cat urine. She made an effort to sound indifferent, however, when she answered. "Please, don't fuss. We understand and we'll be quite comfortable."

Samuel's expression contradicted her words, but she signaled him with a quick frown that she hoped he'd interpret.

Caroline looked none too pleased, but she led them to the sitting room and opened the door. "Can I fetch you a cup of tea?"

"Thank you, no." Cecily smiled at her. "If you would finish the gown right away, I'll be happy to pay you a little extra for your effort."

"Then I shall see to it right away." After one more doubtful look at both of them, she sped off in the direction of her sewing room.

"Better let me go first." Samuel stepped into the room and looked around. He sounded relieved when he added, "Looks clean enough to me, m'm, though it smells a bit."

Cecily followed him in and shooed a cat off the nearest chair. Several more stalked around the room, and a couple of dogs lifted their heads to scrutinize the visitors, then went back to snoozing by the fire.

"She likes her animals, doesn't she," Samuel observed, looking around the room. "I've never seen this many cats and dogs in one person's house." He bent over to stroke the nearest dog—a large black animal with only one ear. "She must love animals a lot."

"Yes," Cecily said quietly. "I'm sure she does."

"I just can't believe she—"

"Shshh!" Cecily put a finger over her lips.

Samuel snapped his mouth shut.

Giving him a warning look, Cecily said loudly, "It must

be comforting to have so many animals around when one lives on her own, like Miss Blanchard."

Taking his cue from her, Samuel straightened. "I'm sure it is."

Still talking, Cecily moved over to the sideboard and pulled out one of the drawers. She shuffled through the contents and, finding nothing, she closed the drawer and opened another.

She found what she was looking for in the third drawer. Moving a stack of envelopes aside, she caught a glimpse of glittering gold. Carefully, she picked up one of the small gold stamps and held it out to Samuel. Lowering her voice, she whispered, "The signature of the Christmas Angel."

Samuel stared at her. "I just can't believe it!"

"Shshh!" Cecily held up a warning finger. Crossing the room to the empty chair, she sat down. "She can't know we suspect her. Be very careful what you say and how you say it."

Samuel looked as if he wanted to cry, but he nodded and bent down again to stroke the dog.

The sound of a door closing alerted Cecily. "Samuel, just listen to everything I say, and don't interrupt or contradict." She had no time to say more, as the door opened and Caroline entered, carrying the gown over her arm.

"Here it is, Mrs. Baxter." She held up the shimmering gown. "I hope it is satisfactory."

"I'm quite sure it will be." Cecily bent down to pat the black dog on the head. "This is a fine animal."

Caroline handed the gown to Samuel, who now sat poker-faced and silent. "Yes, he is. I found him wandering around the streets in Wellercombe. Poor thing was nothing but skin and bones when I found him."

"Well, he certainly looks healthy enough now." Cecily stood, and Samuel jumped to his feet. "We must be off. We have a very important appointment this afternoon."

Caroline looked as if she was unsure how to answer that.

Ignoring her, Cecily continued, "I noticed the other day that wheel on the wall in your dressing room. I assume you are interested in the occult?"

Caroline shifted uneasily from one foot to the other. "I have a passing interest, that's all."

"Ah, I see." Cecily moved closer to the door. "Then you must have heard of my friend Mrs. Madeline Prestwick?"

The seamstress seemed unsettled by the question. "I have heard talk of her, yes."

"Most people consider her a witch, you know."

Samuel had his back to Caroline, which was fortunate, since an agonized look crossed his face.

Cecily ignored him and smiled at Caroline, who looked just as aghast. "I'm sure—" she began, but Cecily interrupted her.

"She does have remarkable powers. In fact, she has promised to use them to help me find the Christmas Angel."

Caroline's face turned ashen. She seemed unable to turn her gaze from Cecily's face, but felt behind her for the arm of a chair before falling down on it.

Cecily avoided looking at Samuel, who was now staring in dismay at the hapless seamstress. "Madeline is going up to Putney Downs today to the woods nearby the spot where Thomas Willow was killed. There she will conduct a private séance, some sort of ritual that will give her the name of the

Christmas Angel. Once she has it, she will bring it to me at the Pennyfoot where P.C. Northcott will be waiting for the news."

Caroline opened and closed her mouth, as if seeking words that wouldn't come.

Samuel cleared his throat, and Cecily gave him a sharp nudge. "Come, Samuel. We must get back to the club with as much speed as possible, so that we can be there when Madeline returns with the name of our infamous killer."

She headed for the door, saying, "Thank you for finishing my gown today. I shall enjoy wearing it at the Welcome Ball."

Caroline seemed in a daze as she followed them out to the hallway. She barely managed to acknowledge Cecily's farewell before shutting the front door in her face.

"How terribly rude," Cecily murmured, as she walked down the path to the gate.

Samuel leapt ahead of her to open it. When he spoke his voice was full of despair. "She just doesn't look like a dangerous killer."

"Most people don't." Cecily paused at the carriage, waiting for him to open the door. "I'm sorry, Samuel. I know you like her but—"

Samuel shook his head. "You know, lots of people buy those stamps. I saw them in the toy store the other day. A whole pile of them. Anyone could buy them."

"It isn't just the stamps, Samuel. On our first visit I smelled something awful burning in the sewing room, like human hair. Also, Lady Marion told me that Miss Blanchard was at the Bellevue estate delivering her gown the morning Henry Farnsworth died." She swept an arm toward the house. "It's because of those animals, Samuel. She rescues them, and punishes those who ill-treat them."

Samuel jutted out his jaw. "I don't believe it. I don't believe she's capable of killing all those men."

Cecily climbed aboard the carriage and settled her skirt around her ankles. "Given enough reason and the right circumstances, everyone is capable of killing. We all have our dark side. Thankfully the vast majority of us know how to control it. Anyway, it's out of our hands now. The plan has been set in motion and we shall soon see if I am right."

Samuel looked far from happy as he closed the door. Cecily leaned back and braced herself for the jerk of the carriage as he urged the chestnut forward.

They had barely reached the edge of the lane before a horse and cloaked rider passed them at lightning speed. Cecily watched them disappear around the bend ahead and slowly let out her breath.

Now that everything was set, she could think of all sorts of reasons why it could go wrong. The bait could be ignored, or dealt with in a way she hadn't thought about, or, in the worst-case scenario, Madeline could be killed before help could get to her.

Cecily deliberately shut off her thoughts along that line. She had learned from experience never to try to second-guess an adversary. She knew what she had to do now, and the rest was up to providence.

Thanks to Gertie's help with the dishes, Pansy arrived at the final dress rehearsal with plenty of time to spare. She was thankful she had no lines to speak, since she was certain she would forget every word in her excitement.

Standing in the wings, she watched Doris perform, knowing without a shadow of a doubt that she would never be as good as her. She would just have to do the best she could and hope she didn't mess things up too much.

Now that she could fly, she could really get into the part of Tinker Bell. She remembered something Mrs. Fortescue had told her. *Believe you really are the person you are playing.*

Pansy closed her eyes. She was Tinker Bell—Peter Pan's protector and friend. A beloved fairy, capable of magic. Soon the ballroom would be full of toffs, all watching her fly. All watching her big dying scene.

She heard her cue and floated forward, ready to take on the world. This was what she wanted to do for the rest of her life. She wanted to be an actress, performing in front of huge appreciative audiences. She wanted to hear applause and know it was for her. She wanted to travel to exciting places, and she wanted to be really famous, with people clamoring for her autograph.

"Tinker Bell!"

The thunderous roar snatched Pansy out of her daydream. A smattering of giggles dragged her focus back to the stage. Peter Pan stood in front of her, hands on hips, glaring at her with a ferocious scowl.

Mrs. Fortescue hovered in front of the stage, staring up at her. "We are all waiting for you, Tinker Bell, to fly onto the ship. I suggest you attach your wings, however, before you fall flat on your face."

Several of the children started giggling again, and were

immediately hushed by a fierce stare and a sharp flap of Phoebe's hand.

Pansy's face grew warm as she realized she'd forgotten to have her wires attached before she came out onstage. The footman who was supposed to help her with it stood in the wings, waving the contraption at her.

"Sorry, Mrs. Fortescue." She skipped back to the wings and waited for the footman to attach the wires. From now on, she promised herself, she'd concentrate on the performance. The daydreams would have to wait for another time.

CHAPTER
❄ 19 ❄

Cecily waited until the carriage was clear of the town before tapping on the window that separated her from Samuel.

He reached back and slid the windowpane across, calling out, "Yes, m'm?"

"Make sure you take the next turn out to the Downs, Samuel."

There was a long pause, then her stable manager's voice, heavy with apprehension, answered her. "Are you quite sure you want to do this, m'm?"

"Yes, Samuel, I am quite sure, and hurry. As fast as you can."

"Very well, m'm." The carriage swayed to one side as Samuel guided the chestnut into the turn, then they were rattling up the cliff path to the Downs.

All Cecily could hope was that they would not be too

late. She would never forgive herself if something happened to Madeline.

Gazing out the window at the sands below, she tried to reassure herself. She had gone over the plan carefully with everyone. All the pieces were in place. Surely it would work as she had envisioned?

Curling her fingers into her palms she leaned forward, as if urging the carriage to go faster. By now Madeline would be at the edge of the woods, waiting for a dangerous killer to approach.

If her friend had rung P.C. Northcott as instructed, the constable should also be waiting within a short distance, waiting to pounce on the killer the moment Madeline appeared to be in danger.

Over ruts and bumps the carriage bounced, jolting Cecily up and down and side to side, snapping her teeth. Barely aware of the bruising ride, her gaze was glued to the edge of the forest.

They were nearing the spot where Thomas Willow had died. Dark clouds had gathered angrily overhead. The change in the weather had brought a thunderstorm in from the sea. The wind whipped the carriage as it bounded across the cliffs, and rain now streamed down the windows.

Cecily could hardly see, squinting through the rivulets of water obstructing her view. Somewhere out there in the mist, Madeline was waiting. Somewhere out there a killer stalked, intent on murder.

Vaguely Cecily could see the outline of trees, and then a flash of color. "Stop!" She pounded on the window. "Stop, Samuel!"

The carriage rocked violently as Samuel dragged on the reins. The chestnut, taken by surprise, reared up on its hind legs, whinnying its outrage.

The carriage halted. Without waiting for Samuel, Cecily flung open the carriage door. Madeline was there, on the far slope of the Downs, facing the cloaked rider. The hood had fallen back, and even at that distance, Cecily recognized the auburn hair.

There was no sign of the constable. She looked in vain for the stocky figure wearing the dark blue uniform. Samuel leapt down from his seat, his eyes wide with apprehension. "She's there. Where's the bobby?"

"He was supposed to be here. I can't see him anywhere."

Samuel took one look and started racing across the grass. Cecily took off after him, cursing her stupidity in thinking that she could rely on Sam Northcott.

The Christmas Angel had swallowed the bait, but the constable was not where he was supposed to be. Now it was up to her and Samuel to save Madeline.

Samuel closed in, just as Caroline turned, her hand raised and her gleaming knife poised to strike.

Cecily screamed, and stumbled across the wet grass, the wind tearing at her hat and the rain beating her face. She saw Madeline raise both hands, fingers outstretched, her long, wet hair streaming behind her.

Her voice rose with the wind, calling out words Cecily didn't understand. Samuel leapt toward Caroline, reaching for the hand that held the knife.

The woman neatly sidestepped, giving Samuel a shove. He tumbled forward and cracked his head on the massive trunk of an ancient oak. With a grunt he collapsed and lay sprawled on the ground.

Cecily no longer had breath to scream. She could only stand there, watching as Caroline, poised above Samuel's fallen body, raised the knife above her head.

"You will die, wretch!" she yelled, grasping the knife with both hands. "No one can stop the angel of mercy! The animals need me!"

Cecily willed Samuel to get up, but he lay still, unconscious from the blow to his head.

Madeline called out again, her face lifted to the heavens. There was a loud crack, and a bolt of lightning flashed down from above and slashed across the knife, sending it spinning from Caroline's hand.

The seamstress screamed and fell to her knees, clutching her hand to her chest.

From behind Cecily came the sound of pounding hoofs and rattling wheels. Out of the rain came a horse and carriage, with Kevin Prestwick flailing a whip, and P.C. Northcott seated beside him, one hand firmly holding on to his helmet.

Cecily dropped to her knees by Samuel's side, thankful to see him stirring. Behind her she heard the doctor's worried voice, asking if Madeline was hurt.

Northcott announced that he was arresting Caroline for the attempted murder of Samuel.

"She tried to kill me," Caroline insisted. "Keep that witch away from me!"

Dr. Prestwick examined Samuel, who by now had opened his eyes and was trying to sit up. "He'll be fine," the doctor announced, then turned his attention to Caroline's hand.

"It's badly burned," he said, as Northcott dragged the defiant woman to her feet. "I'll take you both down to the constabulary and I'll treat her there." He looked at Madeline. "Samuel can take you home on his way back to the Pennyfoot."

She nodded, then took a step toward Caroline, who shrank back. "You will tell them the truth," she said, her dark eyes glittering with a strange, fierce light. "You will tell them everything. For if you don't, if you leave out one single word, I promise you will find yourself facing a far more terrible fire that will consume you until you are nothing but ashes."

Caroline flinched and allowed the constable to lead her over to the carriage.

Kevin paused, his probing gaze on his wife's face, then he gave her a brief nod and turned to follow Northcott to the carriage.

Cecily called after him. "Why was Sam with you? He was supposed to be here to protect Madeline."

The doctor paused. "The constable had another accident on his bicycle. Hit a rock and buckled the front wheel. He should ride in a carriage from now on. I passed him on the road and offered to give him a ride."

He looked back at Madeline. "I never dreamed when I saw him that he was on his way to save my wife from a killer." He shifted his gaze to Cecily. "You would have had much to answer for had she come to any harm."

"I know," Cecily said quietly. "I'm so sorry."

"It's all right, Cecily." Madeline walked over to him and laid a hand on his arm. "It was my idea, and it was worth everything to capture the Christmas Angel."

Frowning, he dropped a quick kiss on her forehead, and left.

Samuel climbed to his feet. "What happened?"

"Caroline is on her way to jail." Cecily took his arm. "Are you all right?"

Samuel grimaced and rubbed his jaw. "My pride's hurt more than anything. She was too fast for me."

"Do you feel like driving the carriage home?"

"Of course." He grinned at Madeline. "Glad to see you're okay. I reckon your husband turned up just in the nick of time."

"Yes, I suppose he did." Madeline smiled at Cecily. "All's well that ends well, as they say."

"Yeah. It could have been a lot worse." Samuel headed a little unsteadily toward the carriage, followed by the two women.

"Thank you, Madeline," Cecily said, as Samuel drew out of earshot. "That's another of my lives you have saved."

Madeline smiled. "You may want to slow down, Cecily. You'll run out of lives one day."

"I'm inclined to agree with you. I almost cost you yours today."

"Nonsense. You saved my life. If you and Samuel hadn't distracted that awful woman when you did, I might not have been able to defend myself in time."

"Then the lightning bolt *was* your doing."

Madeline's expression was inscrutable. "Let us just call it divine intervention. It will avoid a lot of awkward explanations."

Cecily had no time to answer before they reached the carriage, where Samuel waited to open the door. Drenched to the skin, she climbed inside, thankful to be under a dry roof again.

CHAPTER
❋ 20 ❋

"How awful! You could have been killed!" Pansy stared at Samuel in horror, chilled by the story he had just told her.

"Yeah, if it weren't for the bobby and Dr. Prestwick turning up," Samuel agreed. "They saved my life, as well as madam's and Mrs. Prestwick's, too."

Pansy shivered, hugging her shoulders. It was always cold in the stables, but right then, after listening to Samuel's tale, she felt colder than she'd ever felt before. "I'm just glad you're safe," she said, moving closer to hug him.

His arms around her immediately made her feel warmer. Tess came up to them and nuzzled Pansy with her nose. Laughing, Pansy knelt to hug the dog, too. "So Caroline Blanchard was the Christmas Angel, like madam thought."

Samuel patted Tess's head. "Yeah. I still find it hard to believe. She didn't look like a killer."

"Will she go to prison?"

Samuel shrugged. "I dunno. I suppose that will be up to a judge and jury to decide."

"What will happen to all her cats and dogs if she goes to prison?"

Samuel looked miserable. "I dunno. I hope they can all find good homes."

Pansy glanced around the stables. "I don't suppose they could stay here."

"Madam would never allow that. She wasn't too happy about me keeping Tess."

Pansy gave the dog another hug. "Well, I'm glad she did let you keep her." She scratched Tess's ear. "What would we do without her now?"

Samuel grinned. "We?"

Red-faced, Pansy stood up. "You know what I mean."

"Do I?"

Aware he was teasing her, she went on the defensive. "Well, I've got something to tell you. We had the final dress rehearsal for *Peter Pan* today and Mrs. Fortescue said I'm the perfect Tinker Bell."

The amusement drained out of Samuel's face. "You're really enjoying being in that pantomime, aren't you."

Pansy clasped her hands together and closed her eyes. "Oh, yes. It's the most exciting thing I've ever done in my life. When I'm up there, I'm in another world. I feel important, special, like everyone's watching me and loving me. I've never felt like that before."

She opened her eyes to see an agonized expression on his face. It was gone so quickly she thought she might have imagined it, but something in his eyes told her he wasn't as happy for her as she'd expected him to be.

Catching his sleeve, she said earnestly, "You must come and see me, Samuel. At the performance. You must see me being Tinker Bell."

"Of course I will."

His voice was gruff, as if he was having trouble getting the words out.

"It's what I want to do for the rest of my life." She was talking fast, words spilling out in her excitement. "I want to be onstage in London and Paris and Rome." She waved a hand in the air. "All over the world."

He still had that strange look on his face. It was as if he was pulling away from her, shutting himself off so she couldn't reach him.

Worried now, she shook his arm. "I want you to be proud of me, Samuel. I want you to look at me the way you look at Doris."

It was out before she'd known she was going to say it. Samuel pulled away from her, shaking her hand free, turning his back on her.

Tears formed in her eyes, dribbling down her cheeks. "What is it, Samuel? Why are you so cross with me?"

"I'm not cross with you." He hunched his shoulders. "I'm disappointed, that's all."

"Disappointed? I don't understand."

He turned back swiftly, grabbing her shoulders with rough hands. "Doris did that to me," he said, his voice harsh with anger. "She let me fall in love with her and then she abandoned me for the stage. I couldn't compete with all those toffs waiting for her every night at the stage door. They made me feel I wasn't good enough to lick their boots."

Sobbing, Pansy tried to free herself from his grip. "I'm sorry, Samuel. But that wasn't my fault."

"You're doing the same thing, don't you see?" He let her go so suddenly she almost fell. "You'll go off with her to London to be on the stage, and I'll never see you again."

Pansy stared at him, her heart pounding and her tears drying on her cheeks. "Are you saying you'd miss me?"

"Course I'll miss you!" He threw a hand up in the air. "I love you, don't I. I can't stand the thought of you breaking my heart the way Doris did."

"Oh, my." Pansy drew a deep breath, then let out a shriek that made Tess bark. Throwing herself at Samuel, she clung to his neck. "I love you, too, Samuel, and I would never leave you to go on the stage. *Never!*"

Samuel seemed to have trouble finding his voice. "Really?"

"Really." She looked up into his face. She'd been wrong. Being onstage wasn't the most exciting feeling in the world. Being in Samuel's arms, hearing him say he loved her—that was the most wonderful, thrilling feeling she'd ever known. She was going to remember it for the rest of her life. "Happy Christmas, Samuel."

He gave her the most beautiful smile she'd ever seen. "Happy Christmas, my love."

"Where the devil have you been?" Baxter stared in horror as Cecily hurried over to the fire and stood shivering in front of it. "You look like you've been swimming in the ocean."

"I've been up on Putney Downs." Cecily couldn't seem to stop her teeth chattering, though whether it was from the cold or the drama she'd just been through, she couldn't tell.

"What on earth for?" Frowning, Baxter approached her. "You're soaking wet. What were you doing up there?"

She gave him a weak smile. "Catching the Christmas Angel."

"Good Lord! Tell me what happened. No, get out of those wet clothes first, then tell me what happened. I'll send for some hot cocoa."

Feeling a little steadier, Cecily headed for the boudoir. "Tell them to put some brandy in it. Oh, and I'd like some of Mrs. Chubb's mince pies. I feel like celebrating."

By the time she had changed out of her wet and muddy clothes and into a warm woolen frock, she was feeling quite exhilarated. A dangerous killer was safely behind bars, the snow had gone, and Christmas was a week away. The Pennyfoot was ready for the Christmas guests, and all was well with her world.

Joining Baxter in the sitting room, she accepted the steaming cup of cocoa he handed her and sniffed it to make sure the kitchen staff had added the brandy.

The welcoming warmth sliding down to her stomach was most satisfying, and she sat down with a sigh of pleasure in front of the fire. Baxter had stoked it, and flames licked the shiny black lumps of coal, creating a smoldering red glow of heat.

"Now," Baxter said, as he sat opposite her, "tell me what happened."

She told him, leaving out the moment when Madeline called forth her powers to create the lightning bolt that saved them. "It was a miracle," she said instead. "Madeline called it divine intervention."

"I'm inclined to agree." He tilted his head on one side. "Are you telling me everything?"

"Everything I know." Cecily stared into the fire. "I was so certain Lester Salt was the killer at first. I don't know how I could have been so misled."

Baxter finished off his mince pie and leaned back. "So when did you realize it wasn't Lester Salt?"

"When I learned that his book on mysticism wasn't what I thought. Until then I was convinced he was practicing black magic. Then he told me that Caroline Blanchard had told him that Thomas Willow's dog refused to leave his side when he died. He'd already told me that he rang the constabulary when the dog returned without Thomas, so how would Caroline have known that about the dog unless she'd been there?"

"Good point." Baxter laced his fingers together. "Still, she could have seen someone else kill Thomas and been too afraid to say anything."

"She could have, but she didn't. I should have known when I was thinking about Henry Farnsworth shooting pheasants. Everyone said that Jimmy Taylor had a nasty temper. I'm guessing that Caroline saw him beating his horse and perhaps threw the rock at him to make him stop."

"So you think she didn't mean to kill him?"

Cecily shrugged. "I don't know. Whether she did or not, she must have realized he was dead, and took a lock of his hair to send his soul to the devil for tormenting his horse."

Baxter nodded. "That makes sense. But what about the others?"

"Lester Salt told me that Thomas kicked his dog. Colin Mackerbee slaughtered pigs. Henry Farnsworth shot pheasants. The foxhunters killed foxes. I think that with Jimmy's death, Caroline went on a rampage of revenge—cutting off locks of hair and sending the souls to hell."

"So how in blazes did you end up on the Putney Downs?"

Cecily told him about the plan she'd devised, knowing that if Caroline Blanchard was the killer, she'd have to silence Madeline before she could tell everyone the true identity of the Christmas Angel.

"She called herself the angel of mercy," Cecily said, staring into the flames. "That must have been why she left the angel stamps on her victims' heads."

Baxter's expression was one of alarm. "Good Lord, Cecily! You could all have been killed."

Cecily leaned forward and patted his hand. "Yes, well, we weren't, darling, so all's well. Sometimes one has to take extraordinary measures to catch a killer as devious as the Christmas Angel. Madeline assured me she could defend herself. I had complete faith in her abilities."

Baxter groaned. "I hate to think what you will get into next."

"I hope there won't be a next." Cecily stretched her toes closer to the fire. "Of course, if Sam Northcott hadn't fallen off his bicycle again, he would have been there to protect Madeline."

Baxter made a sound of disgust in his throat. "That idiot needs to find better transportation. I've lost count of the number of times he loses his bicycle."

"Well, perhaps after this he'll get one of those newfangled motorcars you're always complaining about."

Baxter grunted. "Heaven preserve us. Knowing North-cott, he'd drive the dratted thing right into the lobby. He has to be the most incompetent constable on the force. His clumsiness could have cost you all your lives."

"Well, fortunately for us, that bolt of lightning took care of things. I don't think Kevin was very happy with Sam. Or me, for that fact. Madeline was nice enough to tell him the whole thing was her idea."

Baxter shuddered. "When I think what could have happened to—" He broke off as a light tap on the door interrupted him. "Now what?" Grumbling to himself, he walked across the room to open the door.

Cecily heard one of the maids announce, "P.C. Northcott is in the library. He wants to speak with madam."

"Tell him we will be there shortly." Baxter closed the door and strode back to her. "Northcott," he said, his tone thick with disgust. "I'll speak with him. You stay here and rest."

"No." She put down her cup and rose. "I want a word with him. There are questions yet to be answered."

She thought about the questions as she led the way down the stairs to the lobby. She had spent so much time looking for a link between the victims, instead of searching for a motive.

It had been there right under her nose. She had just been too blind to see. Was she losing her powers of deduction? Was she taking far too much for granted, instead of digging beneath the surface of lies to find the truth?

If so, then she would be well to heed Baxter's wishes, after all. For without the sharp edge that had always served her so well in the past, she would be a danger not only to herself, but to everyone else around her.

She put her depressing thoughts aside as they entered the library. Sam Northcott was in his usual spot in front of the fire, rocking back and forth on his heels.

He saluted her when he saw her. "Very commendable, Mrs. B. We would not have caught her without your help."

"Well, don't get too reliant on my wife," Baxter said, wagging a finger for emphasis. "I don't relish the idea of her putting herself in danger for your benefit."

Northcott puffed out his chest. "For the benefit of mankind, sir. A dangerous killer was h'apprehended because of your wife's commitment to the law." He coughed. "Though I was a little surprised it were Caroline Blanchard."

Cecily sighed. "Yes, it took me a while to see her as a killer. Am I right in thinking that she threw the rock that killed Jimmy Taylor?"

"Yes, you are, m'm. Right as rain. She admitted as much when I talked to her a while ago. Said she saw him beating his horse. She said she was filled with a terrible anger and threw the rock to stop him. He fell off the wagon and hit his head going down on the wheel. That's what killed him."

Cecily felt a stab of sympathy for the seamstress. "And the locks of hair?"

Northcott smoothed a hand over his bald head. "I don't rightly understand all that mumbo jumbo, m'm. Miss Blanchard said something about throwing them on the fire and speaking to the devil, but by then she was talking a lot of nonsense." He touched his forehead with his fingers. "Not quite right in the head, m'm, as I see it."

"Did she say why she left the stamps on their heads?"

Northcott looked uncomfortable. "She said as how she had some in her pocket, and when she bent over Jimmy Taylor, they fell out and one stuck on his forehead. She thought it were some sort of sign, so she left it there and that's when she decided to take his hair."

"Ah, that explains it. She must have decided to leave the same sign on all her victims. What will happen to her?"

Northcott shrugged. "That's up to the courts. If she's as daffy as I think she is she'll probably be sent to an institution." He shivered. "I don't envy her that, m'm. I've seen some of them places. Horrible, they are."

Cecily tried not to imagine Caroline Blanchard locked away in a mental asylum. "What about her animals? Will they be looked after?"

"We'll try to find them homes, m'm, though I don't know how soon we can do that. Might be a while. At least until after Christmas."

Cecily struggled with her good sense for a moment, then said quickly, "We can house them in the stables until they find homes. I'm sure my staff won't mind taking care of them."

She heard Baxter make a choking sound and ignored him. "Well, thank you for telling us all this, Sam. I suppose you'll be on your way to London now?"

"Yes, m'm. Me and the missus will be off in the morning." He glanced at the mantelpiece where the clock ticked away. "Well, I'd better be on my way. I don't suppose . . ."

She understood at once. "I'm sure Mrs. Chubb can find you a sausage roll or two on your way out."

"Very kind of you, I'm sure, Mrs. B." Northcott got to his feet. "I did want to thank you, m'm, for all your help. Because of you, the missus and I can have a good Christmas holiday. She'll be grateful to you, I know."

"I'm glad, Sam." Cecily waited for Baxter to get up before rising herself. "Have a very happy Christmas."

"You, too, m'm." He looked at Baxter. "And you, sir."

"Likewise," Baxter mumbled.

As the door closed behind the constable, Cecily sank onto her chair. "I can't tell you how happy I am that's over. Now I can focus on Christmas."

Baxter grunted. "I can't believe you invited a horde of cats and dogs to run all over the place. What on earth prompted you to do that?"

Cecily shrugged. "I couldn't just leave them in the house to starve. The staff will look after them. I'll make sure they're not allowed in the club."

"I should think not. Our first guests will be arriving tomorrow."

"Including Arthur Balfour." Cecily smiled. "Imagine having Britain's prime minister as our guest. That should give the Pennyfoot's reputation a boost. The maids will have a fine time fighting over who waits on him."

"Well, let's hope we get no more mass murderers lurking around, or we'll be spending next Christmas alone." He raised his chin to stare at the ceiling. "Though, come to think of it, that might be rather nice."

She laughed. "You know you'd be bored to death."

"After all that's happened around here lately, boredom might be a welcome change."

"Nonsense." She linked her arm through his. "Come, darling. Let's enjoy our last night of peace in our suite before the hotel is full of clamoring guests."

They climbed the stairs together, with the scent of the glistening fir tree mingling with the aroma of nutmeg and cinnamon rising from the kitchen below.

Once more, Cecily thought, as they turned onto the landing, she had brought a villain to justice. It had been a hard-won battle, with too many missteps along the way.

Her confidence had been shaken. She felt she was losing her edge, and she wasn't at all certain that if she were to face another villain, she'd be able to outwit him.

Right now, however, she would put all such thoughts out of her mind. It was Christmas, and she had all the time in the world to enjoy it.